KU-060-901

THE CONVENIENT FELSTONE MARRIAGE

Jenni Fletcher

This is a work of fiction. Names, characters, places, locations and incidents are purely fictional and bear no relationship to any real life individuals, living or dead, or to any actual places, business establishments, locations, events or incidents. Any resemblance is entirely coincidental.

This book is sold subject to the condition that it shall not, by way of trade or otherwise, be lent, resold, hired out or otherwise circulated without the prior consent of the publisher in any form of binding or cover other than that in which it is published and without a similar condition including this condition being imposed on the subsequent purchaser.

® and ™ are trademarks owned and used by the trademark owner and/or its licensee. Trademarks marked with ® are registered with the United Kingdom Patent Office and/or the Office for Harmonisation in the Internal Market and in other countries.

MILLS & BOON

All rights reserved including the right of reproduction in whole
or in part in any form. This edition is published by arrangement with
Harle~~quin Books S.A.~~

This i   DUMFRIES &   ~~nd~~
incide   GALLOWAY   ~~l~~
life in
establ   LIBRARIES   is
entire~~ly~~

DUMFRIES & GALLOWAY LIBRARIES	
AS366246	
Askews & Holts	Jun-2017
AF	£4.99

This b   y of
trade ~~~~   ~~ted~~
witho~~ut~~   ; or
cover   ar
condit~~~~   ~~ent~~
purch~~a~~

® and   ~~er~~
and/or ~~~~   ~~h the~~
United ~~Kingdom Patent Office and/or the Office~~ for Harmonisation in
the Internal Market and in other countries.

Published in Great Britain 2017
by Mills & Boon, an imprint of HarperCollins*Publishers*
1 London Bridge Street, London, SE1 9GF

© 2017 Jenni Fletcher

ISBN: 978-0-263-92583-8

Our policy is to use papers that are natural, renewable and
recyclable products and made from wood grown in sustainable
forests. The logging and manufacturing processes conform to the
legal environmental regulations of the country of origin.

Printed and bound in Spain
by CPI, Barcelona

Jenni Fletcher was born on the north coast of Scotland, and now lives in Yorkshire with her husband and two children. She wanted to be a writer as a child, but got distracted by reading instead, finally writing down her first paragraph thirty years later. She's had more jobs than she can remember, but has finally found one she loves. She can be contacted via Twitter, @jenniauthor.

A previous book by Jenni Fletcher in
Mills & Boon Historical Romance

Married to Her Enemy

Visit the Author Profile page at millsandboon.co.uk.

To M&M with lots of love.

Chapter One

North Yorkshire—July 1865

'But I don't want to marry him!' Ianthe Holt felt as though she'd just been slapped in the face. 'How could you even suggest such a thing?'

'Because it's a good idea, that's why!' Her brother, Percy, threw his head back against the carriage seat with a sigh. 'And I didn't say that you *had* to, just that you ought to consider it.'

'He's twenty years older than me!'

'Thirty, more like.'

'Then how could you… How could I…?'

Ianthe spluttered the words, barely resisting the urge to kick her brother violently in the shins. There was a great deal more about Sir Charles Lester than simply his age that bothered her, not that Percy would ever believe that. Good idea or not, the Baronet was the last man on earth she wanted to marry. Even the sight of him these days gave her goosebumps, yet here she was, trapped in a train compartment, every burst of steam and thud of the pistons taking her closer towards him.

Silently she gritted her teeth and stared out of the window, trying to soothe herself with a view of the countryside rolling past. Arguing with Percy these days was pointless, and an outright refusal would only make him more stubborn. No, she had to try and stay calm, however much she wanted to scream.

Not that the rugged terrain was doing anything to steady her nerves. She was used to city life, to houses and shops and factories. This Yorkshire landscape was so different it felt strangely unnerving, as if the whole world had suddenly become bigger and wilder, as if she were losing control of every aspect of her life.

'You said we were going to visit Aunt Sophoria.'

'We are, but Charles has a house near Pickering too. I didn't lie.'

'You didn't say you'd been arranging a wedding behind my back!'

'*Discussing*, not arranging. Look, sis, you don't have to do anything you don't want to, but you might try to like him. He's quite sincere, you know, asked permission for your hand and everything.'

'He asked *you*?' Ianthe swung around incredulously, calm resolve forgotten. 'I'm twenty-one! I don't need your permission to marry.'

'I'm head of the family.'

'You're my brother, Percy, my *little* brother! I'm perfectly capable of making decisions on my own.'

'I thought it very good of him to come to me first.'

'Oh, don't be so pompous! You never used to be. That's his influence, too.'

'And you never used to be such a dowdy old spinster. You know you were quite pretty before you went to Bournemouth, but now it's impossible to tell behind that high collar and that awful hair. Do you have to scrape it back so tightly? You look such a prig.'

'You know I don't care for appearances.'

Ianthe twisted her face away quickly, catching an unwelcome glimpse of her reflection in the carriage window, of nondescript brown hair and matching, wide-set eyes. Doe eyes, her father had called them, though they seemed to have grown even bigger since his death. Now they looked almost unnaturally large in her narrow face, making the rest of her features appear too small by comparison.

'And do you have to wear grey *every* day?' Percy seemed to be warming to his theme. 'It's depressing.'

'We're only just out of mourning!'

'Exactly, *out* of mourning. I'd have thought you'd want to wear colour again. Personally, I don't know what Charles sees in you.'

'I wish he wouldn't see anything! And you needn't be so unchivalrous. We're not alone.'

She threw a pointed glance towards the man sitting opposite. He'd been asleep when they'd entered the compartment, his dark head resting casually against the windowpane, but Percy was doing nothing to keep his voice down and the last thing she wanted was an audience. Her situation was mortifying enough without it being aired in public.

Besides, she wasn't at all certain that their travelling companion was quite as unconscious as he'd first appeared. During Percy's last tirade, she thought she'd glimpsed a slight shift in his expression, an almost infinitesimal furrowing of his brows, as if he were offended on her behalf.

Had she imagined it or was he listening?

She narrowed her eyes, studying his profile as she watched for any further flicker of movement. Even asleep, he was quite strikingly handsome, with a straight nose, chiselled cheekbones and square jaw all framed by black, neatly trimmed hair. His skin was lightly tanned, as if he spent a lot of time outdoors, though judging by the expensive cut of his clothes he was also a gentleman—though surely a gentleman wouldn't eavesdrop quite so blatantly?

She must have imagined it.

'What?' Percy followed the direction of her gaze. 'Oh, he's asleep. And I doubt he'd be very interested in our little domestic drama even if he weren't.'

'You should still keep your voice down.'

'Why? If he wakes up, we can ask his opinion. I'm sure he'll agree with me. No man wants a wife who looks like an old maid.'

'I don't want anyone else's opinion. And don't you dare ask!'

'I'm only trying to help. If you don't marry Charles then I've done my best and that's that. You'll have to find someone else on your own and you'll never catch a husband looking like that. *Ow!*'

Ianthe shot her brother a venomous glare, slowly retracting the elbow she'd just jabbed violently into his ribs. She knew exactly how her appearance made her appear. That was the whole point. She didn't like her grey clothes or dowdy hairstyle any more than he did, but at least she couldn't be accused of drawing attention to herself. She couldn't be accused of anything untoward at all. This was who she was, who she *wanted* to be now, whether Percy or any other man liked it or not.

But his words still hurt, especially since the old Percy would never have been so cruel as to insult her. Since their mother's death from consumption the previous year, followed by their father's grief-stricken demise soon after, her brother's whole character seemed to have changed for the worse, his sunny disposition darkening the more time he spent with Sir Charles. Now she felt as though she hardly knew him at all. If she could only reach out to the old Percy, appeal to his better nature somehow...

'I just wish you'd told me the truth about this trip.' She tried not to sound too accusing. 'Can't we be honest with each other?'

Percy heaved a sigh. 'Look, Charles asked me not to tell you he'd be here. He said he wanted to surprise you, show you his house or something before he proposed. He spends most of his time in London, but he seems very proud of the place. That's why I didn't say anything until we reached Malton.'

'Because you knew I'd take the first train home, you mean.'

'That, too. But now we're here, can't you just look on it as a holiday? It must be at least ten years since we last visited Aunt Sophoria.'

'Twelve.'

Ianthe found herself relenting slightly. Their aunt hadn't been well enough to attend either of their parents' funerals, though her letters of condolence had been tender and thoughtful, even inviting her to move north, though Ianthe had known that her aged, impoverished relative could hardly afford to keep herself, let alone anyone else. Given what had happened afterwards, however, now she rather wished she'd accepted…

In any case, the thought of spending some time with Aunt Sophoria now was the one bright point on her horizon. Her memories of childhood holidays spent with their mother's sister were vague, but happy. Mostly she remembered a mass of lace and blonde ringlets enveloped in a cloud of sweet-smelling perfume.

'I'll be glad to see her again.'

'And she's agreed that you can stay as long as you want.'

'What do you mean?' The nostalgic feeling evaporated at once. 'I thought we were only staying a week.'

'Well…' Percy squirmed in his seat. 'The truth is, London's expensive. I can't afford lodgings for us both any more. And Charles thinks it's more appropriate for you to live with Aunt Sophoria anyway.'

'*Charles* thinks that?'

'Yes, but I agree. I should have seen the propriety of it sooner.'

'So you mean this—all of this—was *his* idea?'

'I suppose so, though it really just goes to show how much he cares for you. He's a capital fellow. You know Father thought so, too.'

'Father never suggested I marry him! And you know how Mother felt. She didn't even like being

in the same room with him if she could help it.
She always took me away, too.'

'Oh, you women and your prejudices!' Percy
rolled his eyes in exasperation. 'All I know is that
he's been very good to me this past year. He's
helped me out a lot with expenses.'

'You owe him *money*?'

'Just a little, though you needn't look so disapproving. It's not easy supporting both of us. I
know Father didn't mean to leave us in such a
sorry financial state, but he did. I had to pay the
bills somehow.'

'You can't blame Father.' Ianthe stiffened defensively. 'You know he was heartbroken after
Mother died.'

'He was irresponsible, letting all his invest-
ments go to ruin and leaving me to carry the
burden.'

'Burden?' She flinched. Was that all she was
now?

'I didn't mean it like that.' Percy at least had
the decency to look shame-faced. 'All I'm saying is that we need to be practical. We don't have
the income to carry on as we are. Marriage is the
only solution for a woman in your position and as
far as I can see you're not overwhelmed with suitors. That's why I brought you here to see Charles.'

Ianthe felt a roiling sensation deep in the pit
of her stomach, something between fear and disgust. She'd had her suspicions about the Baronet's

intentions—had made her own feelings on the subject abundantly clear, or so she'd thought—but she still hadn't expected him to stoop so low.

This was all a trick. No, worse than that, a trap. Sir Charles had manipulated Percy into bringing her here, cutting her off from her home and friends, isolating her in a remote northern town with only an impoverished maiden aunt for company, probably assuming that she'd be forced to marry him.

Well, she wouldn't be manipulated so easily. There had to be another alternative.

'I'll find employment.'

'Don't be ridiculous. After what happened last time?'

'That wasn't my fault!'

'So you keep saying. It's just a good job the family were discreet or your reputation would have been ruined. I'm only glad Charles didn't hear of it.'

Ianthe folded her arms mutinously, heartily wishing the opposite. 'It's not likely to happen again.'

'No.' Percy's gaze swept over her critically. 'I suppose not. But if getting a job doesn't work out, what then? You'll have nothing to fall back on. Marrying Charles is your best option, you must see that. You'll have money and protection and children, too, I suppose.'

'Children?' She spluttered the word in hor-

ror. The way Sir Charles looked at her was bad enough. The thought of him touching her made her skin crawl. As for having children...she wasn't exactly sure what that entailed, but she definitely didn't want to find out.

From a practical perspective, however, Percy was right—the Baronet was her best option. Life as a governess had been far more dispiriting than she'd expected and, after what had happened in Bournemouth, the thought of finding another position made her stomach twist with anxiety. *If* she could find another position... It had been hard enough the first time and it wasn't as if she could ask for references! If word of what had happened there got out, she'd be lucky ever to find employment again.

Besides, no matter how hard she tried, how severely she dressed or how distantly she behaved, nothing she did ever seemed to deter Sir Charles. He'd always looked at her strangely, ever since she was a child and he'd introduced himself as an old friend of her mother's, but since her death those looks seemed to have become more intense than ever. He'd gone abroad for a few months after the funeral, but since he'd come back, around the same time she'd returned from Bournemouth, he seemed to be always around Percy, always there, always watching her. There seemed to be no escaping him these days. She was tired of resisting, tired of trying to hide. And if Percy owed him money…surely it was her duty to help repay the debt, no matter what the cost to herself?

'This must be Rillington.' Percy leapt up as the train slowed to a halt. 'I'm going to get a newspaper. All this arguing is giving me a headache.'

'Wait!' She grabbed his hand as he passed by, making one last desperate appeal. 'There's just something about him. I can't explain it…'

'Well, whatever it is, it shouldn't bother you for long. Charles must be fifty at least.'

'Percy!' She dropped his hand at once. 'You shouldn't say such things! Someone might hear you.'

'Oh, I can't win!' He flung the compartment door open and jumped out. 'I won't be long. Just promise me that you'll think about it and be sensible.'

'If I do, will you promise to tell me the truth from now on?'

'Of course!' He was already striding away. 'Just remember, thirty years! You'll be a rich widow soon enough.'

Ianthe glared after him, seized with the impulse to follow, to grab her bag, leap down onto the platform and run away. But where would she go? Percy and her aunt were the only relatives she had left and now it seemed even they were conspiring against her. She fell back against her seat, watching her brother's retreating back, silently resenting his freedom. He never worried about how he behaved or how indiscreet he sounded. He never worried about censure at all. How could the rules for men and women be so different? At least no one else had been around to overhear his last remark.

She gave a sudden guilty start, sitting bolt upright again as she met the steely gaze of the man sitting opposite. He hadn't moved, hadn't so much as lifted his head, but he was wide awake now, looking straight at her with an expression of brooding, almost ferocious intensity. This time there was no mistaking the frown on his stern features. He looked furious.

'You're awake.' She found herself stating the obvious.

'As you can see.'

She blinked, taken aback by the scathing tone of his deep, northern-accented voice. He was leaning back in his seat without making even the slightest attempt to sit up, as if she were so far beneath his contempt that there was no need for propriety, the look in his eyes even more insulting than his manner. She felt her mouth turn dry. Besides Sir Charles, no man had looked at her so intently for a long time. In her new, drab garb she'd started to think herself almost invisible to the opposite sex, but now this stranger's pale gaze seemed to bore straight through her.

Quickly, she glanced out of the window, but

there was no sign of Percy. Typical of him to be indiscreet and then leave her to clear up the mess! Clearly this man had overheard some, if not all, of their conversation after all. Now it looked as though he were about to rebuke *her* for it. Well, she was in no mind for a lecture, especially not today.

'Sir.' She lifted her chin up defensively. 'I beg you to forget anything you might have overheard. It was a private conversation.'

'Then perhaps you ought not to have held it in a public carriage.'

'A gentleman ought not to eavesdrop.'

'I could hardly help it. I should think the whole locomotive could hear your brother's voice.'

She felt her cheeks flush scarlet with mortification. Even if that were true, which she was afraid it might be, he ought not to mention it. What kind of a gentleman was he?

'My brother shouldn't have been so indiscreet. But as you doubtless heard, I already reprimanded him.'

'Was that a reprimand?' Grey eyes regarded her mockingly. 'It sounded as if you were more afraid of having your little scheme overheard.'

Scheme? She opened her mouth to protest and then closed it again. Now that she thought of it, she'd only told Percy to be quiet. She hadn't contradicted him at all. No wonder this man assumed the worst, though he still had no right to chastise her. They hadn't been introduced and she was a lady sitting on her own. They shouldn't even be talking, let alone arguing.

She folded her hands primly in her lap. 'I do not have a scheme, sir.'

'Except to marry a man you dislike for his money and then wish for his imminent demise. What would you call that but a scheme?'

'I'd say you know nothing about it. And since you care so little for good manners, I might add that appearances can be deceptive. You, for example, look like a gentleman, yet you very clearly are not.'

'Perhaps not, though I've been called far worse, I assure you.'

'I don't doubt it. But my affairs are none of your business.'

'On the contrary.' A shadow darkened his face. 'I think it every man's business to know that women like you exist.'

'*Women like me?*' An icy chill raced down her spine. What did *that* mean? How could he know what kind of woman she was? How could he possibly tell?

'Schemers. Deceivers. Women who say one thing to a man's face and another behind his back.' He let his gaze drop contemptuously, as if he were studying her from head to toe and finding her wanting. 'You don't even have the decency to speak well of your quarry. At least I

know what I am. You still think yourself a lady,
I suppose?'

He turned his face away, staring out of the
window as she gazed into thin air, speechless
with shock. How was it possible? After everything she'd done to alter her appearance, to alter
herself, how could he still look at her and call
her a schemer?

She caught her breath, struggling against the
old familiar feelings of shame and self-loathing.
She'd been called a schemer once before, had
tried to plead her innocence then, too, not that it
had made any difference. Was everything they'd
said about her in Bournemouth true, then? Was
there something so bad, so inherently corrupt in
her nature that even a stranger could see it?

No! Her mind resisted the idea. And even if
there was, it wasn't intentional. She wasn't the
one scheming against Sir Charles. She didn't
want anything to do with him at all. He was the
one scheming against *her*! And how dare this
stranger speak to her so abominably, as if she
were the most shame-faced fortune-hunter he'd
ever laid eyes on. Whoever he was, he had no
right to judge!

'Yes,' she began angrily, 'I do call myself a
lady. At least as much as you're a gentleman. And
if you'd been paying closer attention or given me
the slightest benefit of the doubt, you'd know that

I have no desire and certainly no intention of marrying Sir Charles!'

'*Sir* Charles?' The stranger turned his head sharply at the end of her speech, having continued to stare out of the window for most of it. 'You mean Charles *Lester*?'

Ianthe bit her tongue, realising her mistake a few seconds too late. Was it possible that they hadn't mentioned his identity earlier? No, now that she thought of it, Percy always referred to him as Charles, while she avoided his name altogether. Not that there was any point in denying it now.

She nodded cautiously as the stranger ran a hand through his hair, muttering something indistinguishable under his breath.

'Do you know him, sir?'

'We're acquainted.'

'Oh.'

She waited, hardly knowing whether to feel guilty or relieved. For once, it seemed as though Percy's behaviour would have consequences. If this man were acquainted with Sir Charles, then doubtless he'd tell him everything they'd just said. On the other hand, embarrassing as it was, it would solve her dilemma. After such a public condemnation, the Baronet would probably never want to see her again.

Perhaps it hadn't been such a terrible mistake after all…

'In that case…' the stranger leaned forward suddenly, resting his forearms on his knees as he bent closer towards her '…I believe I ought to retract my last comments. I overheard half a conversation and reacted badly. I believe I came in somewhere around the time you were denouncing your brother as pompous and then I could hardly intrude without embarrassing you.' He frowned, as if admitting something against his will. 'But it was wrong of me, I ought to have announced myself. I wasn't trying to listen, but your brother's last words…' He shook his head regretfully. 'I apologise unreservedly.'

Ianthe blinked in bewilderment, stunned by such a marked transformation. The stranger's voice was still terse, but the ferocious scowl and derisive curl of his lip were gone, as if the focus of his anger had simply shifted elsewhere. What had happened? A moment ago he'd seemed to despise the very sight of her and now he was apologising? The only difference was that he'd learnt the identity of her suitor.

The realisation was distinctly unsettling.

'You have a poor opinion of Sir Charles then?' She hardly dared ask.

'None that I'd care to repeat.'

'Under the circumstances, I believe I have a right to know.'

He shook his head, looking out of the window with a brooding expression. 'As I said, we're only acquaintances. Most of what I know is second-hand and I don't care for gossip.'

'You just called me a schemer, sir,' she snapped. 'I don't see why you should start being reticent now.'

He looked back towards her then, his gaze newly appraising, and she found herself smoothing her hands over the folds of her dress self-consciously. What was he looking at? What was he thinking? Not that she cared what he thought of her, but the piercing gleam in those ironclad eyes disturbed her somehow. Still, if he thought he could avoid giving her an answer, he could think again...

She lifted her chin, determined not to yield. 'If you want me to forgive you, then you might at least have the decency to tell me the truth.'

A single black eyebrow quirked upwards. 'What does it matter if you intend to refuse him?'

'It matters because my brother spends a great deal of time in his company. If there's something unsuitable about Sir Charles, then I'd like to know about it.'

He nodded his head slightly, her words seeming to convince him at last. 'Very well, then. I think he's a lecher and a gambler, though rich enough, I grant you. I wouldn't blame any woman for objecting to such an alliance.'

'Even a woman like me?'

A muscle jumped in his jaw. 'Forgive me, I

misspoke. My anger was mainly directed at your brother, but when I opened my eyes, he'd already gone. I'm afraid I took my temper out on the wrong person. I beg you to forget what I said.'

'Forget?' She stared at him incredulously. 'You think it so easy to forget such words?'

'No. Perhaps not.' His gaze flickered momentarily. 'My only excuse is that I've had a difficult morning. I felt provoked.'

'And that's supposed to be an apology?' She gave a curt laugh. Difficult morning or not, he had no right to vent his bad temper on her. She already had Percy's insults to contend with. She didn't need some stranger's as well!

'It's an explanation. You have to admit your brother's words were callous in the extreme.'

'My brother is young and sometimes foolish, but he wants what's best for me.'

'By forcing you to marry a man like Lester? Yes, he sounds an ideal brother.'

'He's not forcing me to do anything! You don't know anything about it. *Or* us. Our financial circumstances are such that—'

She stopped mid-sentence, wondering why she was even bothering to argue. None of this was his business. There was no need to defend either herself *or* Percy. Except that she felt a strange desire to explain herself, if only to get the matter clear in her own mind.

'My brother wishes to see me settled and financially secure, that's all. Not that I'd expect a man of means to understand that.'

The stranger's lips twisted scornfully. 'Not all men are born with means. Some of us make our own way without selling our sisters.'

'How dare you!' She felt her temper snap, her voice rising with anger. How dare he suggest something so monstrous, as if Percy would barter her off simply to pay back his debts and free himself from the responsibility of providing for her! Even if there *was* a grain of truth to the accusation, she refused to believe that her brother was so heartless! He was just young, that was all…

'I speak as I find.'

'Then you're no gentleman, sir. You're a disgrace to the word! And I'd be grateful if you'd keep the rest of your thoughts to yourself.'

She swung away, chest heaving, half-relieved, half-dismayed by her outburst. Not that he didn't deserve such censure, but if he was no gentleman, then she was certainly no lady to behave in such an unrestrained, uncontrolled manner. Maybe what they'd said about her in Bournemouth was true after all…

'Tell me, is it marriage itself you object to or Sir Charles in particular?'

She turned back towards him, eyes widening in disbelief. Why was he still talking? Why couldn't he just leave her alone? He sounded infuriatingly calm, not the slightest bit offended by her insults.

'I believe I asked you to be quiet, sir.'

'No, you asked me to keep my thoughts to myself. Hence my interest in yours.'

'You're impertinent!'

A hint of sardonic amusement crossed his features. 'I think we passed impertinent a long time ago. But since we've already established that I'm not a true gentleman and since I'd like to make amends for my behaviour, I have a proposal for you.'

'A proposal?' She repeated the word suspiciously.

'A business proposition, if you prefer. Something that might benefit both of us.'

Out of the corner of her eye, she caught a glimpse of Percy strolling back along the platform towards them, whistling and swinging a newspaper in one hand. There was no time for this. Whatever the stranger's proposal was, it was too late to hear it. She had to conclude this bizarre, indiscreet, utterly inappropriate conversation as quickly as possible.

'I've no interest in anything else you have to say, sir.'

'You won't hear me out?'

'My brother is returning. I beg you to say no more on the subject. On *any* subject.'

'Shame.' He looked nonplussed. 'I was prepared to offer you an alternative to Sir Charles.'

She froze. Was he offering her employment? He sounded sincere, but why would he offer to help her? Was this some kind of cruel joke or just another veiled insult?

'What kind of alternative?' she couldn't resist asking.

'What I said, a business proposition.'

'I know nothing of business, sir. I was a governess.' She regarded him dubiously. 'Do you *need* a governess?'

'Yes, as it happens. Though I was thinking of something a little more permanent.'

'A companion for your mother, perhaps?'

'My mother is dead.' He leaned back in his seat, adopting the same casual posture in which she'd first seen him.

'Your sister, then?' She glanced anxiously out of the window. Percy was only a few paces away.

'I don't have a sister, so far as I know anyway.'

'Then what?' she burst out in exasperation as Percy's hand reached for the door handle. Why couldn't he just get to the point? 'What do you *need*, sir?'

'The position is with me.' He smiled suddenly, transforming his features from simply striking to quite devastatingly, heart-stoppingly handsome. 'I need a wife.'

Chapter Two

Robert Felstone was aware that he'd been acting badly.

He'd boarded the train in a ferocious temper that had only deteriorated the further they'd travelled. He hadn't intended to listen, had feigned sleep in order to be alone with his own troubled thoughts, but the conversation taking place opposite had first disturbed and then enraged him. After Louisa's refusal of his marriage proposal that morning every word had felt like a fresh insult.

He'd tried his best to ignore it, but the unseen woman's antipathy towards her suitor had struck a raw nerve. Was that how Louisa had talked about him behind his back? Had she been secretly repelled by his visits even as she'd batted her eyelashes so convincingly?

The memory of their interview still made his blood boil. If it hadn't been for Louisa's flirting, he would never have even considered proposing, yet she'd had the nerve to imply—no, more than that, to actually *say*—he wasn't good enough. He'd thought success in business had earned him a place in society, a modicum of respect at least, but apparently that wasn't the case. He was just as disreputable now as he'd always been. He was the only fool who hadn't known it.

Back on the train, half-listening, half-fuming over his rejection, he'd become increasingly irate, interpreting every word from his own injured perspective, taking the side of the beleaguered suitor before finally venting his anger on the unfortunate would-be bride. He'd been offensive, improper and unforgivably rude, as if Louisa's comments about his past had actually stripped away the veneer of respectability he'd worked so hard to attain.

It was only when he'd learned the mysterious suitor's identity that he'd finally come to his senses, anger turning at once to agreement. Lester's name had changed everything, but by then the damage had been done. He'd done what he'd always sworn he would never do and judged a woman without knowing her whole story, as if he had any right to play judge and jury.

And then he'd proposed. What the hell was he doing?

He leaned back in his seat, folding one leg casually over the other as he watched the rapid interplay of emotions on his travelling companion's face. Judging by the combination of shock and outrage, a passer-by might reasonably assume he'd just propositioned rather than proposed to her. Which in one sense, he supposed, he had. They hadn't even been introduced and here he was suggesting a far more intimate relationship. No wonder she looked so appalled. He didn't even know her name.

'Just in time.' The brother bounded back into the carriage just as the stationmaster's whistle blew. 'I say, sis, are you hot? You look like a beetroot.'

'I…' She looked vaguely surprised to see him. 'A little warm, that's all.'

She raised both hands to her cheeks, still peering warily through her fingers as if afraid they were trapped in a carriage with a madman. Robert felt tempted to laugh. Given his recent behaviour, it was a reasonable assumption. He was almost starting to question his sanity himself. He'd spent twenty-six years specifically *not* thinking about marriage and now he'd made two proposals in one day.

Was he out of his mind?

He frowned, seriously considering the question. Had his pride been so badly injured by Louisa that he'd felt the need to propose to the very next woman he met? Or was he so unaccustomed to hearing the word *no* that he'd had to keep going until he got the answer he wanted? It was just the kind of reckless, impulsive behaviour he might have expected from his younger self, not the sensible, respectable man of business he was today. After all the time and thought he'd put into deciding whether or not to ask Louisa, was he really prepared to jump to the furthest extreme and marry a complete stranger?

What if she said yes?

The brother dropped into the seat opposite and Robert gave a polite nod, wishing he could throw a fist at his jaw instead. Now that the woman's situation was clearer he felt angrier towards the youth than ever. If he were really friends with Lester, then surely he knew what kind of a man he was, especially where women were concerned. What kind of brother actively encouraged his sister to marry such a reprobate?

The idea of offering her an alternative had come to him out of the blue, somewhere around the time she'd demanded to know his real opinion of Charles Lester. It had been an impulse, a desire to make amends for his insulting behaviour, combined with a determination to put Louisa behind him and get his affairs settled once and for all, but then he was accustomed to trusting his impulses. His business instincts had never steered him wrong before, and wasn't marriage a business? When one deal didn't work out, he moved on to another.

It wasn't as if he'd ever expected to marry for love. Growing up with his mother had taught him the folly of that particular emotion. He'd done his best to act the lovesick swain for Louisa, though in truth he'd found the pretence as tedious as the rest of their courtship. Perhaps that had been his mistake, trying to speak a language he didn't understand. *Business*, he did understand. Business, he was good at it. In his domain, no one could ever accuse him of not being good enough.

In which case, why not take emotion out of the equation and treat marriage strictly as a business arrangement? He had neither the time nor inclination for a new courtship, and this woman seemed more than a little reluctant to wed Sir Charles. It was the perfect business proposal, a mutually beneficial arrangement for them both. He was in the market for a wife, she for a husband. He'd thought to make a society match, but since Louisa had made it abundantly clear that no lady of any social standing would have him, asking this stranger had seemed the obvious thing to do.

Somehow, insanely, it still did.

Even if she *was* the strangest-looking damsel in distress he'd ever seen. With his eyes closed, he'd assumed the brother's insults had been exaggerated to hurt her feelings, but first impressions made it difficult to argue. It *was* hard to imagine what Sir Charles saw in her. Her clothes were so old-fashioned they seemed to belong to another era, every item a drab, uniform grey that did nothing for her wan complexion. Her collar was so high it looked as if it must surely constrict her breathing, while the rest of her gown was completely shapeless, hanging loose around her waist with almost no definition at all. Combined with an ancient-looking poke bonnet, woollen gloves, a shawl that might better serve as a dishcloth and a pair of heavy lace-up boots, she seemed determined to look as severe and dowdy as possible.

Ungallant as it sounded, she wasn't exactly the bride he'd envisaged when he'd set out that morning. Louisa, with her golden curls and indigo-blue eyes, was the most exquisitely beautiful creature he'd ever laid eyes on. This woman looked as though she never even glanced in a mirror. Side by side they might resemble an old crow next to a glamorous swan.

After Louisa's rejection, on the other hand, the very contrast was appealing. Besides which, there was no trace of meanness in her face, no hint of Louisa's sulkiness or petulance. It was a pleasant face, albeit a trifle too thin, a fact accentuated by the severity of her hairstyle, scraped back so tightly that he could hardly distinguish the colour, a nondescript shade somewhere between blonde and brown. But her skin was clear, her lips full and wide, and there were even faint lines curving upwards from the corners of her eyes as if, difficult though it was to imagine, she was accustomed to laughter. Overall, she might be quite pretty, if she hadn't clearly resolved to be otherwise.

'It's only twenty minutes to Pickering.' The brother seemed blithely unaware of any tension in the compartment. 'So the porter says.'

'A little longer.' Robert interrupted smoothly, glad of the chance to prove his respectability, if not his sanity, at least. 'Forgive my intrusion, but the new deviation line to Whitby has only just opened. It's a longer route so it's caused a few delays along the branch line, but some of the porters still forget.'

'The new line takes longer than the old one?' The youth sounded scornful. 'That doesn't sound like progress.'

Robert allowed himself a cynical half-smile. What was it the sister had called him? Pompous. The word seemed particularly apt.

'It's much safer than the old rope-worked system at Beckhole. It's a steep hill and there have been several bad accidents there over the years. The new route is safer.'

'Ah…well, when you put it like that.' The youth nodded sagely. 'Are you connected to the railway, sir?'

'I'm on the board of directors.' Robert smiled, gratified to see the woman's head twist slightly towards him, as if she were reviewing an earlier opinion.

'Indeed? Then I'm glad to meet you. My name's Percy Holt.'

'Robert Felstone, delighted to meet you.'

'Felstone? Have we met before, sir? Your name seems familiar, but I can't place it.'

'I don't think so. Unless…perhaps you visit the area often?'

'No, not for a long time, though we used to come every summer as children. Our mother was from Pickering. We're going to stay with our aunt there now.' The youth gestured towards the woman almost as an afterthought. 'This is my sister, Miss Ianthe Holt.'

'A pleasure, Miss Holt.'

He offered a hand, wondering if she would take it. She could hardly refuse to acknowledge him without telling her brother what had just happened and, from what he'd observed of their relationship, he didn't think she was about to do that. Besides, for some strange reason he found himself actually wanting to touch her, to find out if she were really as buttoned-up as she seemed. She looked so strait-laced that he felt an unexpected desire to ruffle her up.

'Mr Felstone.' She extended a hand, letting it drift vaguely in his direction before retracting it again quickly.

Robert felt a powerful urge to laugh. He wasn't accustomed to women expressing anything other than gratitude for his attention. Even Louisa, insincere as she'd apparently been, had seemed flattered by it. This woman looked as though she wanted to throw him from the train. Was she still angry over his earlier comments or did she simply doubt the sincerity of his proposal? he wondered. And in the latter case…how could he convince her?

'Ianthe. That's an unusual name.'

He flashed his most charming smile. Even during his penniless youth, he'd quickly discovered the disarming effects of his good looks upon women. Since earning his fortune, these seemed to have increased tenfold, though he suspected this woman might prove more of a challenge.

'It's from a poem.' Her expression didn't alter.

'Ah. There are gaps in my education, I'm afraid. I never studied poetry.'

'You amaze me.' She didn't bother to hide the sarcasm. 'It teaches men refinement, I think. Or at least how to speak to a lady.'

'Ianthe!' Percy sounded shocked. 'Forgive my sister, Mr Felstone. We've travelled all the way from London today. She must be tired.'

'On the contrary—' she glared at her brother acerbically '—I'm feeling quite fresh. There's no need to speak for me.'

Robert bit back a smile. No, it seemed the prim and proper Miss Holt—he was glad to know her name at last—wouldn't be so easy to charm at all. Somehow the thought made her all the more appealing. But the train was already slowing into Pickering station. If he was going to convince her, he didn't have much time.

'Wait a minute!' The brother held up his newspaper suddenly, pointing to the headline. '"Felstone's of Whitby awarded new naval contract." I knew I recognised your name from somewhere! Are you connected to the shipbuilding family, sir?'

'I am that family, I'm afraid. All there is of it anyway.'

'So you're on your way to Whitby?'

'Eventually, though I'm staying in Pickering for a few days. There's to be a public gala and private ball celebrating the official opening of the new railway line tomorrow. I'd be happy to add your names to the invitation list if you wish?'

'I don't travel with a ball gown, sir.' Miss Holt sounded distinctly unimpressed.

'Well, I'd be delighted.' The youth threw her an icy look. 'I'm afraid my sister prefers books to dancing these days. I expect she'd rather visit the castle.'

'Indeed?' An image of Sir Charles flashed into Robert's mind. 'You like old things, then?'

Doe eyes flashed back. 'I enjoy history, Mr Felstone. I don't enjoy being mocked.'

'I'm quite serious, I assure you, Miss Holt. I'm rarely anything but.'

She made a scornful sound. 'I find that hard

to believe from a man whose manner can change so completely. Just now, for example, I had the impression that you were angry and yet here we all are, the best of friends.'

'Make enquiries in the town about me if you wish.'

'You overestimate my interest, sir.'

'Ianthe!' The brother's mouth dropped open. 'What's the matter with you?'

'With me?' She swung towards him, two crimson spots appearing high up on her cheekbones. 'You're the one who can't keep his thoughts to himself! This is all *your* fault.'

'My fault? I apologise, Mr Felstone, I don't know what she's talking about, but I'm sure she meant no offence.'

'I'm sure she did not.' Robert waved his apology away as the train gave a final burst of steam and shuddered to a halt.

'And I'm sure I did!'

She stood up abruptly, grabbing a carpet bag from the rail above her head and swinging it in front of her like a shield. 'Good day, Mr Felstone. I doubt our paths will meet again. Our stay is of only a very short duration and our diary is fully *engaged.*'

'Ah.' Robert bent his head in acknowledgement. She could hardly have made her answer any clearer. 'In that case I wish you well. Whatever you decide.'

She didn't reply, flinging open the compartment door and storming furiously away.

'I say…' The brother jumped down after her, turning at the last moment with a look of apology. 'Sorry about that. Women, you know. But if you're serious about the ball, I'd be very grateful.'

Robert nodded absently, a faint smile playing around his lips as he watched her grey dress disappear into the crowd. Common sense told him he ought to feel relieved by her refusal. He knew almost nothing about her, and hadn't the brother mentioned some impropriety? Still, it was hard to imagine anything too shocking about her, nothing scandalous for certain. And there was definitely something about her, something that grabbed and held his attention. He wasn't sure—couldn't even imagine—what it was, but it made him reluctant to concede defeat so easily. She was… He strove for the right word… Interesting.

He picked up his top hat and suitcase and stepped down from the carriage. The platform was crowded, heaving with passengers and luggage, the walls and metal-beamed ceiling decorated with banners for the approaching gala. He made his way steadily through the throng, nodding to various acquaintances without stopping to speak, his mind preoccupied with the image of a woman in a grey dress.

'Ah, Felstone, you're here at last!' A cheerful-looking man with a shock of unruly blond hair accosted him the moment he stepped into the station office. 'Come and read this speech, will you?'

Robert smiled and put down his case, leaning against a desk as he scanned quickly through a sheath of papers. 'It's good, Giles. Just don't forget to thank us all for our patience.'

'Too long, then?'

'Maybe a page or two, but I'm sure you'll do a splendid job.'

The other man made a harrumphing noise. 'I wish I shared your confidence. Couldn't you do it instead? You're far better at public speaking than I am.'

'You're the engineer.'

'Exactly. I'd rather be working on the line than talking about it. Why does everything we do have to be celebrated with banners and bunting?'

'Not to mention a ball.'

Giles groaned aloud. 'Don't remind me. Kitty's been talking about it non-stop all week. By the by, she told me something very interesting about you at breakfast.'

'Really?' Robert kept his gaze fixed on the papers.

'Seemed to think you were on the verge of matrimony with Louisa Allendon.'

'Trust me, Giles, if I were you'd be the first to know.'

'So it's not true, then? Pity. Kitty was quite

excited. Thought we could have dinner parties or something.'

'Then I'm sorry to disappoint her, though as it happens, she was half-right. The lady simply decided against me.'

'She refused you?' Giles's eyebrows almost vanished into his hairline. 'But she's been flirting with you for months!'

'I had that impression, too, but it appears I'm not quite respectable enough. Not respectable at all, apparently. Certain things about my past—my parentage—were disagreeable to her.'

'Ridiculous!' Giles looked outraged on his behalf. 'It's not as if any of it was your fault!'

Robert smiled and put a hand on his friend's shoulder. 'It was foolish of me to think anyone had forgotten. It seems wealth and success allow access to society, not acceptance.'

'The woman's a fool!'

'In any case, I'm sure Kitty will be able to tell you everything in a few days, probably more than I know myself. In the meantime, we have a gala and ball to endure.'

He strode across to the window, putting the subject firmly behind him, searching the street below for any sign of a grey dress. Where had Miss Holt been going when she'd stormed away? The brother had mentioned an aunt…

'Is that Charles Lester?' His gaze sharpened suddenly.

'Mmm?' Giles came to stand at his side. 'Oh, yes, he arrived in town yesterday. I played cards with him in the Swan last night. Seemed very pleased with himself despite the fact he was losing.'

'What about?'

'Didn't say. Something about a woman, most likely.' Giles did an abrupt double take. 'I say, don't be too bothered.'

'What?'

'You were scowling. I said, don't be too bothered about Louisa.'

'Oh. No, I wasn't thinking about her.'

He moved away from the window, turning his back firmly on Charles Lester. The Baronet represented the very worst of his class. Arrogant, entitled, not to mention a notorious womaniser. His reputation was near legendary, almost as much as his own father's had been, his conquests usually women without protectors or ones poor enough to be paid off afterwards. The orphaned, impoverished Miss Holt seemed to fit the bill exactly, though the brother had definitely said he wanted to marry her. Not that she seemed like his usual type of woman. Like *anyone's* type, for that matter.

Still, the thought of the strait-laced Miss Holt in Sir Charles's clutches made him feel inexplicably angry. After his own behaviour that morning, he felt strangely protective towards her, as if he'd somehow become responsible for her well-being. Not that he could help her if she wouldn't let him. He'd asked her to marry him, for pity's sake! He could hardly make any more amends than that…

'I say, are you sure you're all right?' Giles peered at him thoughtfully. 'You seem preoccupied. Nothing wrong at the shipyard, I hope?'

'No, they don't need me for a few days.' His lips curved wryly. 'It's just a new proposal I'm working on.'

'Need any help?'

'No, though there is something Kitty could do.'

'Whatever you need. You know she's half-smitten with you.'

'Only half?'

'Very funny. It's not fair that some men have good looks and fortune.'

'Not enough for Louisa Allendon, apparently.'

'I always thought she was flighty. What did you see in her anyway? Besides her more obvious attractions, I wouldn't have thought the two of you well suited.'

Robert drew his brows together, surprised by his friend's acuity. Now that he thought about it, it was hard to remember what his exact motives had been. He'd simply had the feeling that it was time to marry and Louisa had been beautiful, charming and accomplished, not to mention well connected.

'It seemed a good match, socially. She's from

an old family and you know her father was close friends with mine...'

His voice trailed away as he realised what he was saying. Was that the real reason he'd proposed to her, then, to prove a point to his dead father? Fool. It was too late for that, five years too late. The very idea was ludicrous. Not to mention grossly unfair on Louisa. If it hadn't been for the manner of her refusal, he might have owed her an apology, too.

How could he have been so blind?

'Ah.' Giles sounded sympathetic. 'Well, she couldn't have done any better, if you ask me.'

'You're a good friend.' Robert pushed the memory of his father aside, burying it along with any thought of Louisa. As for what she'd said, what the whole of society apparently said about him behind his back, he wasn't going to accept *that* so lightly. He wasn't going to accept it at all.

'Did you know that old Harper's thinking of selling?'

'Eh?' Giles looked startled by the sudden change of subject. 'You mean his shipyard?'

'So I hear.'

'Well, I never. I thought the old boy would go on for ever. Though you know what he's like. He'll never find a buyer he approves of. No one's ever going to be good enough.'

'Especially not me.'

'He's traditional. He definitely won't sell to a bachelor, I'm afraid. Family values and all that.'

'That's what I thought.'

Robert rubbed his chin thoughtfully. He already owned the largest shipyard in Whitby. If he bought Harper's, then he'd have one of the largest on the east coast, in the country even. It was doable, not to mention a way of proving his worth *without* society's help. He smiled slowly. If Louisa and society didn't think he was good enough to join them, then he'd demand their respect instead—show them all just what an illegitimate upstart son could achieve *without* their help. He'd be the perfect model of respectability, with more power and influence than his father had ever had.

And he'd start by marrying the most sensible, respectable-looking woman he could find, one that Harper would definitely approve of.

Miss Holt. He'd never seen a woman *less* likely to cause scandal. She was exactly the sort of wife he needed, a helpmeet, not an ornament, one who could fit unobtrusively into his busy life with the minimum of fuss or distraction, leaving him free to deal with his expanding business concerns. She wasn't flirtatious or hysterical or highly strung, hadn't burst into tears or tried to ingratiate herself with him when he'd accused her of being a schemer. On the contrary, she'd given as good as she'd got, had a mind of her own and no fear of speaking it. No, the more he thought of it, the more the strait-laced, straight-talking Miss Holt seemed to be just what he needed, a far more suitable bride than Louisa had ever been.

But she'd said no. As proposals went, it was hard to imagine one going much worse. He could hardly blame her for refusing him. No reasonable woman would accept such a proposal from a stranger who'd just insulted her to her face.

On the other hand, a desperate one might. Just how desperate to avoid marrying Lester was she? he wondered. He had a day to find out. Time enough to convince her to reconsider. And he knew exactly how to start.

'I'll see you tonight.' He clapped a hand on Giles's shoulder, already making for the exit. 'Is Kitty at home?'

'I think so, but what about the speech?'

'We'll discuss it at dinner. I have something important to do first.'

Giles looked taken aback. 'With my wife?'

'I need some information.' Robert threw a grin over his shoulder. 'Then I need to take her shopping.'

Chapter Three

'Are you awake, dear?'

Ianthe opened her eyes, momentarily blinded by the expanse of colour that greeted her. Where was she? In a bedroom she didn't recognise, daubed and draped in such an overwhelming shade of rose-petal pink that she could hardly distinguish one object from another. With the sun streaming in through open curtains, the whole room seemed to be blushing.

'Ianthe?'

She rubbed her eyes, disoriented after such a deep sleep. She had the vague impression that the curtains had been closed only a moment before, but who had opened them? Who was that calling her name? The voice seemed to come from close by...

She yelped, catching sight of a small face, half-hidden beneath a huge frilly nightcap, peering down at her.

'Aunt Sophoria!'

'Oh, good, you're awake.' The face beamed. 'I didn't mean to startle you, but I was starting to worry.'

Ianthe put a hand to her chest, trying to calm her now frantically pounding heartbeat. 'How long have I been asleep?'

'Almost since you arrived.'

Her aunt bustled across the room and then back again, bearing a cup of tea in one hand and a plate of macaroons in the other, before perching precariously on the side of the bed.

'Here we are. I bought these as a treat for us last night, but since you were indisposed, we'll have them for breakfast instead.'

'Thank you.' Ianthe accepted the tea gratefully. 'I'm sorry I ruined our arrival, Aunt, but Percy and I had the most dreadful quarrel.'

'So I gathered. You were quite overwrought when you got here.'

'Oh...' Her cheeks flushed as memories of the day before came flooding back. She'd collapsed into her aunt's arms on the doorstep, still reeling from the shock of Percy's deception and Mr Felstone's so-called proposal. 'I'm sorry.'

'Nonsense! You've given the neighbours something to talk about. They'll be thrilled.' Hazel eyes twinkled mischievously. 'So I sent you off to bed and Percy to stay at the Swan. I had intended for him to use this room while you shared with me, but it seemed like you needed some peace. Besides, I didn't like the way he was talking to you. Takes after your father's side of the family, that one.'

Ianthe smiled, trying to imagine her brother in such a vibrantly pink bedroom. Now that she was getting used to the colour, she was starting to like it, as if she were a little girl back in the nursery. It felt like a safe haven, a space of her own again—a home. That was all she wanted in life now, a place to hide from the world. But she still owed her aunt an explanation for her behaviour. If only she knew where to begin...

'It wasn't entirely Percy's fault, Aunt. I behaved very badly.'

'Oh, I doubt that. Have a macaroon.'

'You don't understand.' She took a deep, faltering breath. 'He wants me to marry Charles Lester.'

'Lester?' Aunt Sophoria paused with a biscuit halfway to her lips. 'That vain old buffoon? Don't be ridiculous.'

'You don't like him?'

'Never have, never could. He used to hang around your mother when she was a girl, too. I used to chase him away then. What on earth is Percy thinking?'

'They've become close this past year. That's why Percy brought me here. They arranged it together.'

'Ah. I did wonder about your brother's sudden enthusiasm for visiting me after ten years. So Lester's in on it, then?'

Ianthe lifted her shoulders and then dropped them again despairingly. 'Percy says he's going to propose, but I don't understand it. I've done nothing to encourage him and it's not as if I have money or connections. It can't be love, I'm sure of it.'

'Love?' Her aunt chewed on a macaroon thoughtfully. 'No, love isn't a sentiment I'd associate with Charles Lester.'

'He scares me, Aunt.' She gave an involuntary shudder, trying to put all the things she'd scarcely dared think about into words. 'He watches me so intently all the time, like he's hungry, but as if it's not really me he's looking at either. It's like it's me, but not me that he wants. I don't know how else to explain it.'

Aunt Sophoria screwed up her mouth for a moment before patting her hand reassuringly. 'Well, if you don't like him then that's an end to it and we'll tell your brother so together. As for Lester, don't worry, I know how to handle him.'

Ianthe put down her tea, flinging her arms around her aunt's neck with a sob of relief. 'Oh, thank you, Aunt. I was so afraid you'd agree with Percy.'

'As if I ever could!' Aunt Sophoria gave her

a tight squeeze. 'Honestly, men! I ought to box both their ears.'

Ianthe laughed before sitting back again with a guilty expression. 'That wasn't all I was upset about, I'm afraid. You see, there was another man on the train.'

An image of Mr Felstone's sternly handsome features flashed before her eyes, making her hesitate. Perhaps it was better *not* to tell her aunt about him. In the cold light of day the whole thing sounded ridiculous, as if she'd simply imagined it. Was it *possible* that she'd somehow misunderstood his proposal? That she'd been so angry that she'd somehow…misheard?

She frowned, thinking over their argument. No, he'd definitely called her a schemer before he'd asked her to marry him. A business proposal, he'd called it, though surely he couldn't have been serious. No sane man would suggest such a thing to a woman he'd only just met, no gentleman certainly. And yet…he'd seemed sane. He'd even seemed like a gentleman. So why had he said it? At the time she'd assumed that he'd been mocking her, taking advantage of their isolated situation to make fun of her dowdy appearance. Now, after a solid night's sleep, she felt more confused than ever.

'You mean Mr Felstone?' Aunt Sophoria picked up the last macaroon and popped it between her lips.

Ianthe's mouth dropped open. 'How do you know that?'

'Percy told me that part.'

'So you know I quarrelled with him, too?'

'Oh, yes, but I wouldn't worry about it. Mr Felstone's very civil, nothing if not a gentleman. I'm sure he won't hold it against you.'

'Civil?'

'A bit stern, perhaps, but charming when he wants to be. The older I get, the more invisible I seem to become, especially to men, but Mr Felstone's always very attentive. He's considered quite the catch around here despite his background, not that anyone's managed to land him just yet.'

Ianthe gaped at her aunt, slack-jawed in disbelief. *Civil* and *charming* were the last words she would have used to describe him. Did the man have an evil twin, perhaps? If he were even half the gentleman her aunt seemed to think, then surely he wouldn't have made fun of her so callously, not unless...

She shook her head, resisting the idea. It was impossible. His proposal *couldn't* have been genuine...*could* it?

She racked her brains, searching for another alternative. 'But is he quite sane, do you think?'

'Sane? I should think so. He's a self-made man, owns the biggest shipyard in Whitby, not to mention a whole fleet of merchant vessels. I think he might have something to do with the new iron-works, too, not to mention the railway. I don't suppose one can be mad and achieve all that.'

'Oh.' She didn't know what else to say, relieved that she hadn't mentioned his proposal after all. She had the distinct impression that her aunt wouldn't be quite so sympathetic if she denounced him, too. Though if all of that were true, why on earth had he proposed to *her*? Surely such an eligible bachelor could have his pick of available women. She felt a stab of resentment. He *must* have been mocking her after all. As if insulting her weren't bad enough…

'You know, his birth caused quite the scandal,' Aunt Sophoria continued blithely. 'His father was Lord Theakston.'

'What's so scandalous about that?'

'Nothing at all,' her aunt chuckled, 'except that his mother wasn't Lady Theakston. She never had any children, poor woman. They might have made up for being married to him, the old rogue.'

Ianthe leaned forward, intrigued despite herself. 'So who was his mother?'

'One of the housemaids. Not the first he dallied with either, nor the last, but once Lady Theakston found out she was having a baby, she turned her out on to the street.'

'But that's awful!'

'It was, not that Theakston himself did anything to stop it. No one knew where she went after that. Then twelve years later, she and the boy popped up out of the blue in Whitby, he gets himself a job at old Masham's shipyard, the old man takes a shine to him and before anyone knows it, he owns the whole place. The mother died soon afterward, and there was some kind of reconciliation with his father, but something must have gone wrong. I know they quarrelled before the old man died anyway.'

'Oh.' She *still* didn't know what to say.

'Do you know…?' Aunt Sophoria tilted her head to one side suddenly. 'You look so much like your mother this morning. I couldn't see the resemblance last night, but now it's quite uncanny. I could almost believe you were her again.'

Ianthe smiled, relieved at the change in subject. 'My father always said we were doubles.'

'So you are. My poor girl, this past year must have been very hard for you, losing your parents so close together.'

She bit her lip, trying to stop it from trembling. 'He just seemed to give up without her.'

'They always had too much romantic sensibility, the pair of them.'

'Aunt!'

'They did. He ought to have pulled himself together.'

'Surely you don't blame him for dying?'

Aunt Sophoria screwed up her mouth as if torn

between two conflicting opinions. 'No. I suppose not.'

Ianthe stared at her in shocked silence for a moment before bursting into peals of laughter. 'Father always said you were wicked.'

'Did he? How wonderful. I'm the black sheep of the family, you know.' Her aunt smiled mischievously before heaving herself back to her feet. 'But now I think it's time to get up. I unpacked your bag, I hope you don't mind, though there wasn't much there. It's all very respectable, but...' Her face fell and then lit up again suddenly. 'Would you like to borrow something of mine? I have a pink taffeta that would suit you perfectly. I could do your hair, too, if you like. I do so hate these new flat styles.'

Ianthe bit her tongue. The idea of wearing something belonging to her aunt was more than a little alarming. On the other hand, Percy would doubtless waste no time in bringing Sir Charles to call and, if her drab, old-fashioned attire didn't deter him, Aunt Sophoria's wardrobe just might...

'That sounds like a wonderful idea.' She wrenched the bedcovers back with a smile. 'Perhaps I could do with some colour.'

It didn't take long for Ianthe to regret her decision. Descending the stairs in her aunt's idea of a day gown was far more problematic that she'd imagined. There were so many layers and decorative flounces she had to keep a tight hold on the banister to stop herself from falling and breaking her neck.

She stopped on the landing halfway, studying her reflection in a heavy gilt-framed mirror, wondering whether to burst into laughter or tears. Her aunt's old, steel-rimmed crinoline made her look as if she were wearing several dresses at once, while her puffed sleeves were embellished with enough lace to make a whole other skirt. Her hair, meanwhile, was piled so high on her head that she looked as if she had a bird's nest sitting on top—the whole frizzy arrangement held in place with an oversized day-cap, fastened beneath her chin with an elaborate bow. She looked like some kind of confection, a pink cake topped with white frothy icing.

For a meeting with Sir Charles, she looked perfect.

'Ah, there you are!' Aunt Sophoria met her in the hallway as she finally reached the bottom of the stairs. 'You have a visitor.'

'Already?' Ianthe's heart sank. Apparently Sir Charles wasn't wasting any time.

'He's been waiting ten minutes. And of course Betsy isn't here this morning. I'll have to make the tea myself. Will he want cake, do you think?'

'No! I mean, I'm sure he won't be staying long.'

'We still have to be courteous, dear.' Her aunt

squeezed her hand reassuringly. 'Didn't I tell you it would be all right? Now, run along in. You can't keep a man like that waiting.'

'But you said…'

Ianthe felt a twinge of resentment as her aunt vanished through a side door. So much for promising to help her—she'd left her to face Sir Charles alone! On the other hand, at least this would get the interview over with. The events of the day before, upsetting though they'd been, had at least clarified her feelings. She wouldn't marry him, not for money, not for protection, not even for Percy. She had to make that clear once and for all.

She gave the door a firm push, sweeping into the parlour with a determined flourish.

'Good morning, S—'

She stopped short as she caught sight of the man standing with his back towards her. He was taller and more imposing than Sir Charles, his broad shoulders encased in a smart, three-quarter-length navy coat trimmed with royal-blue velvet, the crisp white collar of his shirt contrasting vividly with his thick, black hair.

'Mr Felstone?' she gasped, annoyed by the catch in her own voice.

'I'm afraid so.' He turned around, his expression flitting between surprise and amusement before he seemed to master himself. 'Thank you for seeing me, Miss Holt. Under the circumstances, I would have understood if you'd refused.'

Ianthe stiffened, fighting the urge to turn tail and run. As if everything that had happened yesterday wasn't bad enough, now he had to see her like this? In her aunt's cluttered parlour he looked even more handsome than she remembered, while she looked like some kind of doily! Well, there was no point in trying to hide her outlandish appearance now. He'd already seen the worst. She had to brazen it out, no matter how embarrassing.

'I didn't expect to see you here, Mr Felstone.'

'Ah.' He seemed to guess the truth. 'You were expecting Sir Charles perhaps?'

'Yes.' She regarded him warily. 'How did you find me? I don't think I told you where I was staying.'

'You didn't, but I have a friend whose wife is fortunate enough to know everything that happens in Pickering.' He raised an eyebrow inquiringly. 'But I can leave if you prefer?'

For a moment, she was tempted to agree. After yesterday, he was the last man—*almost* the last man, she corrected herself—that she wanted to see. On the other hand, her aunt clearly held a very different opinion. She wouldn't appreciate her throwing him out, no matter how much she wanted to.

'It's not my house.' She shrugged. 'You may do as you please.'

'You're very kind.'

She glanced at him suspiciously, but he looked

utterly calm and contained, a whole different man to the one who'd insulted her just yesterday, in complete control of his words and temper. If only she could say the same about herself.

She pressed her lips together, trying to decide what to do next. The polite thing would be to ask him to sit down, but she was in no mood to be polite. Under the circumstances, it seemed ludicrous to resort to conventionalities. Besides, the room itself made it difficult to concentrate. After her monochromatic bedroom, the parlour was a tumultuous riot of colour, crammed with enough furniture for a room twice the size. A cursory glance revealed at least twelve different places to sit. Even the wallpaper was cluttered, decorated with sprigs of cherry blossom interlaced with tendrils of crimson fruit. Combined with a flower-patterned carpet it gave the distinct impression that her aunt was trying to establish a garden indoors. The effect would have been overpowering even without Mr Felstone standing in the middle.

What was he doing there? She felt a fresh burst of exasperation. After she'd bade him goodbye so definitively on the train—or thought she had—she hadn't expected to see him again at all. If he'd come to mock her again then she'd have no compunction about picking up the nearest ornament and flinging it at his head.

She glanced around the room, searching for

suitable weapons, her gaze settling finally on a large box on the table.

'What's that?'

'A peace offering. You said you didn't have a gown for the ball.'

'So you brought me one?' She frowned, surprise vying with irritation. Peace offering or not, the gesture was hardly appropriate. She didn't want anything from him—nothing except his departure.

'Forgive the impertinence, but I mentioned your situation to my friend's wife, who was happy to offer a loan. You're around the same size so I believe it should fit. If you wish to borrow it, that is.'

Ianthe made her way warily across the parlour, lifting the lid and trying not to gasp as she caught a glimpse of the satin fabric inside. The dress was beautiful, a silvery light grey, simply cut with a round neckline and not so much as a flounce or ruffle in sight. She ran her fingers over the sumptuous material, resisting the urge to press it against her cheek. Such a gown would be a joy to wear. It also looked suspiciously new.

'I recall your brother mentioning that you like grey.'

'It's lovely.' She tore her fingers away reluctantly. 'Your friend's wife is very generous, but I can't possibly accept.'

He ignored her objection. 'I also managed to

procure an invitation for your aunt. I noticed her name wasn't on the guest list.'

'For Aunt Sophoria?' She spun around eagerly. That was an even better present than the dress, though she'd no intention of forgiving him so easily, no matter how churlish she sounded. 'That was very thoughtful. My aunt will enjoy herself, I'm sure, though she hardly needs me to chaperon her.'

'What don't I need, dear?' Aunt Sophoria bustled into the room at that moment, barely visible behind a giant tea tray.

'Allow me.' Mr Felstone stooped to relieve her at once. 'I was just telling your niece that I've arranged invitations for you both to the ball this evening. If you care to attend, that is.'

'The ball?' Aunt Sophoria's face lit up instantly. 'Well, we'd be delighted, wouldn't we, Ianthe? Do take a seat, Mr Felstone.'

'Thank you, Miss Gibbs.'

He looked around as if searching for an available seat, and Ianthe felt a smug sense of triumph, pleased for once to see him at a disadvantage. Despite the preponderance of furniture, nearly every chair was hidden beneath some form of lace-based frippery.

'Allow me.' She smiled condescendingly, uncovering a small sofa beneath a pile of cushions.

'My thanks.' He caught her eye with a flash of amusement in his own. 'Won't you join me?'

The smile dropped from her face at once. Getting dressed, the thought of sitting down had somehow never occurred to her. She'd worn hoops in the past, of course, but never such a vast crinoline. Now she wondered how her aunt managed. Awkwardly, she reversed towards the opposite sofa, bending her knees slowly as she tried to make her progress look as natural as possible.

'Sugar lumps!' Her aunt's sudden cry made her freeze halfway down.

'What's the matter, Aunt?'

'I forgot the sugar lumps.' Aunt Sophoria was already back on her feet. 'Do pour Mr Felstone some tea, dear. I won't be long.'

Ianthe stared at the teapot in horror. If she offered him tea then she'd have to stand up again! She cast an anxious glance towards him, but he seemed oblivious to her distress, apparently engrossed in the porcelain figure of a small dog at his feet.

She cleared her throat. 'Would you care for some tea, Mr Felstone?'

He glanced up, the shadow of a smile passing his lips. 'I think perhaps we ought to wait for your aunt.'

She dropped the rest of the way into her seat with an unladylike thud. What was he still doing there? He'd made his peace offering, as he called it. If he was waiting for her to forgive and forget, he could wait all day. Silently, she stared down at her hands, her fingerless, crocheted gloves folded neatly in her lap. Why couldn't he just put her out of her misery and leave?

'Miss Holt.' His deep voice broke the silence at last. 'Yesterday I behaved in an appalling manner. I'm afraid that my temper has a tendency to get the better of me. My apology was churlish and my proposal somewhat less than chivalrous. I beg you to forgive me.'

She looked up again quickly, glancing towards the parlour door in alarm. She didn't want her aunt to overhear *that*!

'Very well. We'll say no more about it.'

'Just one more thing and I'll be silent. Before you left, you accused me of mocking you. I assure you that I wasn't.'

'No?' She couldn't keep the scepticism out of her voice.

'No. You may not think me a gentleman, but I do have some sense of decency. Why would I joke about such a thing?'

'Because, as my brother so delicately observed, I'm not the kind of woman men generally propose to.'

'None the less, I was quite sincere.'

Ianthe curled her hands into fists. He sounded genuine, but he couldn't be. More likely he was simply regretting his behaviour and attempting to cover his tracks, pretending that his proposal had been real in order to protect his reputation. It would serve him right if she said yes!

'Mr Felstone...' she pulled herself up haughtily '...if you're afraid of me spreading gossip about you then I can relieve your worries at once. I assure you, I have no intention of telling anyone else about your proposal.'

'I'm not worried at all. I'm quite accustomed to being talked about.'

'Then if you think you've compromised me...'

'I don't.'

'Then I don't understand you, sir! Why would a man of fortune, apparently in full possession of his faculties, make such an offer? Unless it's your custom to propose to complete strangers?'

'It's not my custom, as you say, to propose at all. Up until a few months ago, I'd never given the matter any thought.'

'Then why...?'

'I'll be blunt, Miss Holt, since you seem to favour that approach. I'm a busy man. I like business and I like my work, but I don't enjoy the social obligations that come with it. Lately, I've felt I might be better placed if I had a wife to assist me.'

'So naturally you asked me?'

'Naturally, I asked a woman of my acquaintance who I was led to believe would favour my suit. She didn't. When we met on the train, I was returning from that interview. I won't deny that injured pride played a part in my proposal to you, but I was perfectly serious. I still am. When I learned of your predicament in regard to Sir Charles, I saw an arrangement that might suit us both.'

'My predicament, as you call it, is none of your business!' she snapped. How dare he talk about her private affairs so familiarly, never mind the arrogant presumption that she needed his help! She didn't need him or any other man to save her! She could save herself from the Baronet...just as soon as she figured out how.

'I do not need rescuing, sir.'

'I never said that you did.' He sounded infuriatingly calm. 'I'm simply offering you a solution.'

'But you don't know me!' She sprang back to her feet, crinoline forgotten. Where was Aunt Sophoria? Surely it wasn't so hard to find sugar lumps!

'How well do any couple know each other before they marry?'

'Better than this!'

He shrugged. 'I'm sure over time we would develop a regard for each other. You strike me as a sensible, respectable woman, and I want a respectable wife. My life has been more than eventful enough.'

'Oh.' She flinched inwardly. Sensible and respectable were good. They were what she wanted, how she strove to appear, yet somehow the words still felt like an insult. Besides, he didn't know her at all if he thought she was sensible. Sensible women didn't elope with their employer's sons!

'You cannot hear yourself, sir. You say that you want a sensible wife and yet your proposal is quite the opposite. Forgive me for thinking there must be some other reason behind it.'

His lips curved in an appreciative smile. 'It seems that I've underestimated you, Miss Holt. The truth is that I'm an ambitious man. Yesterday I was forced to confront certain facts about my position, or lack of it, in society. And since I cannot progress in that direction, I've decided to progress in another. I want my shipyard to be the biggest and best on the east coast. To achieve that, I need to buy out one of my neighbours, a certain Mr Harper. He's an old man and willing to sell, but he's somewhat…traditional. He doesn't approve of me or my background, and he definitely won't sell to a bachelor. Hence my need for a bride.'

'*Any* bride?'

'Not any, but one he'll approve of, yes.'

'How flattering. What if he hears that you proposed to someone else yesterday?'

'He might hear rumours, but if I announce our engagement before they reach him, he'll dismiss them as just that—rumours.'

'And you don't think he'll be suspicious if I

simply appear out of the blue?' She shook her head incredulously. 'Why not ask someone else you already know?'

'Because I need an engagement to be convincing. I go away on business often enough to make a long-distance courtship plausible. He won't know that we've only just met.'

Ianthe drew her brows together thoughtfully. Put like that, it sounded almost convincing. It would put an end to Percy and Sir Charles's plotting, not to mention give her a new start, a new home, somewhere to call her own again. And she *was* a new woman after all. Perhaps she *could* be the sensible bride he wanted. It might be tempting, if it weren't so preposterous.

'Unless you have some personal objection to me?' His face darkened abruptly. 'Perhaps you've heard of my background? My parentage?'

She blinked, taken aback by the flash of steel in his grey eyes. 'Your parentage is irrelevant, sir. If I thought that birth were any indication of breeding then I'd have married Sir Charles already.'

'Then perhaps you dislike me personally?'

'I think you're moody and ill-mannered. Other than that, I've no objection to your character.'

'I might have used the same words to describe you this morning. With the addition of stubborn, that is.'

'I am not st—!' She stopped mid-word, gritting her teeth at the irony.

'Quite.'

'What about love then?' She inched her chin up. 'Or do you think that doesn't matter in marriage?'

'I believe that's your poetry speaking again.'

She felt a stab of bitterness. Did any man think of love? Not Percy or Sir Charles or this man either, apparently.

'I assure you, it's quite possible to marry for love. My parents did.'

'That was fortunate for them, though for my own part, I've never had the benefit of any such example. My father wasn't known for his finer feelings and my mother only came to regret them. I've seen the effects of your so-called love, Miss Holt. I'm not capable of forming such an attachment myself. If that's what you're waiting for, then I'm afraid I can't help you. What I'm proposing is a practical arrangement, not a romantic one.'

'Practical?' She gave a sceptical laugh. 'Yesterday you condemned me as a schemer and yet today you tell me I ought to be practical? Make up your mind, Mr Felstone.'

'There's a great deal of difference between marrying a man you despise and simply being practical.'

'You've given me every reason to dislike you.'

'True, but at least we know where we stand.' He gave a wry smile. 'Things can only get better.'

Ianthe bit her lip. That was definitely true. Unconventional as his arrangement sounded, it did make a kind of sense. But how could she possibly agree to marry a man she'd known for less than a day? He didn't scare her like Sir Charles, but she knew even less about him. At least with the Baronet she already expected the worst. This man was an unknown quantity, more attractive and yet potentially even more dangerous.

Besides, the thought of marrying *without* love went against all of her old cherished ideals and dreams. Even if she didn't expect it for herself any more, she hadn't changed so completely. She still believed in the possibility of love, even if not for herself...

'Mr Felstone...' She started to speak and then stopped, disturbed by a knock on the front door, by the sound of her aunt's voice followed by Percy's, then another man's... She caught her breath in panic.

'Sir Charles, I presume?' Mr Felstone looked utterly unperturbed, pulling himself casually to his feet. 'In that case, I'll take my leave. I'll be staying at the Swan until Thursday. If you wish to discuss any part of my offer, I'm more than happy to do so. If not, I promise never to mention it again.'

'Wait!' She swung around, as panicked now by

the thought of him leaving as she'd been by his presence half an hour before. She'd been prepared to face Sir Charles then, but now she needed time to recompose herself. As if such a thing were possible with Mr Felstone's proposal still ringing in her ears! Her head was still spinning from the fact that he actually meant it. How could he throw her into such confusion and then abandon her now?

Besides, it occurred to her that his presence there might actually be useful. Even if she had no intention of accepting him, Sir Charles wasn't to know that. If he found them together, alone and unchaperoned, the situation might look just compromising enough to deter him. And if not... Mr Felstone would make an intimidating rival, even to a baronet. If anyone could scare him off, surely it would be him.

If she could persuade him to stay. Which meant changing everything about her behaviour so far.

'I mean, please wait!' She stepped in front of him, effectively blocking the way. 'I'll think about your offer, but don't go!'

Chapter Four

$\sim\!\!\sim\!\!\sim\!\!\sim\!\!\sim$

'You want me to stay?'

Robert studied her face, trying to understand what she was really asking him. Her expression had just run the gamut of emotions from dismissive to panicked to imploring in less than thirty seconds. He'd been about to quit the field, certain that she'd been about to reject him—again—but now she was actually pleading with him to stay. Why?

'There's no need to leave on Sir Charles's account.' Her voice quavered slightly. 'You haven't had tea yet.'

He knit his brows suspiciously. She was trying to smile and failing, her strained features barely concealing an undercurrent of fear. Clearly she hadn't been exaggerating when she'd said she didn't want to marry Sir Charles, but *fear*? Aversion was one thing, but this…this was something else entirely. Was she afraid of him, then?

'Please.' She threw a nervous glance over her shoulder when he still didn't answer. 'Just for a few minutes.'

'You don't want to be alone with him?' He felt vaguely disturbed by the idea. 'Your aunt and brother are here.'

'It's not that...'

'You want to make him jealous?'

Her eyes flew to his. 'Yes. If he sees us alone together...'

'He might not like the competition?'

She held his gaze in guilty silence for a few moments before shaking her head. 'I shouldn't have asked. I'm sorry.'

'Don't be. I'm flattered.'

'Then you don't object?'

He gave a small shrug, surprised to find that he didn't object at all.

'Not if you think it might help, though it might not be the wisest course of action. Some men like a challenge.'

'I don't know what he likes!' Brown eyes flashed tempestuously. 'But I've tried everything else!'

Robert cocked an eyebrow, surprised as much by her vehemence as by the words themselves. What did *that* mean? That she'd tried 'everything else'? *What else?*

His gaze dropped to her extravagant pink dress, so wildly different to her sensible grey outfit from the day before. She seemed to have gone from one extreme to the other. There was nothing remotely sensible about her appearance now. When she'd entered the room he'd thought he'd made a mistake and had the wrong woman. She looked like a younger version of her flamboyant aunt, the ridiculous lace cap on her head framing her face like the petals of a huge flower. Not that there weren't still points to admire. The tight bodice accentuated curves that had been largely hidden the day before, revealing a surprisingly statuesque figure, shapely waist and ample, round breasts...

He forced his attention back to her words. *I've tried everything else.* Was her outlandish appearance all a façade then, some kind of bizarre attempt to repel Sir Charles? That would explain why she'd looked so embarrassed to see him instead. After charging into the parlour so defiantly, her cheeks had turned almost the same colour as her dress, though he had to admit the effect had been unexpectedly alluring.

'I'm more than happy to play the rival suitor, Miss Holt.' He made an ironic bow. 'Shall I stand here or languish at your feet?'

She shot him a cutting look, opening her mouth to retort before clamping it firmly shut again as the tall, suavely dressed figure of Sir Charles Lester appeared in the doorway.

'Ianthe.' The Baronet strode forward at once,

grasping her hands and raising them both to his lips, seemingly oblivious to anything unusual in her appearance. 'You look just as lovely as ever.'

Robert regarded the other man critically. In his mid-fifties, the Baronet had an air of casual, confident authority, with a strong athletic figure and abundance of silver-blond hair. There was nothing obviously untoward or overtly threatening about his appearance, but the hard edge to his features gave him away. It was the same edge he recognised from his father's face, the same look of a man accustomed to wanting—and getting—his own way.

And in this particular case what the Baronet wanted was obvious. The way he was clutching Ianthe's wrists put him in mind of a falcon digging its talons into a small bird. As for her... She was standing completely immobile, her whole body stiff and rigid, as if simply awaiting an opportunity to get away.

He tensed, seized by an instantaneous rush of dislike, barely resisting a compulsion to grab the other man by the collar and throw him out on to the street.

'Felstone.' Sir Charles addressed him without turning his head. 'I didn't think you were the type to make calls on ladies.'

Robert held his temper with an effort. The Baronet's tone was dismissive, though if he thought he could be chased away so easily, he could think again.

'I make the occasional exception. When the company's so pleasant, that is.'

'Indeed?' Sir Charles dragged his gaze away from Ianthe's face at last. 'Percy told me you met on the train yesterday.'

'That was my good fortune, yes.'

'And here you are again today.' Green eyes narrowed unpleasantly. 'Isn't there any work to be done for the gala?'

'Plenty, I should imagine.'

Robert flung himself back down on the sofa, throwing one leg casually over the other with the air of a man determined to stay put. Antagonising a man with the Baronet's influence didn't make particularly good business sense, but then his behaviour seemed to have become increasingly reckless since meeting Miss Holt. Good business or not, he wasn't going to abandon her now, not when she'd just begged him to stay. As for the man's ill manners, he'd be more than happy to take issue with those...

'And we're quite delighted that you called, Mr Felstone.'

Sophoria Gibbs pushed past the Baronet so roughly that Robert almost laughed out loud. He'd always suspected that the old woman's eccentricities belied a sharp mind, but he'd never been so certain of it until that moment. It seemed he wouldn't have much work to do to get her on side. If he asked, she'd probably help him haul Sir Charles out on to the street.

'Let me do the tea, Aunt.' Miss Holt extricated herself from the Baronet's clutches at last, rubbing her wrists together as she moved towards the table.

Robert's eyes narrowed. Even from where he was sitting, he could see faint red marks, indentations left by Sir Charles's fingers. How hard had he been holding her? His gaze shifted towards the Baronet, but the other man looked completely absorbed, his eyes following her every movement around the room with a look of alarming intensity.

'Mr Felstone, how d'ye do?' The brother strode into the room finally, throwing himself into a chair without waiting for a reply. 'I hope you're in a better mood today, sis.'

'There's nothing wrong with my mood, Percy,' she answered stiffly, pointedly handing Robert the first cup of tea.

'No? You were in a fearsome temper yesterday.'

'Well, I'm not now.'

'In that case, I hope you'll permit me to escort you to the ball tonight?' Sir Charles threw Robert a sharp look. 'Percy told me about your offer, Felstone, but I'd already arranged invitations for both himself and Miss Holt.'

'And their aunt, no doubt?'

Robert smiled benignly as the Baronet's smug expression faltered. 'I'm afraid not. I thought the evening might be too much for Miss Gibbs.'

'I can still out-dance you, Charles.' The old woman made a cackling sound. 'It's just a good thing Mr Felstone thought of me.'

'In any case—' Sir Charles ignored her '—I've also taken the liberty of arranging a gown for you, Ianthe. White Parisian silk. Your mother had one just like it. I think it should look very fetching on you.'

Robert watched as she came to a sudden stop in the centre of the room. Moving around the small space distributing tea, she'd put him in mind of a tennis ball, being batted about between players. Now she seemed to be hovering over the net, trying to decide which way to fall or whether to abandon the court altogether.

For a tense moment she didn't answer, smoothing her hands over the front of her pink taffeta as if trying to make up her mind about something. Then she pulled her shoulders back and lifted her head all of a sudden, meeting the Baronet's gaze squarely.

'Thank you for the offer, but I already have a gown.'

'Since when?' Percy sounded indignant.

'Since Mr Felstone was good enough to bring me one.'

Robert smiled innocently, leaning back in his chair as four sets of eyes swivelled towards him.

'Well, how kind of you!' The aunt was the first to speak.

'Very.' Sir Charles sounded less than pleased.

'It was my pleasure, though the credit really belongs to Kitty Loveday. She offered the loan. I'm simply the delivery boy.'

'Her husband works for the railway, doesn't he?' The Baronet's tone was scathing.

'He's an engineer, yes. As well as a good friend and one of the cleverest men I know.'

'Why, Katherine Loveday!' Aunt Sophoria's face broke into a wide smile. 'You used to play with her when you were children, Ianthe. She never stopped talking even then, but she was always a kind girl.'

'She still is.' Robert gave an approving smile. 'I'd be glad to reintroduce you tonight, Miss Holt.'

'Isn't a ball a bit frivolous for you, Felstone?' Sir Charles's expression was now openly antagonistic. 'I thought you lived to work. Or are you trying to distance yourself from business at last?'

'I've no intention of doing anything of the kind. I'm fortunate enough to enjoy what I do. But I can have an evening off occasionally.'

'Will Louisa Allendon be attending, then?' Sir Charles gave a look of feigned innocence. 'I thought you were spending all your spare time with her.'

Robert clenched his jaw, tipping his head slightly to acknowledge the hit. 'I've no idea where Miss Allendon intends to spend her evening.'

'No? What a shame. Though I did hear she didn't like the smell of the shipyard. Too close to the fish market, perhaps. You must be feeling quite let down there.'

'Would you care for something to eat, Mr Felstone?'

Ianthe's voice prevented him from answering. He looked up to find her standing beside him, holding out a plate of miniature cakes with a distinctly apologetic expression, as if she were worried about the impact of the Baronet's words. He raised an eyebrow, strangely touched by her intervention, though on the other hand, perhaps she was right to be worried. If he stayed another minute, he might make even more of a scene than he had yesterday.

Besides, he decided, he'd already done what she'd asked him. He'd definitely succeeded in making Sir Charles jealous. What she did next was up to her...

'No, thank you.' He swallowed the rest of his tea and stood up. 'I'm afraid Sir Charles is right and I have work to do. The gala will be starting shortly.'

'Of course, we mustn't keep you any longer.' She gave what looked like a genuine smile. 'Thank you for calling.'

'Miss Holt.' He held out his hand and she took it, willingly this time, placing her smooth hand in his rough one with a smile that faded the instant their fingers touched.

He felt a jolt, as if someone had just shoved him hard in the chest, accompanied by a strange scorching sensation that seemed to pass through her fingers and up his arm, rendering him speechless. He saw her eyes widen in response, heard her sudden intake of breath, though somehow he couldn't release her. He didn't want to release her. He wanted to pull her closer. As close as he could...

'Mr Felstone.' She found her voice first, averting her gaze as she slowly tugged her hand away.

He cleared his throat, hardly trusting himself to speak as he made a formal bow to her aunt and then strode determinedly out of the parlour, barely pausing to scoop up his hat before charging out on to the street and almost slamming the door behind him.

What the hell had just happened?

He stopped on the doorstep to take a deep breath. One moment he'd been thinking about dragging the Baronet outside by the scruff of his expensive collar, the next he'd felt an almost visceral shock as his fingers had touched Ianthe's. How could simply touching her hand have had such a powerful effect? She wasn't unattractive, despite her unusual fashion sense, but he wasn't attracted to her...was he? He frowned, alarmed by the possibility. *That* wasn't what he wanted, wasn't part of the business arrangement that he'd proposed. He wanted sensible and respectable. He had a business to build, not to mention a shipyard to run. The last thing he needed was a woman to distract him. Louisa had taken up enough of his time already.

But then he'd been angry, after all. He'd been tense, his blood fired up by Sir Charles's comments about Louisa. Whatever he'd felt had probably just been temper, nothing to do with *her* at all...

He clamped his hat on his head and turned his steps in the direction of the station, walking so fast that he almost bumped into a couple walking arm in arm in the other direction.

'Why, Robert!' A pair of inquisitive blue eyes framed with dark curls peeped up at him from beneath an elaborate spoon bonnet. 'Fancy meeting you here!'

'Kitty.' He forced a smile, still wrestling with his bad temper. In truth, he should have expected this, should have known he couldn't enlist Kitty's help with the gown and then expect her to keep away. Clearly his edited account of meeting Miss Holt on the train wasn't enough to satiate her curiosity. 'And Giles, too. What a coincidence. I thought you'd be on your way to the gala by now.'

'So did I.' Giles rolled his eyes.

'Bit of an odd route you're taking, then. You *do* remember that the station's at the bottom of the hill, not the top?'

'Quite.'

'We're taking a stroll to calm Giles's nerves.' Kitty fluttered her eyelashes innocently. 'Though we're heading back down now if you'd care to join us?'

'With pleasure. If you're sure that Giles has walked enough, that is?' he couldn't resist teasing, extending an arm to let Kitty hook her spare hand around it. After two years, he'd learned that there was no point trying to keep secrets from his friend's wife—all but a few important ones, anyway—though he still had no intention of making her interrogation easy.

'So?' They'd only gone a couple of steps before she started. 'Did Miss Holt like the dress?'

'I think so.'

'And?'

'And what?'

'Was your visit a success?'

'In what way?'

'Was she pleased to see you?'

His lips twitched. 'That remains to be seen.'

'She wasn't too tired from her journey?'

'Apparently not.'

'Oh, for pity's sake!' Giles burst out impatiently. 'Just tell her what happened and have done with it. You know we'll never have any peace until you do.'

'Giles!' Kitty looked aggrieved. 'You know I don't want to pry.'

'And you know perfectly well that you do. Just ask him.'

'I'll do no such thing.' Kitty lifted her button nose in the air. 'Since you both think so ill of me.'

'I assure you that we think nothing of the kind.' Robert shared a conspiratorial look with his friend. 'But as I told you, it only was a brief visit to deliver the dress.'

And to ask her to marry me, he added silently. Not that he was about to tell Kitty that. He might as well take out an advert in the local paper. As to how it had gone... Honestly, he had no idea. Miss Holt might prefer him to Sir Charles, but that wasn't saying much. That moment when their fingers had touched had seemed to affect her, too, but then she'd been the one to pull away. She hadn't even looked at him when he'd left, had seemed no closer to accepting his proposal, though after the way his own body had reacted, he wasn't entirely sure he wanted her to any more. That had definitely *not* been part of his proposal. On the other hand, the thought of leaving her at the mercy of Sir Charles made his fists curl instinctively. No matter how unnerved he'd been by their exchange, he couldn't do that...

He dragged his thoughts back to the present, aware of Kitty still watching him.

'As it happens, you're already acquainted with Miss Holt. Her aunt says you used to play together.'

'Really?' Kitty's face brightened again. 'Wait, you mean, *Ianthe* Holt? Why, of course I remember her! Her mother was Phylidia Gibbs, Sophoria's little sister, the one who married an artist and moved to London. Oh, she was the most beautiful woman I ever saw! No wonder you like her, Robert, if she takes after her mother.'

Robert hesitated, wondering how to answer such a statement truthfully. 'She looked somewhat like her aunt today.'

'Well, I'm sure she's perfectly charming. Maybe I should call, since we're already acquainted?'

'No!' Giles intervened hastily. 'Leave Robert to it.'

'But maybe I can help, like I did with the dress?'

'You were very helpful.' Robert agreed tactfully. He'd enlisted Kitty's help in buying the gown, partly to avoid gossip, partly because he had no idea how to order women's clothing, specifying the material, style and colour and then leaving her to do the rest, promising it as a gift with the sole proviso that Miss Holt borrow it first. That way he hadn't lied. Disingenuous as it was, the dress was technically on loan. Not that Kitty was capable of keeping any secret for long. If she called on Miss Holt that day, the truth would be out before they ever reached the ball.

'I could tell her all the good things about you.' Kitty sounded alarmingly eager.

'As opposed to the many bad ones?'

'Just leave it be, Kitty. You'll see her tonight.' Giles threw him an apologetic look. 'Sorry, Robert, you know my wife won't be happy until she's married off every eligible bachelor in Yorkshire.'

'Well, I think it's exciting.' Kitty pouted. 'When was the last time Robert took an interest in any woman? He didn't even tell me about Louisa Allendon.'

'Can't think why not.'

'So this is different, don't you think?' She heaved a sigh. 'I wish you still talked about me that way, Giles.'

'What way?' Robert glanced down in surprise. He didn't remember saying anything particularly noteworthy about Miss Holt, let alone in any particular *way*.

'It wasn't so much what you said as the fact that you said it at all. You know, you two can be very boring talking about trains and boats all the time. It made a refreshing change. You said she seemed very respectable.'

'So you did!' Giles broke into a grin. 'I wouldn't call that very romantic, though.'

'It wasn't supposed to be.'

'But I could *make* it sound romantic. If you let me call on her, that is.'

'I doubt there'll be time after the gala.' Robert struggled to be diplomatic. 'Besides, she had other guests when I left.'

'Oh?'

'Her brother and Sir Charles Lester.' He tried not to growl the name.

'Oh, I remember Percy!' Kitty beamed again. 'Though I wonder what Sir Charles was doing there. They say he's been acting very strangely of late. How does she know him?'

'A family friend, I think. What do you mean, strangely?'

'Making extravagant purchases, that sort of thing. He's had the whole of his house redecorated, bought a new carriage, new horses, too. They say it looks like he's getting married, not that anyone believes it.'

Robert frowned thoughtfully. That clinched it, then. At least the Baronet's intentions towards Miss Holt were honourable, though his behaviour seemed somewhat pre-emptive. He seemed to be making preparations for a wedding *before* asking the bride. Had he even considered that she might refuse him?

In which case, how would he react when she did?

'So you'll introduce me to her tonight?'

'Mmm?'

'You'll introduce me to Miss Holt tonight?'

'Of course.' He smiled at Kitty's persistence. 'Though first we ought to go and listen to your husband's speech.'

Giles harrumphed loudly. 'You two remember that, do you? I thought my nerves had been entirely forgotten.'

'Don't be silly, darling.' Kitty released Robert's arm to squeeze both of hers around her husband's waist. 'You'll be marvellous. And I promise not to say another word about Miss Holt until dinner.'

Chapter Five

Ianthe ran her hands over the satin bodice of her borrowed gown with a sigh of pleasure. Whoever Mr Felstone's friend was, she had exquisite taste.

The design was beautiful in its very simplicity, plain but fashionable, with low sloping shoulders, short lace sleeves and a tight-fitting bodice that ended in a point at her waist. Below that, the material flared out like a silk waterfall, hemmed at the edges with white lace, though not enough to detract from the gorgeousness of the fabric itself. The whole thing fitted so perfectly that she could almost imagine it had been made specifically for her. If she'd been able to choose a gown for herself, she could hardly have done any better.

She gave an enthusiastic twirl in front of the mirror, the dress itself seeming to lift her spirits. After months of dressing in unrelenting black and dark grey, the lighter shade was a relief, the silvery tint perfectly complimenting the paler threads in her hair and giving them a vibrancy she wasn't accustomed to. Under its heady influence, she'd actually been tempted to shun her usual severe hairstyle in favour of more fashionable ringlets, though she'd finally settled on a sensible loose chignon instead, held in place with a hairnet. After all, Sir Charles would be at the ball and she'd no wish to encourage him by seeming frivolous. Not to mention Mr Felstone…though he'd said that he liked sensible.

Would he like her appearance tonight? she wondered.

She caught her breath, recalling the sudden, unexpected and strangely thrilling sensation that had flared in her chest and then raced through her body as their fingers had touched. It had only been a few seconds, but her stomach had seemed to swoop and then dip alarmingly. Had he felt it, too? His expression had seemed to freeze for a moment, though he'd given no indication of any deeper feeling. If anything, he'd looked almost angry when he'd left. Probably she'd simply imagined it and he hadn't felt anything, yet she had. She most definitely had.

That it had happened at all was disturbing. She'd entered her aunt's parlour feeling one way towards him and come out again feeling another entirely. Not that she knew what it was. She was still too shocked by his proposal to know *what* she felt beside confused. She'd been grateful to him for staying when she'd asked, but surely the sudden connection between them hadn't simply been gratitude? She'd never felt anything quite so disorienting before, not even with Albert...

Not that it mattered, she told herself firmly. She still had absolutely no intention of accepting his offer, especially not now. Whatever she'd felt when they'd touched, she had no intention of making a fool of herself by repeating the experience. It certainly wasn't something a sensible, respectable woman ought to feel. It was more like one of the baser urges Albert's mother had accused her of. The new Ianthe wouldn't stoop to such urges—nor would Mr Felstone want her to. If it was sensible and respectable he wanted, then he ought to take the next train back to Whitby and leave her alone. If it hadn't been for Albert, she *might* have considered his proposal, but now it was utterly out of the question. If she accepted his offer then she'd be honour-bound to tell him the whole humiliating truth about her past. And she had absolutely no intention of doing that.

In which case, she really ought *not* to be wearing his loaned gown, but it was impossible to resist. She'd never worn anything that looked and felt quite so gorgeous. And she was making a point to Sir Charles, she told herself. That was her real reason for wearing it—nothing to do with Mr Felstone at all. Whatever he thought of her was irrelevant. She couldn't—*wouldn't*—accept his offer and she'd tell him so tonight. She'd be calm and collected and not the least bit distracted. Just as long as he didn't touch her... Her stomach flipped over again at the thought. Perhaps a ball wasn't such a good idea after all.

'You look beautiful, dear.' Aunt Sophoria clasped her hands together admiringly as she entered the parlour. 'Your Mr Felstone will be very impressed.'

Ianthe gave her a remonstrative look. 'He's not *my* Mr Felstone, Aunt.'

'No? He doesn't make calls on any other young ladies in Pickering as far as I know.'

'Maybe he's discreet.'

'Good gracious,' Aunt Sophoria chuckled. 'You sound like me. And I thought you were a romantic like your mother.'

'I used to be.'

She regretted the words the instant they were out of her mouth. Why had she said that? She didn't want to think about who she used to be... Not to mention that Aunt Sophoria was now looking at her with a distinctly inquisitive expression.

'Do we have to go tonight, Aunt?' She turned her face away evasively.

'Not if you don't want to, dear. Is something the matter?'

'No. It's just... I haven't danced in so long. Balls, dances, entertainments like that...they seem to belong to another life somehow.'

'To when your parents were alive, you mean? Enjoying yourself doesn't mean that you've forgotten them.'

'I know, but it's not who I am any more.'

'Oh, my dear, you've been in mourning. It takes time to recover, but you're too young to hide away from the world. You were always such a happy girl. You will be again.'

Ianthe smiled weakly, wishing that were true. For a while she'd thought that it might be, that she could find happiness again with Albert, but look at how that had turned out... She'd left Bournemouth more unhappy than ever. She wasn't about to open herself up to that kind of hurt and humiliation again, not for anyone.

'You won't want to wear grey for ever, dear.'

'I will!' She pursed her lips tightly, trying to hold back the sudden onslaught of emotion. 'When I wear grey, people leave me alone. *Most people* anyway. That's all I want now, to be left alone.'

'Oh, my dear, why don't you tell me what happened?'

She stiffened at once. 'My parents...'

'Apart from that. There was a man, I suppose. There's usually a man.'

'I...' Ianthe bit her lip, the words on the very tip of her tongue. Surely, if anyone would understand about Albert, it was her aunt. It would be a relief to tell someone, to let it all out and ask whether what they'd said about her was true. But she still couldn't bear to talk about it, not yet.

'No?' Aunt Sophoria patted her cheek kindly. 'Well, when you're ready to talk, we can talk. In the meantime, we have a ball to attend.'

'But you said we didn't have to go!'

'That was before. Now I think it's the best thing for you. Besides…' she patted her blonde curls with a coquettish wink '…I think I look rather fetching, don't you?'

Ianthe smiled affectionately. Her aunt was wearing a white chiffon gown unsuitable for a woman half her age, yet somehow she carried it off.

'I think you look lovely, Aunt.'

'And we won't let Sir Charles ruin your evening. Let him have one dance and that's it. You won't be short of partners, I'm sure.'

Ianthe nodded doubtfully. Personally, she thought that any evening with Sir Charles was ruined already, but there seemed to be no way of avoiding him. He'd stayed for another half hour after Mr Felstone had left—until Aunt Sophoria had finally shooed him and Percy away—his behaviour just as disconcerting and confusing as always. She'd hardly spoken to him, let alone offered any encouragement, yet the looks he'd given her had been more intense than ever.

But perhaps her aunt was right. She couldn't simply hide from the world. And surely the new, sensible Ianthe could cope with anything Sir Charles might throw at her, no matter how uncomfortable he made her. If she couldn't avoid him, then she'd have to make her feelings clear once and for all.

She shook her head, wondering how it had happened, that she had two suitors, neither of whom she had any intention of marrying. If only Albert had shown half as much persistence as either! But it was no good. She *couldn't* marry one and she definitely *wouldn't* marry the other.

Whatever happened, she decided, she'd settle her future that night.

One hour later, Ianthe looked around the assembly hall with a gasp of delight. The room was fifty feet long, decorated with low-hanging Union Jack banners and baskets of cut flowers, the far wall entirely taken up with a giant papier-mâché model of a locomotive.

'It's lovely!'

'Do you think so?' Sir Charles sniffed haughtily. 'I thought it somewhat provincial myself.'

She threw him a glare. He'd met her at the front door, insisting on waiting for her outside the cloakroom so that they entered the hall together. So much for avoiding him, she thought angrily. They looked like an engaged couple!

'I don't want you monopolising my niece all night, Charles.' Aunt Sophoria gave him a stern look as she headed towards the chaperons' chairs. 'Or I'll make you dance with me instead.'

Ianthe put on a fake smile, wondering how to extricate herself as the Baronet escorted her around the edge of the hall, craning her neck as she searched for a glimpse of black hair in the crowd. Not that she wanted to see Mr Felstone, she told herself, but since she *had* to be there, she might at least talk to him. It would be infinitely preferable to being introduced to yet another of Sir Charles's acquaintances. His possessive behaviour was bad enough, but the way people were looking at her, as if she were some kind of rare bird, was even worse. What was going on? She felt as though everyone else in the room were in on some secret she herself was excluded from.

'Care to join us in a game, Mr Holt?'

She spun around in alarm as she heard one of the Baronet's friends address Percy. *That* was the last thing she needed. Her brother had been gambling too much over the past year, usually with little success. The man propositioning him looked older, more experienced and decidedly richer.

'Won't you dance with me first?' She put a restraining hand on Percy's arm.

He looked incredulous and she laughed, hooking her arm through his playfully. 'Why not? We haven't danced together in years. Please?'

'Oh, all right. One dance.'

She smiled with relief, making a brief curtsy to Sir Charles before pulling her brother away.

'Don't you have a dance card?' Percy looked at her quizzically as the orchestra struck up a waltz.

'Yes.' She tapped her reticule. Not that anyone had put their names in it yet. A few of Sir Charles's friends had seemed on the verge of asking for a dance, before a look from him had seemed to dissuade them.

'No takers, eh?' Percy shrugged. 'Not that it matters. You've already hooked Charles.'

'Mmm…' She tried to sound nonchalant. 'Speaking of Charles, perhaps you shouldn't play tonight.'

'What, you mean cards? Oh, I won't, not much, though it's good of his friends to invite me.'

'Do you have enough money?'

'Charles will spot me if I run short.'

'I thought you already owed him money.'

'Is this why you wanted to dance?' Percy's eyes narrowed suspiciously. 'So you could lecture me?'

'I just don't want you to get into trouble.'

'Well, I won't.' He spun her away from him roughly. 'And I don't need my sister nagging me about money either.'

Ianthe glanced around nervously. As usual, Percy was doing nothing to moderate his opinions and his raised voice was already starting to attract attention. 'I only want to help.'

'If you really want to help, then you know what to do.'

'That's not fair!'

'I'm serious. Charles is going to ask you to marry him tonight.'

'Tonight?' She almost tripped over his feet.

'Yes, and I expect you to be sensible. If you refuse him then I wash my hands of you.'

'Percy!' She gasped aloud, heedless of the heads now turned towards them. 'You don't mean that!'

'Don't I?' He turned on his heel, throwing her a petulant look before stalking angrily away, leaving her stranded and partnerless in the middle of the dance floor.

Ianthe stood frozen with shock, feeling as though she were caught in a trap. Surely Percy didn't mean it, wouldn't really disown her? But then she'd never have thought that he'd deliberately embarrass her in public either. People were already staring, some sympathetically, others nudging each other and smirking. She clenched her fists, resisting the urge to sink down in a heap and start crying. Percy might have humiliated her, but she wasn't going to show everyone how much he'd upset her, not here in front of an audience. At the very least, she had to get off the dance floor.

She took a step forward and then stopped. Sir Charles was standing straight ahead on the very edge of the dance floor as if he were simply waiting for her to come to him, thin lips curving in a smile that sent chills down her spine. *This* was the real trap. And there was nowhere to run, no other option, none except…

Strong fingers closed over hers suddenly, spinning her around as another hand clasped her waist.

'What…?' She looked up in panic, pulse quickening as she met a pair of familiar grey eyes.

'I saw that your brother was indisposed.' Mr Felstone gave her a dazzling, white-toothed smile before throwing a withering glance at a particularly inquisitive couple beside them, enough to make all the other dancers lower their eyes at once. 'If you'll permit me the honour of a dance, that is?'

She nodded mutely, too surprised to answer, feet moving instinctively to the music as her mind struggled to keep up. Where had he come from? In her turn around the room, she hadn't caught so much as a glimpse of him, however much she'd told herself she hadn't been looking. Now the very touch of his hand seemed to steal her breath away—not to mention his appearance, starkly handsome in elegant black-and-white evening clothes. The swooping sensation in her stomach was back with a vengeance, as if her insides were dancing along to the music as well. She wouldn't have believed such a feeling was possible, not with Percy's threat to disown her still fresh in her mind, and yet the sensation was even more powerful than before. How could she feel so upset and so giddy at the same time?

'Thank you.' She managed to croak out the words at last.

'It's my pleasure. As I said earlier, I'm glad to be of service.'

She made a sound somewhere between a laugh and a sob. 'I didn't think I'd need your help again so soon.'

'Miss Holt?' He looked genuinely concerned. 'Are you upset? Shall I escort you to the cloak-room?'

'No.' She shook her head firmly. If she started to cry, she didn't know whether she'd be able to stop. 'I'd rather stay here.'

'I'm pleased to hear it.'

He smiled gallantly, and she dropped her gaze at once. She'd forgotten quite how handsome he was when he smiled. The effect was quite disconcerting. Never mind that the way he said the words was almost tender, his deep voice curling around each syllable like a caress. She was seized by the irrational thought that he ought to read poetry. He'd be good at it.

She cleared her throat awkwardly. 'I ought to thank you for earlier, too, for staying when I asked. I'm indebted.'

'There's no debt. Considering my behaviour yesterday, it was the least I could do.' He nodded his head to where the Baronet was still standing on the edge of the dance floor, watching them with an enraged expression. 'I see we were half-successful. We made him jealous, though not enough to chase him away completely. He won't take his eyes off you.'

'No.' She shivered. 'He does that.'

'Watches you?' He frowned thoughtfully. 'He doesn't look very happy with either of us. You say he was friends with your parents?'

'My father really. Though he knew my mother first, from when they were young. Not that she liked him.' She hesitated for a moment, before deciding to go on. 'I heard my parents argue about him once. My mother didn't want him to visit any more, but my father said she was imagining things. I didn't hear what, but the words stayed with me.' She gave a small shudder. 'Sir Charles used to stare at her like that, too.'

'If I didn't know better I'd have thought you were already engaged.'

'What?' She tensed at once. 'What do you mean?'

'He seems very possessive.'

'And you think I'm to blame?'

'I didn't say that.'

'You think I've encouraged him?'

'Not at all.' His brows knit together sternly. 'I was commenting on his behaviour, Miss Holt, not yours.'

'I think I'd remember agreeing to marry someone!'

She clenched her jaw, fuming inwardly. Even if he hadn't meant to imply anything about *her* behaviour, the very idea was enraging. Everyone else in the room was likely thinking the same thing, too. That was probably the reason why no one else had asked her for a dance. Mr Felstone was the only one willing to risk the Baronet's displeasure.

Perhaps she was venting her anger on the wrong man after all...

'You've done a wonderful job here.' She gestured around the room, shifting the subject back to more neutral territory. 'It's so inventive.'

'I'm glad you think so.' He was still frowning. 'Though my involvement was mainly financial. I'm afraid my flower-arranging skills are sadly lacking.'

'Well, it looks beautiful. And the music...' she gestured towards the orchestra '...they're very good.'

'They are. You're an excellent dancer, too, Miss Holt, for someone who claims not to like it.'

'Thank you. I used to enjoy it.'

'Used to?' He raised an eyebrow. 'Am I such a terrible partner, then?'

She felt her lips quirk upwards, unable to suppress a smile. 'Not at all. I meant when I was younger.'

'As opposed to your great age now? I wouldn't put you in the chaperons' section quite yet.'

She caught her breath, squirming beneath the intensity of his gaze. She ought to end this, ought to make an excuse to get away. The fluttering sensation in her stomach was showing no sign of abating. If anything, it was only getting stronger. This was exactly what she'd been afraid of and yet, now that she was here, she didn't want the dance to end. The new, sensible Ianthe didn't approve of dancing, but she didn't want to listen to the new Ianthe any more. The dress, the surroundings, the music, the man she ought to resist—all of them seemed to be conspiring against her. She *wanted* to be her old self again, to forget all her anxieties about Percy and Sir Charles for a few moments and just dance.

What could possibly be the harm in that?

She tipped her head back, surrendering to the rhythm of the waltz, trusting herself to his hands as he guided her expertly around the dance floor. She felt a rush of excitement, as if her body had been asleep and she were waking up from a dream, reacting to every sound and sensation anew. She felt light-headed, relishing the warmth of his body through his coat, the solid strength of his shoulder beneath her kid glove. And yet she wanted to feel more, to lean closer, to put her head on his shoulder and feel the press of his body against hers. If they could only keep on dancing like this for ever...

The music stopped and she opened her eyes with a jolt. He was still holding on to her, looking down into her face with surprise and something else, some emotion she couldn't quite put her finger on, but something that made her sway instinctively towards him. Something that reminded her of Albert.

She jerked back abruptly, the new Ianthe reasserting herself. This was the moment when she ought to tell him that she couldn't marry him, no matter how grateful she was for his help or how alive he made her feel... She ought to tell him right now. If she could only find the words...

'You look different, Miss Holt.' His voice sounded even deeper than before. 'You seem to be a different woman every time I see you.'

'Different?' She echoed the word, vaguely crestfallen. 'Don't you like the gown?'

His brow creased slightly. 'Gown? Yes, it's very fetching.'

'Oh.' She pursed her lips. Wasn't it respectable enough for him, then? Not that he'd any right to criticise when he was the one who'd brought it!

'I meant it as a compliment, Miss Holt.'

'Thank you,' she answered stiffly. 'You'll have to thank your friend for lending it to me.'

'You can thank her yourself. Here she is.'

The words had barely left his mouth before a

woman in cobalt-blue satin accosted them, enveloping her in a hug almost before she had a chance to turn round.

'Dear Miss Holt, how wonderful to see you again. I know you won't mind my being so forward, but you look just the same as I remember. You remember me, don't you? I'm Kitty Loveday, formerly Tremain. This is my husband, Giles.'

'Of course.' Ianthe returned the embrace cautiously, struggling to keep up with the flow of words. 'I'm delighted to make your acquaintance again.'

'Robert has told us so much about you.' The tall peacock feather in Kitty's hair bobbed up and down enthusiastically. 'I don't think I've ever heard him talk for so long about anything that wasn't a ship or a train. I can tell he's quite smitten with you.'

'Smitten?' She stole a swift glance sideways, though judging by the scowl on his face the feeling had been quite transitory.

'And that gown looks simply breathtaking on you. I so wished I could have worn it myself, but Robert insisted.'

'Kitty...' His voice held a note of warning.

'But why didn't you?' She glanced down guiltily. 'I'd never have borrowed it if I'd known.'

'Why, isn't it obvious?' Kitty giggled. 'He can be very cunning, you know...'

Ianthe shook her head in confusion. It wasn't

obvious at all. Nothing about this evening was obvious—why she'd come, why Percy was behaving so differently, why her own body seemed to be wilfully betraying her better judgement? As for why Mr Felstone would have insisted on Kitty lending her a dress that she wanted to wear, she had no idea. None of it made any sense, though whatever Kitty was getting at, she had a feeling she might not want to know. Neither of her male companions were looking particularly pleased with her.

'How do you like Pickering, Miss Holt?' The husband, Giles, came to her rescue.

'I haven't seen much of it so far.' She smiled gratefully. 'It's been a long time since I visited.'

'You're from London, I believe?'

'Yes. Wimbledon.'

'Me, too. I came north for work and never left.'

'Thanks to me.' Kitty linked her arm through his.

'Thanks to you.' He smiled and Ianthe felt an unexpected pang of jealousy. Despite Kitty's indiscreet manner, the way they looked at each other was genuinely affectionate. It was the way she'd thought, *hoped*, she might have been with Albert. Before she knew better.

'So if you're both from London and I'm from Pickering, then it's only Robert who won't tell us where he's from.' Kitty gave a sly smile. 'Though perhaps he will if *you* ask him, Ianthe?'

'Me?' She shook her head uncertainly. 'If he doesn't wish to tell, then I doubt I'll be able to persuade him.'

'Oh, but do try. He's so secretive, it drives me to distraction. I can't think why he won't say.'

'Because it's not very interesting.' He sounded stern again suddenly. 'You already know my mother left Levisham before I was born and we moved to Whitby when I was twelve. I don't see why any further details are necessary.'

'I'm only curious.'

'Then I'm sorry to disappoint you, Kitty. Again.'

'But if you just give us a clue…'

'You expressed an interest in the decorations, Miss Holt.' He spoke over Kitty, extending an arm out towards her. 'Would you care to take a closer look?'

Ianthe looked at his arm, torn between wildly conflicting emotions. As much as she wanted to escape Kitty's questions, she found physical contact with him equally disconcerting. On the other hand, while she was with him, Sir Charles seemed to be keeping his distance. Surely that was a good enough reason to stay by his side?

'I'd be delighted.' She placed a hand on his biceps tentatively, trying not to react as an immediate jolt passed between them.

'This way then, Miss Holt.'

They made their way in strained silence around

the room. The decorations were as impressive up close as they'd been from a distance, though she found it hard to appreciate them with her angry companion standing so close beside her. His obvious bad mood was starting to affect her nerves. She'd been afraid of him bringing up the subject of marriage again, but he seemed in no mood to talk at all. He was still scowling, as if Kitty's questions had struck a particularly raw nerve. Surely a little conversation wouldn't go amiss... At last she couldn't bear the silence any longer.

'I don't think she meant to upset you.'

'Mmm?' His scowl deepened momentarily, as if he'd forgotten she was there. 'Oh, I know. Her heart's in the right place, but she's just...'

'Inquisitive?'

'That would be the polite way of putting it. If it weren't already so blindingly obvious, I'd warn you not to tell her any secrets.'

She stiffened immediately. 'What makes you think that I have any?'

'Doesn't everyone?'

'Do you?' She turned the question around.

'Most of my secrets are already public knowledge.'

'They can't be so bad, then.'

'That depends on your perspective.' He gave a bitter-sounding laugh. 'There's very little about my past that people around here don't know. Most of what they say is true, though you should know that I've no intention of discussing any of it either now or in the future.'

'Oh.' She started, taken aback by the sudden granite tone of his voice. His eyes, too, were hooded, as if shutters had been deliberately drawn over them. On the other hand, his words brought a glimmer of hope. A husband who didn't want to talk about his past could hardly expect his wife to reveal too much about hers. In which case...*could* she consider his offer? The thought made her breathing quicken erratically.

'Perhaps some secrets are best kept hidden?' She tried to keep her tone light.

'There's no perhaps about it. There are some things about my own past I'd rather not know. I prefer to look to the future. Unless I can learn from the past, I'd rather not look back.'

She turned her face aside, mind racing with the implications of his words. If there were some things he preferred not to know, then maybe there was no need for her to tell him about Albert. No need for him ever to know. If she could be the wife he wanted *now*, could that be all that mattered?

'Have I shocked you, Miss Holt?'

She kept her face averted so that he couldn't read her expression. In truth, it was her own thoughts that shocked her. His proposal wasn't romantic, but it might be the escape she was looking for—an arrangement that would benefit both of them—wasn't that what he'd said? She didn't want to be rescued any more than she wanted to be coerced or threatened, but if her brother really disowned her then she'd have little choice but to accept one of her suitors, and if she had to choose one…

And surely the strange physical reaction she seemed to feel around him would pass? After all, it was only physical. She didn't dislike him any more—not after he'd come to her rescue twice in one day—but she wasn't about to do anything so foolish as fall in love with him. After what had happened with Albert, she'd no intention of falling for any man's charms ever again.

In which case, she might as well *consider* his offer…

'Not at all, Mr Felstone. I was simply thinking about your proposal. I was wondering whether, as a man of business, you'd be prepared to negotiate…'

Chapter Six

'I'm *always* prepared to discuss terms, Miss Holt.' Robert concealed his surprise with an effort. 'What exactly did you have in mind?'

'You said that you wanted a business arrangement.' She spoke slowly, as if choosing her words with care. 'I'd like to know what exactly that would entail.'

'Very well, then. Perhaps we should sit down?'

He led her into the supper room, glancing back over his shoulder towards Sir Charles. He was still standing on the edge of the dance floor, watching them with a look of ill-concealed, simmering fury. Robert narrowed his gaze, vaguely disturbed by the intensity of the other man's expression. This was more than just jealousy. This looked like something more, something darker. He was looking at Ianthe as if she were a possession he wanted back. At him, as if he wanted to shoot him.

Well, at least there were some benefits to not being considered a proper gentleman, he decided, turning his back contemptuously. Sir Charles probably assumed, quite rightly, that he was more than prepared to fight back.

'Would you care for some punch, Miss Holt?'

She nodded, and he led her towards a small table, stalling for time as he tried to gather his scattered thoughts. Whether she needed a drink or not, he certainly did. What *did* he expect from a wife? To be honest, he hadn't thought that far ahead, though now the question raised distracting possibilities. He wasn't accustomed to being caught off guard, especially in contract negotiations, but she seemed to be full of surprises this evening.

Her appearance, for one. He'd intended the dress as a gesture, simply selecting a style and colour he'd thought would suit her. He *hadn't* expected her to look quite so good in it. The shoulderless style accentuated the sleek, smooth curve of her neck, not to mention the way her breasts swelled distractingly over the top of her bodice. She'd done her hair differently, too, arranging it in a softer style than before, making her gaunt features appear less severe and yet, paradoxically, her eyes even more huge, like umber-brown orbs that seemed to glow with amber flecks in the candlelight.

His eyes had been drawn towards her the moment she'd entered the hall, though it had taken a few more seconds for him to actually recognise her. She seemed to have gone from virago to vision in just one day. At first he'd kept to the back of the room, keeping out of sight as he'd battled an unexpected surge of jealousy, trying to work out the relationship between her and Sir Charles. Judging by the Baronet's proprietorial manner, a casual observer might reasonably have assumed they were engaged already. Certainly everyone else in the room seemed to think so. Only she seemed resistant to the idea, the tension in her face obvious even from a distance.

She'd practically dragged her brother out on to the dance floor, though whatever their argument had been about had been enough to drain the colour from her face in an instant. Not for the first time, he'd thought that what the youth needed was a good sound smack in the jaw, though seeing him abandon her so cruelly, he'd revised that opinion to a thorough beating instead. Seeing her standing alone, the object of laughter and ridicule, he'd rushed to her aid with the sole intention of offering comfort. He hadn't been thinking about marriage, hadn't intended to bring the subject up at all.

He certainly hadn't expected her to do it. Was she seriously considering it, then?

He poured her a glass of punch before filling his own to the brim. After their dance, he needed to calm more than his thoughts. The way her body had softened beneath his touch, yielding to his embrace as they'd whirled breathlessly around the room, had been surprising and enticing in equal measure. He'd actually found it a wrench to let her go at the end.

He hadn't been exaggerating when he'd said that she seemed like a different woman. She thought he'd been talking about the dress, though he'd actually been studying her face, trying to reconcile its carefree expression with that of the severe-looking woman he'd proposed to on the train. The features were the same and yet every-thing else about her seemed completely different. How could he ever have thought she looked se-vere? At second, or more accurately *third* sight, she was one of the prettiest women he'd ever laid eyes on.

'So this business arrangement...' She peered at him over the edge of her glass. 'What are your terms exactly, Mr Felstone?'

'Robert.' He pulled out a chair opposite her. 'If we're discussing marriage, then I think you can start using my first name.'

'Very well.' She glanced around the room, as if afraid of being overheard. 'Then you may call me Ianthe.'

'Ianthe.' He leaned forward, resting a forearm on the table. 'Then to answer your question, I ex-pect my wife to attend social functions with me, to make calls and arrange the occasional dinner party. Beyond that, you may do as you please.'

She dipped her head thoughtfully. 'That sounds acceptable. Though I'd like to do more with my time than make calls and arrange entertainments.'

'I'm glad to hear it. I wouldn't stop you from doing anything else that you wanted.'

'I like lectures, music recitals, art exhibitions. Would you permit me to attend such events?'

'Of course. Though I wouldn't have thought...' He paused mid-sentence. He'd been about to say that he wouldn't have thought she'd be interested in such things, but the look on her face was intensely serious.

'You thought what?' She looked offended, as if she'd just read his mind. 'Those things mean a great deal to me.'

'Like dancing?'

She flushed slightly. 'That's different, but, yes. I couldn't give them up, not for anyone.'

'I wouldn't ask you to.'

'Some men would disapprove.'

'Lester, for example?'

Her brow furrowed slightly. 'He once told me that art led my mother astray, not that I knew what he meant.'

'In that case, you may stray as far as you wish. Within reason, of course.'

'So it would be a strictly business arrangement?'

She bit her lip and his gaze followed the movement. Funny, he hadn't noticed how full her lips were before, probably because she pursed them so often. Now they looked luscious and moist and surprisingly tempting, as red as the cheeks that seemed to be darkening even as he watched.

'Robert?'

'Mmm?' He forced his gaze back up.

'I asked if it would be strictly a business arrangement.'

'As I said.'

'Entirely?'

'Ah.' He lifted an eyebrow as he realised what she was really asking him. Truly, she *was* full of surprises. 'You mean would it be a real marriage?'

'Yes.' She dropped her eyes to the table, blushing furiously as she trailed a pattern along the wood with her fingertip. 'I mean…I understand that most men want heirs?'

He raised his cup and drained the remainder of his punch in one mouthful. Generally, he preferred to keep *that* part of his life separate from his day-to-day existence, visiting a certain discreet lady in Malton whenever the need arose, though he supposed such visits would have to stop once he was married. In truth, he hadn't given the possibility of a physical relationship with *her* any thought. He'd proposed largely because he hadn't been attracted to her, however ridiculous that idea seemed to him now. He certainly hadn't expected such thoughts to cross *her* mind, though her anxious expression told him everything he needed to know about her own feelings on the subject.

The realisation was unexpectedly disappointing, though at least he could ease her fears on that score.

'I already have a ward, a boy I'm raising as my heir. I'm teaching him business, though it occurs to me that you might be able to fill in the gaps in his education. Poetry and history, for example.'

'Oh.' Her eyes flew to his with a look of surprise. 'So you *do* want a governess?'

'I suppose so, if that idea's more agreeable to you.'

She didn't answer, resting her elbows on the table and tapping her fingers together with a contemplative expression.

'Is there something else worrying you?' Odd that he actually enjoyed studying her face now. She really was far prettier than he'd first given her credit for.

'No. Yes.' She took a deep breath and then let it out again slowly. 'It's just so…final.'

'Marriage?' He laughed. 'I believe it's supposed to be.'

'Yes, but to do it for *business*. It just doesn't seem a good enough reason.'

'It seems as good as any to me.'

'But what if...?' She hesitated, as if reluctant to voice her thoughts aloud.

'What if...?'

'What about *love*?' She dropped her hands, fixing him with a serious stare. 'You say you're not capable of it, but what if you just haven't met the right person yet? What if you meet them later? Then I'll be in the way. It could all be such a dreadful mistake.'

He gave a shout of laughter, so loud that at least twenty heads swivelled towards them.

'It's not funny!' she hissed across the table.

'It is.'

'I don't see why. People fall in love every day.'

'Some of them even believe it, too.'

'They do!' She folded her arms indignantly. 'How can you be so cynical?'

'Experience, remember?' He cleared his throat, trying to be serious. 'I don't think your question is really aimed at me, Ianthe. I told you, if it's romance you're after, I'm not your man.'

'That's obvious, though I certainly wasn't talking about myself.'

'No?'

'No! I have no expectations on that score, I assure you.'

'Then it seems we're quite compatible after all.' He grinned, but she only glared back at him belligerently.

'And what if your business deal falls through?'

'Why should it?'

'I've no idea, but I should imagine there are lots of ways. But if it does, then you'll have married me for nothing. Have you thought about that?'

'I've considered the risks.'

'Maybe they're bigger than you think.'

He raised an eyebrow. She sounded as if she were trying to warn him of something. She certainly seemed to have thought of every possible obstacle to their union, though she still hadn't said no…

'Perhaps I think you're a risk worth taking, Ianthe.' He put both hands on the table, laying his terms out as straightforwardly as possible. 'Look, I've told you what I want. I intend to own the biggest shipyard on the east coast. I need a respectable wife to help me achieve that. My instincts tell me that's you, but the decision is yours. I'm leaving Pickering tomorrow afternoon. Needless to say, my offer leaves with me.'

'So soon?'

'Unfortunately, yes. I have a board meeting at the station in the morning, but with your permission I'll call at your aunt's just after noon. I need an answer before I return to Whitby.'

'So let me get this straight.' She frowned pensively. 'If you're not married, then your neighbour won't sell his yard?'

'Not to me, no.'

'So you absolutely *need* a wife?'

'Yes.'

'And buying his yard is important to you? As long as that goes ahead, that's all that matters?'

'I suppose so.' Not that he would have put it quite so bluntly...

'And it's me or no one?'

'At this point, yes. Unless you can find me another willing candidate.' He jerked his head towards the ballroom, trying to lighten the tone. 'Would your aunt be willing, do you think?'

Her lips curved upwards. 'More than willing, I think. She's been singing your praises all day.'

'Really?' He beamed. 'I'm flattered.'

'She said you were civil *and* charming.'

'And you thought she was talking about a different man?'

Brown eyes sparked with humour. 'I thought you had an evil twin.'

'Ah...' he chuckled '...you wound me, Miss Holt, though I suppose I deserve that. But there's no evil twin, I'm afraid, just me. You'll have to take me or leave me as I am.'

'Very well.' She pushed her chair back, still smiling. 'Then I'll let you know my decision tomor— Oh!'

A look of consternation crossed her face as she glanced through the archway that led to the card room. Robert turned around at once, expecting to see an altercation at least, but there was only her brother playing poker with a group of the Baronet's cronies.

'You don't like your brother playing cards?' he hazarded a guess.

'It's not that. It's just…he's not good at it. I ought to stop him.'

'Wait!' He sprang up as she started out of her chair, grasping her arm just above the elbow. 'He might not appreciate his sister coming to the rescue.'

She froze, her whole body seeming to stiffen the moment he touched her. So did his, though in a very different way. He could feel her heartbeat accelerate beneath his fingers, tempting him to pull her into his arms, to press his lips against her shoulder, to trail them along the smooth curve of her throat. Would the skin there feel so soft? The desire to find out was surprisingly tempting.

He loosened his hold, trailing his fingertips down to her elbow before he finally let go. Clearly the punch had been stronger than he'd thought.

'I've no intention of embarrassing him.' Her voice sounded breathless.

'I'm sure you do not, but considering what happened earlier…'

He left the sentence unfinished, taking her

flushed cheeks to show that she understood his meaning.

'I have to do something.'

'Then let me go. If I join the game, then perhaps I can persuade him to leave.'

She looked up at him uncertainly. 'He's *my* brother.'

'And if you agree to my proposal, he'll be mine, too. Why not let me help?'

'You don't mind?'

He bit back a grimace. *Mind* was an understatement. He hated gambling with a vengeance, but he wasn't about to let her go marching into the card room either. Even if it hadn't been for her brother's earlier behaviour, Sir Charles was standing beside the door, waiting to close it behind her most likely. What was wrong with the man? He looked like a hunter ready to throw a net over his prey.

'What if you lose?'

He gave her a look that was part-offence, part-amusement. 'I appreciate the confidence.'

'I didn't mean it like that. I just meant that if you do lose, I won't be able to pay you back, not for a while anyway.'

'I wouldn't expect you to.'

'And I can't promise anything else either.' She held his gaze seriously. 'About your proposal, I mean.'

'You'll be under no obligation, Ianthe.' He

frowned at the very suggestion. What kind of man did she think he was? 'Call this my last apology for yesterday. After this, we'll be even.'

'Very well then.' She looked relieved. 'Thank you.'

'Is your brother staying at your aunt's house, too?'

'No, at the White Swan.'

'Then I'll make sure he gets back safely.'

'Promise?'

She grasped at his sleeve, and he nodded, touched by her care for her brother. It was only a pity the youth didn't deserve it.

'I'll do my best, I promise that.' He glanced down at her hand, barely resisting the impulse to cover it with his own. The urge to touch her again was almost overwhelming. But if he touched her now then he'd have to find a way to let her go again as well. Somehow, for some inexplicable reason, he didn't know if he could.

'It might take me a while.' He cleared his throat huskily.

'Of course.' Her hand slipped from his arm as she took a step backwards. 'In that case, I'll go and find my aunt. It's getting late.'

'Good idea.' He inclined his head. 'In that case, don't worry, Ianthe. Trust me.'

'I do.' She looked him straight in the eye with a look that he couldn't interpret. 'I'll see you tomorrow at noon.'

Chapter Seven

Ianthe glanced impatiently at her aunt's front door, pacing up and down as she waited for news. At first she'd tried pacing the parlour, but after bumping into the furniture a half-dozen times she'd finally given up and come out to the hall. She needed to keep moving, needed to do *something* to stop herself from worrying about Percy. Despite his behaviour, she still wanted to know he was all right. She'd hardly slept, wishing that she hadn't left him the night before. What if Mr Felstone—*Robert*, she corrected herself—hadn't been able to get him away from the gambling table? What if he was ruined? What if they were destitute?

What had happened?

The front door opened and she whirled around expectantly, practically jumping upon her aunt as she entered.

'Have you seen him? Have you seen Percy?'

'Good gracious, no.' Aunt Sophoria tugged at the strings of an oversized gingham bonnet with a chuckle. 'He's still asleep, the landlord says. Returned to his room quite the worse for wear apparently, but there's no need to worry. He was the victor last night.'

'Percy *won*?' Ianthe gaped at her aunt in astonishment. Of all the outcomes she'd anticipated, that one had never occurred to her.

'A small fortune, too, by all accounts.'

'But he never wins! I've been so worried!'

'Why?' Aunt Sophoria patted her curls back into place nonchalantly. 'You left him with Mr Felstone, didn't you?'

'Yes, but…'

'Not that he'll be so pleased about that. He's the one who lost.'

'*What?*' The feeling of relief vanished at once. 'You mean *Robert* lost money to Percy?'

'Robert, indeed?' Aunt Sophoria gave her a sly wink. 'Yes, I'm afraid so. The curious thing is that he never usually gambles at all, though now I suppose we know why. Still, a man can't be good at everything. Shall I make tea?'

'No.' Ianthe grasped hold of the banisters, thoughts still reeling. 'Thank you, Aunt, but I think I'll take a walk.'

'Good idea.' Aunt Sophoria bustled off into the parlour. 'I could do with a nap anyway. See you at lunch, dear.'

Ianthe picked up her bonnet and shawl with a deep feeling of guilt. *She* was the one who'd sent Robert into the card room. If she'd known he was an inexperienced card player, she would never have done so. But then why had he volunteered? Why had he risked it? And just how much was a *small fortune*?

She stood outside on the pavement for a few moments, wondering which way to turn. She didn't want to go into town, didn't want to see or speak to anyone until she'd had a chance to clear her head. She needed time and peace to think rationally. With all the worry about Percy, she'd hardly had a moment to consider Robert's proposal, let alone make up her mind.

How long until their interview? The grandmother's clock in her aunt's hallway had said it was just before ten. That gave her another two hours to decide.

She turned her feet in the opposite direction, making her way up the hill and along a succession of side streets towards the castle, impressed as always by the sight of the three giant stone towers standing like silent sentinels over the town. The original fortress was old, dating back almost to the Conquest, though the stone edifice had been added later by Henry III. Six hundred years later, the towers and curtain walls were still standing mostly intact—the same ruins she'd climbed on as a child, though they had more of an air of neglect than she remembered, the original gateway boarded up and half-hidden by weeds.

It had always been a special place for her, the place where her parents had met, where her artist father had spied her mother sitting under the battlements, poetry book in hand, a vision waiting to be painted, or so he'd always said. Entranced by the sight, he'd asked permission to paint her portrait and that had been that. They'd fallen in love that very afternoon, in the space of one sitting.

Ianthe heaved a sigh, starting to relax in the familiar surroundings, remembering the way her father's face had softened and her mother had gazed back adoringly whenever they'd spoken of that first meeting—a story they'd loved to tell as much as she'd loved to hear it, one that had always given her hope for her own future, in the possibility of finding love for herself. Too much sensibility, her aunt had said, and perhaps she was right. Romance had turned to love for her parents, but then not everyone was so lucky...

She climbed over a pile of boulders and sat down on the edge of the old moat, now a ditch filled with nettles and long grass, pulling off her bonnet and placing it on the ground beside her as she thought of her own disastrous love affair. There had been no happy ending for her. Albert had pursued her during his summer break from university, following her around under the pretext of spending time with his younger sisters, quoting Byron, Marvell and Shelley, all of her favourite poets, pledging his heartfelt devotion on a daily basis.

Still in mourning for her parents, she'd been flattered by the attention, pleased to find someone she thought was a kindred spirit in her lonely existence, turning a blind eye to the more selfish, self-centred aspects of his personality. Now she knew that she'd been deceiving herself all along—a realisation that had been almost as painful as the rest of it. She'd been stupidly naive, so desperate to feel something—*anything*—but grief, that she'd willed herself into falling in love with him, as if by recreating her parents' love story she could somehow bring them back. She'd agreed to the elopement against her own better judgement, knowing that his family would disapprove, but believing that love would conquer all.

It hadn't.

Their love affair had started with poetry and ended in bitter, hurtful recrimination. When his family had overtaken them on the road to Scotland, it had taken less than ten minutes for them to turn him against her. He'd stood and listened as his parents had called her a schemer and seductress, every vile name she could imagine, berating her for so long and so vociferously that she'd almost started to believe the words herself. She'd risked her heart, her reputation and her future on a man she'd thought had loved her, but his affections had been worse than fickle. They'd been entirely false.

She'd returned to London and Percy under a grey cloud, heartbroken and humiliated, vowing never to let any man get so close to her again, putting on her grey dress as a sign to the world that *that* part of her life was over. Robert was wrong when he accused her of waiting for romance. The old Ianthe had risked everything for love and lost. Even if she were tempted, the new Ianthe would never be so foolish—wouldn't gamble her heart and happiness on any man again.

In which case, why not accept Robert's proposal? It was a good one, everything her new sensible persona could ask for, even if it was all a pretence. Neither of their hearts was in any danger. He'd been brutally honest about that, telling her he wasn't capable of love—laughing at the very idea—and making it abundantly clear that he'd no romantic intentions towards her, let alone physical ones. She didn't need to provide him with children, didn't need to do anything except put on a respectable façade.

More importantly, *he* was the one who'd said the past didn't matter. And if it really didn't, if he was truly looking to the future, then perhaps there was no need for her to tell him anything about hers either. The only people who knew about the elopement were Percy and Albert's family, none of whom were ever likely to tell.

So long as she was beyond reproach *now*, surely that was all that mattered. The past could stay in the past and she could accept his proposal with a clear conscience...couldn't she?

She pulled her knees up to her chest and rested her chin on top, already knowing the answer. The truth about her elopement wasn't particularly scandalous. She'd shared a closed carriage and a few stolen kisses with Albert, that was all. But Robert had proposed believing her to be someone she wasn't, someone without a past, without any hint of scandal, and *definitely* without the strange urges he seemed to awaken in her, urges that would probably repel him if he ever knew about them.

Not that he'd seemed entirely averse to her at the ball. During their dance—those few moments of weakness when she'd let the old Ianthe free from her self-imposed prison—his expression had shifted to something strangely akin to yearning. He'd accused her of looking like a different woman, but he'd seemed a different man, too. His tall, powerful body had moved to the music in perfect time to hers, the metallic hardness of his eyes turning smoky, as if the iron in them had melted, boring into hers with a nerve-tingling intensity...

She heard a crunch behind her and glanced casually over her shoulder, expecting to see a squirrel or bird and finding Sir Charles there instead.

For a few terrifying seconds her heart seemed to thud to a standstill and then start pounding again, harder and faster as if to make up for lost time. He was standing only a few feet away, staring at her with a voracious expression that made her blood run cold.

She scrambled quickly to her feet, alarm bells clamouring a warning in her head. Something in his expression warned her that things had changed between them. There was nothing elegant or urbane or remotely gentlemanly about him now. Outside the trappings of society, his face looked leaner, sharper and more predatory, the fervent look in his eyes pinning her to the spot.

She dragged in a breath, trying not to panic as she looked around for a route of escape. It was impossible to think that he'd simply found her by accident. She was in a secluded part of the ruins and she hadn't told anyone where she was going. He must have followed her deliberately. Why? What did he want from her? If the look on his face was anything to judge by, she didn't want to find out. She only knew that she had to get away from him as quickly as possible.

Even if the only way out was around him.

'Good morning, Sir Charles.' She tried to brazen it out, keeping her tone as casual as possible. 'It's a pleasant morning for a stroll, is it not?'

'Ianthe.' His voice was a hard monotone. 'I don't like being made a fool of.'

'What do you mean?' Her throat tightened uncomfortably.

'You left the ball very early last night.'

'I was tired.'

'You embarrassed me.'

He took a step forward, and she dug her heels into the grass, resisting the urge to back away. She had a feeling that he'd pounce if she showed even the faintest sign of weakness. Her only choice was to face him down, confront him and hope that she found an opportunity to escape.

'That wasn't my intention, but I had every right to leave when I wanted.'

'What about spending half the evening with Robert Felstone?'

'That would be my business.' She inched her chin up defiantly. 'He's an acquaintance. I don't see how my talking to him reflects upon you.'

'I made introductions on your behalf.'

'I never asked you to.'

She glanced quickly past his shoulder, searching for aid and finding none. There was no one around, no one to see, just crumbling stone walls and a screen of foliage. What had she been thinking, coming here on her own, believing that the romance of the past would somehow protect her? How could she have been so naive? Again! She might as well have sent Sir Charles an invitation. Every instinct told her to get away from him now. If she could just get away from the castle and back on to the street, surely he'd never dare to accost her in public like this.

'Now if you'll excuse me…' she stepped to one side, attempting to curve around him '…I'm late for lunch with my aunt.'

A hand shot out, catching her arm just above the elbow. 'You know I've always taken a keen interest in you, Ianthe.'

She froze, her blood turning to ice beneath his touch. 'There's no need for you to do so.'

'I think there is.' He yanked her towards him suddenly, holding her so close that she could feel the rasp of his breath on her cheek. 'And you're not going anywhere until we understand each other.'

'No!' She tugged on her arm, but his grip only tightened.

'Your mother was wilful, too.' His voice hardened as he watched her impassively. 'Headstrong. Impulsive. Stupid.'

'How dare you!' She stopped struggling and swung her free hand up instead, slapping him hard across the face, but he hardly seemed to notice.

'I loved her anyway. I always did, but I was too young when we met. My parents refused to consider the match so I let her get away. It was the biggest mistake of my life. I won't make the same one with you.'

'*What?*' She gaped at him, too shocked even to fight.

'We loved each other.'

'Liar! She loved my father!'

'The *artist*?' Sir Charles's voice positively dripped with contempt. 'She only thought so at first. By the time she came to her senses it was too late. She wanted me. *We* wanted each other. All these years, we only wanted each other.'

'No!' Ianthe gasped in horror, refusing to believe it. It couldn't be true. If it was, then her whole life was based on a lie. It *wasn't* true! She *wouldn't* believe it. 'You were friends with my father!'

'Like with your brother, you mean?'

'But…' She shook her head, unable to comprehend such duplicity. 'I don't understand. Why would you pretend to like them?'

'To see her.' His gaze softened for a moment, as if he were looking inwards, before focusing intently again upon her. 'And you.'

'Me?'

'If it hadn't been for you, this last year would have destroyed me. When I lost her, I felt as though I'd lost a part of myself, too. That's why I went abroad, to try to find some peace, but I couldn't.'

Even despite their situation, she felt a flicker of sympathy. 'I understand. I've been grieving, too, but she's gone.'

'Not completely.' He coiled an arm around her waist, pulling her against him so tightly that she could hardly breathe. 'There's still a part of her left.'

'No!' Her eyes widened in horror as she realised what he meant. 'I'm not her! I can't replace her!'

'You're close enough. And now that she's gone, there's only you.'

He gave a twisted smile as his lips fell upon hers, plundering her mouth with a ferocity that made her cry out in pain.

'Let me go!' She flung her face to one side, spitting into the dirt.

'You can make it right, Ianthe.' He grabbed the back of her neck, panting against her ear as he twisted her head back towards him. 'You can fix her mistake.'

'Never!'

With a burst of rage, she brought her knee up and kicked him hard in the groin, wrenching herself free as he dropped to the ground with a grunt of pain.

Quickly, she seized the advantage, half-scrambling, half-vaulting over a pile of boulders, skidding on the grass as she bolted headlong back towards the path. For a horrible moment, she felt her shawl snag on the stone, but she let it go, hurtling breathlessly towards the safety of the houses.

He was mad!

She didn't stop running when she reached the street, charging on past the houses, heedless of her appearance, trying to shake off the horror of what had just happened. The truth was more appalling than she'd imagined. So that was the reason Sir Charles never saw any difference in her appearance—because he wasn't seeing *her* at all! Whatever crazed obsession he'd felt for her mother he'd simply transferred on to her! That was the whole reason he wanted her—why he watched her, why he seemed unable to take no for an answer. As for her mother's feelings for *him*... she couldn't think about those just yet. Right now she felt as though her whole world were spinning off its axis. She had to get back to the safety of her aunt's house and hide.

For how long?

She reached the top of the Market Place and skidded to a halt. How long *could* she hide there? She couldn't expect Aunt Sophoria to let her stay for ever. Her aunt had a small enough income without supporting her as well. But what else could she do? Where could she go? She had the unnerving suspicion that Sir Charles would follow her wherever she went. After thirty years of pining after her mother, it seemed unlikely that he'd simply give up now. She couldn't even rely on Percy not to tell him where she was. If she really wanted to escape, then she'd have to break with *him*, too, and she couldn't do that. Even if he *had* threatened to disown her, he was still her brother.

No, she realised, if she couldn't fight or hide, then there was only one thing she *could* do. She could take refuge in plain sight, where Sir Charles could see, but surely wouldn't dare to touch her. She didn't have a choice any longer—had to grasp the only lifeline she had left.

Rightly or wrongly, she had to find Robert and accept him.

Chapter Eight

Robert drummed his fingers on the tabletop, willing the meeting to end. The members of the Railway Board were being particularly long-winded this morning, even more so than usual. At that moment, the possibility of a branch line to Scarborough occupied less of his mind than trying to think up a half-decent excuse to escape.

He threw an impatient glance at the clock. Still an hour until noon. What would Ianthe's answer be? he wondered. He didn't know what to expect. He couldn't even guess how she would look today, let alone what she might say. But if she said yes…

His lips curved in a half-smile. If she said yes, then he could start drawing up plans for expanding the shipyard tomorrow. Harper was prepared to sell—his sources had already confirmed that—and he could offer a better price than any of his competitors. Once he had a respectable bride to show him as well, there'd be no reason for the old man to say no. The sale could go through in a matter of months.

Not that Ianthe was quite the same woman he'd initially proposed to. The way she'd looked during their dance was seared into his memory, heating his blood every time he thought of it, but then he supposed there were worse things than having a wife he was actually attracted to. She still wouldn't distract him from his work, he'd make certain of that. And if a physical relationship were to develop over time, it wasn't likely to affect him unduly. It wasn't as if he were likely to fall in love with her. All things considered, the arrangement should still work out well for both of them.

He was still considering the matter when a clerk popped his head around the door, looking apologetically towards him.

'Excuse me, but there's a young lady here who says she knows Mr Felstone. I'm sorry to bother you with it, sir, but she seems quite distressed.'

'Of course.' Robert pushed his chair back at once, ignoring the sound of aggrieved mutterings from his colleagues. 'Excuse me, gentlemen.'

He hurried outside, striding purposefully along the platform to where Ianthe was standing with her back hunched against a wall, arms wrapped around her waist as if she were trying to make herself look as inconspicuous as possible. She was in the same shapeless grey dress he'd first seen her wearing on the train, but with no shawl or bonnet, as if she'd come out in a hurry. Her hair was uncharacteristically dishevelled, too, with long, wispy tendrils hanging loose over her face that she made no attempt to push back. Just one glimpse told him something was wrong. Her cheeks were unnaturally pale, but the rest of her features were more animated than he'd ever seen them, her eyes darting from side to side as if they couldn't bear to stop moving, while she was chewing her bottom lip so frantically that it actually looked swollen.

Something was definitely wrong.

'Ianthe?' He got straight to the point. 'What's the matter?'

She looked up at the sound of his voice, a fleeting look of panic turning instantly to one of relief. 'Your proposal, does it still stand?'

'What?' He came to an abrupt halt mid-step. 'Yes, of course.'

'Then I accept.' She spoke quickly, as if rushing the words out before either of them could change their minds. 'I'll marry you.'

He tipped his head to one side in acknowledgement, trying not to look too surprised by her answer, let alone her manner of giving it. She looked positively frightened, clasping her hands together in front of her in a futile effort to stop them from shaking. Surely she wasn't frightened of *him*? She'd never given any indication of it before, though he supposed the idea of marriage itself might be intimidating. Given the chaste nature of his proposal, however, he wouldn't have expected such extreme behaviour. Her brown eyes had an over-bright, almost feverish gleam that was downright alarming.

'Then I'm honoured,' he remembered to answer at last. 'Though I thought we were going to meet at your aunt's house?'

'I made my mind up early.' She jutted her chin out defensively. 'I thought you'd want to know.'

'I do. Though might I ask *what* made up your mind?'

A fresh look of panic flitted across her features, fleeting but unmistakable. 'I decided it made good business sense after all. That was the purpose of your proposal, wasn't it?'

'It was.'

'Then we have an agreement.' She nodded emphatically. 'I'll help you convince Mr Harper to sell his shipyard and tutor your ward. In return, you'll provide me with a safe place to live.'

A *safe* place? Robert's eyebrows shot up. What did *that* mean? Why wouldn't she feel safe? There were at least a dozen questions on the tip of his tongue, but he had the distinct impression that she wasn't about to answer any of them. The noise and bustle of the platform seemed to be aggravating her nerves, making her as skittish and highly strung as a young foal. If he pushed her for answers, he had a feeling she might simply run away.

'Then you've made me a happy man, Ianthe. Under the circumstances, I think that my colleagues can manage the rest of the meeting without me. May I escort you home?'

She hesitated, drawing away slightly as he extended an arm out towards her, before swaying back again slowly, placing her hand on his biceps with only the very lightest of pressures. He smiled reassuringly, leading her away from the busy platform towards the station exit. Her hand was still trembling slightly on his arm, though by the way her knuckles were clenched he could tell that she was trying to control it and put on a brave face. Perhaps once he got her into the open air she might relax a little. At least give him some hint as to what the matter was…

'Did you enjoy the ball?' He tried to keep his tone light as they emerged on to Park Street.

'Yes.'

'And your aunt?'

'Yes.'

'It was a great success, so they tell me.'

'Good.'

Robert clenched his jaw in exasperation, his limited supply of small talk exhausted. Now that she'd formally accepted his proposal, she seemed in no mood to talk any further. He only hoped that her aunt would be at home when they arrived. Perhaps she'd know what was going on.

'Where are we going?' Ianthe yanked on his arm suddenly, drawing them both to a halt.

'Back to your aunt's.' He frowned at the note of fear in her voice.

'I don't know this street.'

'It comes out on Burgate, close to her house. I thought you might want to avoid the busier thoroughfares.'

'Why?'

Why? He looked at her incredulously. Wasn't it obvious? 'We can take a different route if you wish.'

'No.' She hesitated briefly before shaking her head. 'I just didn't recognise it, that's all.'

He led them on cautiously, curiosity burrowing a hole in his gut. She was acting as if she were frightened of being alone with him, yet she was the one who'd come to the station, who'd interrupted his meeting, who'd just agreed to spend the rest of her life with him, for pity's sake! It didn't make any sense, unless—he glanced down at her face, searching for clues—unless it wasn't *him* she was afraid of… Unless it was something else, something that had actually frightened her into agreeing to marry him?

He frowned suspiciously. Had something happened to her since the ball then, something that made her feel unsafe? She certainly looked nervous enough. Her cheeks had regained some of their colour, but her expression was still ill at ease, her eyes still glancing around restlessly as if they were searching for something.

Or someone.

His brows snapped together at once. There was only one person he could think of who frightened her, but what could Sir Charles have to do with her behaviour today? He couldn't have followed her home from the ball. He had been in the card room all evening…had still been there when *he'd* left to escort Percy back to the Swan. He wasn't known for having early habits either. It seemed highly unlikely that Ianthe could have seen him that morning. In which case…unlikely and unfortunate as it seemed, her jittery behaviour *must* have more to do with wedding nerves.

His eyes fell on a jeweller's shop down a street to their right and he found himself directing their steps towards it, struck by a sudden idea. If the idea of marriage really alarmed her so much, perhaps the best way to calm her nerves was to face it head-on.

'Do you know how Pickering got its name?' He asked the question casually, feeling her tense the moment he changed direction.

'No.' She sounded panicked again. 'Where are we going?'

He gestured towards the jewellers. 'I'd like to buy you an engagement ring.'

'A ring?' She sounded shocked. 'There's no need. This is a business arrangement.'

'None the less, I'd like to buy you one. To seal the bargain, if you like.'

'Why? We've already agreed on the terms. I've no intention of reneging.'

'Ianthe.' He stopped outside the window, turning slowly to face her. 'My mother never had a ring. I'd like my wife to have one.'

'Oh.' She bit her lip with a look of consternation. 'So it matters to *you*?'

'I'd consider it a personal favour. Besides, as I was saying, Pickering is the town to buy one. According to local legend, an old king called Peredurus once lost his ring here and accused a local maiden of stealing it. Later on, some fishermen caught a pike in the river and found the ring in its stomach. Hence the town's name. Pike ring, Pickering.'

'So the King falsely accused the maiden?'

She gave him a pointed look and his lips quirked upwards. 'Perhaps he simply misjudged her.'

'Then what happened?'

'He married her.'

'Because he felt that he had to?'

'I don't know about that. Perhaps he was trying to make amends. Perhaps he liked her. Or perhaps he just thought she was interesting.'

'Or respectable?'

'Maybe both.'

A shadow drifted across her face suddenly. 'What if she turned out to be neither? At least not in the way that he'd thought?'

Robert arched an eyebrow. There it was again, the feeling that she was trying to warn him about something—something she couldn't actually bring herself to say.

'Perhaps he thought he was a good judge of character. In any case, I don't think he was the kind of king who went back on his word.'

She dropped her gaze, frowning thoughtfully for a moment before peering up at him through dark eyelashes. 'Is that story true or did you make it up?'

'Do you think I'd make up a name like Peredurus? Check the town's crest if you don't believe me.'

He grinned and pushed the jeweller's door open, leading her into a dark room filled with wooden and glass cabinets, each one sparkling with a glittering array of rings, brooches and pendants.

'Take your pick. Anything you like.'

'Anything?' Doe eyes opened wide, seeming to glow with reflected light from the jewellery. 'I don't know what's suitable. Don't you want to choose?'

'You're the one who has to wear it.'

She pursed her lips, peering into the first cabinet they came to and pointing towards a plain band set with a single red stone. 'That one.'

'The garnet?' He looked at her dubiously. 'Is this because I insisted?'

'What do you mean?'

'It must be the plainest ring in the shop.'

'Exactly. Not fussy, just respectable.'

Respectable. There was that word again. He was starting to wish he'd never used it.

'There are bigger rings.'

'I don't want bigger. You said I could choose.'

'So I did.' He heaved a sigh. 'All right, if that's what you really want, but what about that one?' He gestured towards the back of the cabinet, towards a thin, delicately wrought gold band with six small sapphires mounted around a single raised diamond. 'It's still *respectable*, but I think it might suit you.'

'The flower?' She gave an audible gasp.

'May I?' He conferred briefly with the jeweller before picking the ring up and slipping it gently over her finger. 'There.'

'My mother had a ring just like this.' Her voice softened as she gazed at the stone admiringly. 'It broke my heart when Percy sold it. My father always said it was naturally beautiful, just like her.'

'My thoughts exactly.'

'I didn't mean…' Her cheeks flooded with colour. 'That is… It just reminds me of her, that's all.'

'Then we're both convinced. That wasn't so painful, now, was it?'

'No.' She shook her head, a shy smile hovering over her lips. 'I don't want to take it off.'

'Then don't.' He turned to the jeweller. 'Send the bill directly to me in Whitby.'

'Very good, Mr Felstone.' The man looked almost as pleased as she did. 'It's a classic design. An excellent choice, if I might say so.'

'It's perfect.' She was still staring at her hand, her face breaking into a sudden wide smile, like sunshine bursting through clouds. 'Thank you, Robert. I don't think I'll ever wear gloves again.'

'Then let me carry them for you.'

He scooped her things up, determined to prevent anything that might chase her smile away, taken aback by an unfamiliar stirring sensation in his chest. She seemed calmer now, as if the ring had actually soothed her—a whole different woman again, the one he'd danced with at the ball, the one he hadn't wanted to let go...

He held the door open, inhaling the scent of fresh grass as she brushed past him. The happy, wondering smile on her face was dazzling, transforming her features from plain to breathtakingly lovely. For a moment he felt an unwonted impulse to reach down and kiss her, to feel the soft pressure of those wide lips against his. Not that he had any intention of doing so. That would be entirely against the terms of their agreement.

Besides which, he didn't want to frighten her again. Their trip to the jeweller's had gone better than he'd expected, as if all she'd needed was some reassurance, but he still couldn't be certain there wasn't something else bothering her...

'Are you sure you're all right, Ianthe?' He glanced down at her quickly as they walked side by side up the hill towards her aunt's house.

'Yes.' Her answer came too quickly, and he sighed, unconvinced.

'In that case, I'll have my housekeeper make preparations for your arrival. If you wish to prepare a trousseau, you can charge any items you require to my account.'

'No! That is...you've spent enough on my family.' Her face took on an apologetic expression. 'I heard what happened last night. When I asked for your help with Percy, I never imagined that it would cost you so dearly. I'm sorry.'

'You didn't ask me. I offered.'

'I'm still indebted.'

Indebted? A muscle jumped in his jaw. Was that the reason she'd agreed to marry him then, because of the money he'd 'lost' to her brother? He probably should have expected this, though he'd hoped she wouldn't hear about any of it before giving him her answer. Two hundred pounds was a considerable amount, not enough to cause him undue concern, but hopefully sufficient to get the youth out of debt. It hadn't been easy losing convincingly to such a poor player, but he'd been reasonably satisfied with his performance. He certainly hadn't expected it to backfire on him like this…

'There's no debt, Ianthe, I was happy to help. I don't want you to marry me out of gratitude.'

'I'm not!' She seemed shocked by the very idea.

'Good. Apart from anything else, you might find your brother more reasonable now that his finances are in better order. You might not have to marry anyone.'

She lifted her head, looking at him intently for a long, searching moment before her mouth dropped open. 'You lost *deliberately*?'

'I didn't say that.'

'But you did!' Her voice held a note of conviction. 'And the ball gown…it wasn't Kitty's, was it?'

'It is now.'

'But…I don't understand.' Her expression shifted to one of bewilderment. 'Why are you doing all this? Why are you helping me?'

He hesitated. It was a good question, one that he wasn't sure he knew how to answer. Why *was* he so intent upon helping her? Somehow his plans for expanding the shipyard didn't seem convincing enough reasons any more, but how could he explain what he hardly understood himself? All he knew was that he felt a strange desire to protect her, to keep her safe from her brother and Sir Charles, to save her from a marriage she didn't want, to hold her tight in his arms and not let go…

He shook his head. Where had *that* idea come from?

'I told you last night, Ianthe, I think you're a risk worth taking.' The words were out of his mouth before he knew what he was saying.

'I will be.' Her face took on a strangely determined expression.

'Good. Then if you still wish to go ahead, I'll arrange for the banns to be read at once. We can be married in six months.'

'Six months?' She rounded on him as they reached her aunt's doorstep. 'I thought you wanted to be married as soon as possible!'

'I do, but unless we elope to Scotland, I think that's the quickest it can be arranged—Ianthe?' He reached a hand out as her face blanched so quickly he was afraid she was going to faint. 'That was a joke. Are you all right?'

'Yes.' She put a hand to her head, half-covering her face. 'It's just…it's too long.'

'What is? Six months?'

'Yes. I don't want to wait.'

He hesitated, dropping his gaze to her stomach suspiciously. There was only one reason he could think of why she might want to marry in a hurry, though he found it almost impossible to believe. But why else? A respectable woman would never ask to marry in such haste, at least not without some kind of explanation. And an unwanted pregnancy would certainly explain her panicky behaviour that morning, especially if she'd only just realised... Not that it was the kind of thing he could just ask her about. If he was wrong, she'd probably hurl the ring back in his face...

'It might look improper to marry any sooner,' he ventured.

'Why? If this is supposed to be a long-distance courtship, then who's to know if we marry quickly? It can still look respectable.' She sounded defensive again. 'Besides, my aunt can't afford to support me for so long. And you know what my brother wants. I doubt he'll give up on that idea no matter how much money he wins.'

'Surely he won't try to make you marry Sir Charles once we're engaged?'

'I don't know.' A tremor seemed to run through her body as he mentioned the Baronet's name. 'But I can't trust him, not while he's under that man's influence. I have to get away, Robert, please.'

She looked up at him imploringly, and he felt his resolve weaken. Both reasons were convincing, though he still had the feeling that she was holding something back. The edge of desperation in her voice made him uneasy. As much as he wanted to be convinced, surely it was better to wait and be certain...

'Three months, then. I'm afraid that I've too much work at the moment to make it any sooner.'

'Can't you reschedule?'

He frowned. 'I have a lot of people depending on me, Ianthe. A lot of families.'

'Oh.' She looked contrite at once. 'Of course. Forgive me, I was being selfish. Three months is perfectly acceptable.'

'Then we're agreed.' He heaved a sigh of relief. As thin as she was, a pregnancy would surely be obvious in that time. And if he *was* being overly suspicious then so much the better. After all, the sooner they were married, the sooner he could buy Harper's yard.

She nodded and a lock of fair hair tumbled forward, falling loosely over one eye. He reached out impulsively, intending to brush it aside and found himself cupping her cheek instead. To his surprise, she didn't move away. Instead, she tilted her head, half-closing her eyes as she pressed her cheek against his fingers.

'Three months then, Ianthe.' Her skin felt so smooth he had to fight the urge to raise his other hand to join it. 'I consider myself honour bound, but you should not.'

Her eyes fluttered open again. 'I gave you my word. I won't go back on it now.'

'None the less, if you reconsider, a note to

my business address in Whitby will be enough. I don't know how often I'll be able to visit, but with your permission, I'll inform Giles of our engagement. Once he tells Kitty it should be announcement enough.'

'I'm sure.' She gave a knowing smile, drifting away from him gently as she opened the door. 'Won't you come inside? I know that my aunt will be pleased at the news.'

He hesitated, his fingers feeling strangely bereft. The idea of joining her inside was alarmingly tempting. Once they were inside, the door would shield them from view of the street, they'd be alone...

He scowled deliberately. What was the matter with him? He was acting more like a real suitor than a man of business. This was a business arrangement—he had to remember that—no matter how much he wanted to be alone with her.

'I ought to get back to my meeting.'

Her face fell, and he found himself taking her hand, lifting it to his lips as he tried to make up for his brusque tone.

'I'll write to you, Ianthe.'

'Will you?' Her voice sounded faintly husky. 'Then so will I.'

'I'd like that.' He looked down at her hand, knowing that he should drop it and walk away, yet leaning forward instead. What was he doing? He felt as though his mind were watching from a distance, a dispassionate observer as the rest of him moved closer, lured by those captivating doe eyes, a rich shade of toffee brown swirling with coffee-coloured depths...

Their lips touched and he felt a white-hot, tingling sensation, a rush of heat like quicksilver coursing through his veins. Instinctively, his arms swept around her, gathering her into an embrace as her lips moulded to his, even softer and sweeter than he'd imagined, sharing the kiss with equal enthusiasm, as if she shared the sensation, too.

He pulled back abruptly, senses reeling, shocked by the force of his desire.

'Oh.' She staggered against him, pressing a hand to her mouth with a suddenly stricken expression.

'I'd better get back.' He cleared his throat and made a formal bow, trying to make it seem as if their kiss had been a mere formality. As if he hadn't just broken every rule of respectable behaviour. As if he didn't want to do it again...

'Goodbye then, Ianthe.' He didn't know what else to say.

'Yes... Goodbye.' She whirled on her heel, closing the door quickly behind her as if she were afraid he might follow.

Robert looked up and down the street, checking that no one else was around before swearing violently under his breath. That was that, then. He was an engaged man, engaged to a woman he hardly knew, who was definitely hiding something and who'd agreed to marry him for reasons he didn't understand.

And he had absolutely no idea how he felt about any of it.

Chapter Nine

❧❧❧

October 1865

Ianthe lowered the sash on the train window and peered out, letting out a long, deeply held sigh of relief as the port of Whitby finally appeared on the horizon, a cluster of red-and-white houses on either side of a wide cliff-walled harbour. Her new home, where her husband-to-be was waiting.

Finally.

'Not far now.' Aunt Sophoria was positively bouncing up and down with excitement. 'What a shame about the weather, but it can't be helped, I suppose. Look at that view, though! Whitby's always so beautiful whatever the season.'

Ianthe gave a weak smile. Personally she found the weather quite fitting. The grey clouds and lowering drizzle suited her mood far better than the sunshine her aunt seemed to expect. Her boundless enthusiasm, though well intentioned, was starting to grate heavily on her nerves. Judging by Aunt Sophoria's beaming expression, anyone would think that *she* was the bride. Giddy was how a bride was supposed to feel. Not sick to her stomach worrying that the groom had changed his mind.

She chewed her bottom lip, trying and failing to push her misgivings aside. After all, if Robert had wanted to call off the wedding then he'd surely have done so already, not waited until the actual morning, though the lack of communication—*any* communication—from him in the past week had been enough to tear her already ragged nerves to shreds.

His last letter, if it *could* be called anything so formal, had been eight days before, a brief note detailing the arrangements for the day. He'd mentioned train times and a rendezvous point, but there had been nothing personal, not the slightest hint of emotion, nothing to suggest that he was arranging anything other than a business meeting.

Clearly he hadn't been exaggerating when he'd told her not to expect romance. As wedding days went, it was about as unromantic as it could get. Not that it ought to have bothered her. It was a business arrangement after all, but he might have done something to reassure her. He hadn't even sent flowers. Even if she had no right to feel neglected, she still had feelings! What was she supposed to think of such ungallant behaviour?

There was only one possible conclusion she could come to—that he'd changed his mind and was too honourable to go back on his word, hoping that *she'd* call off the wedding instead. As much as she'd spent the past three months trying *not* to think about their kiss—a moment of madness doubtless brought on by the traumatic events at the castle—she knew that her wanton behaviour must have shocked him. It had definitely shocked her. There had been nothing respectable about it. She didn't know which one of them had initiated the embrace…just that they seemed to have moved together at the same time, as if drawn by some irresistible force.

Strange, but after Albert and Sir Charles, she'd assumed that another man's touch would repel her, but the effect had been quite the opposite. One moment, she'd been bidding Robert goodbye, the next she'd practically thrown herself at him—in broad daylight, in the street to boot!

It was almost too shameful to remember and now clearly Robert thought so, too. His absence spoke volumes, demonstrating that he'd realised the truth about her at last—that she was a wanton, a schemer, everything Albert's mother had said… In which case she really ought to give him a chance to back out. If he was only going ahead out of honour, then she'd rather he didn't. No matter how much she needed his protection, she had no desire to marry a man who didn't want her.

She didn't expect love, but she had more self-respect than that.

She plucked at her cloak, rearranging the fabric to distract herself. At least she was dressed like a bride, in a cream-coloured gown with a round neckline, short summery sleeves and a narrow belt decorated with a sprig of orange blossom. To Percy's credit, he'd offered to buy her a new dress, but she'd refused, preferring that he pay off his debts whilst she modified one of her aunt's less flamboyant gowns instead. She'd been secretly pleased with the results, using the excuse of needing a veil to trim away most of the excess lace, leaving just a little to decorate the hem and wrists.

'No more moping around the house for you.' Aunt Sophoria gave her a playful nudge in the ribs. 'It's high time your fiancé showed his face again. He's been busy with business, I suppose, but what kind of an engagement is it when the man doesn't visit?'

A business arrangement, Ianthe thought silently, not that she disagreed with her aunt's assessment. She could hardly remember what Robert looked like. She'd expected to see him at least once before the wedding, but according to his letters he'd been travelling, first to London, then Liverpool and Glasgow, then busy negotiating with Mr Harper. That had been almost *all* he'd written about. She'd learned nothing of importance from his letters, nothing about the man she intended to marry—no more than he'd learnt from her staid, largely weather-based replies.

Not that she had anything else to tell him. Except for a few shopping excursions with Kitty, she'd barely left her aunt's house over the past three months, waiting in a state of heightened nervous tension for something—she wasn't sure what—to happen, but expecting it none the less. The day after he'd left she'd spent practically glued to her aunt's side, afraid of a visit from Sir Charles, though he hadn't come that day or the next.

After a week, relief had turned to a new kind of anxiety, unnerving enough that she'd finally asked Percy where the Baronet was, though he'd been uncharacteristically reticent on the subject. She'd sent him word of her engagement almost straight away, but he hadn't shown his face for another two days, finally showing up with a large black-and-purple bruise over his left eye—another subject he'd refused point-blank to discuss.

When she'd finally summoned up the nerve to ask about Sir Charles, his response had been near venomous.

'But where is he?' she'd persisted in asking anyway, needing to know.

'He said he was going back to London for a while, not that it's any of your business.'

'What do you mean *a while*?'

'I don't know!' Percy's ill temper had hardly diminished since the ball. 'And you've no right to ask. You've hurt him enough.'

'I've hurt *him*?' She felt stung by the injustice of it.

'Yes. He said he expected more of you. So did I for that matter. You've made my life difficult enough as it is.'

'What do you mean?'

But Percy had only shaken his head and pouted. 'Nothing, but he blames me for this whole mess, too, you know. I as good as told him you were willing. You might have thought about that!'

'You had no right to tell him any such thing.'

'In any case, he doesn't approve of your choice either. You know if it were anyone else he might have stayed to fight for you, but Mr Felstone has quite a disreputable reputation. Typical of you to prefer a jumped-up merchant to a baronet! It's no wonder Charles is angry. I'd be offended, too.'

'Good. If he's offended, then I'm glad!'

'In any case, he says he's not ready to see you again yet.'

The words had chilled her to the bone. *'Yet?'*

Percy had refused to discuss the subject any more, returning to London without so much as a by-your-leave and leaving her to wonder and worry on her own, anxiously reliving the events at the castle, both Sir Charles's attack and what he'd said about her parents. Thinking back over her childhood, she'd found nothing to suggest that her mother had been unhappy, let alone pining for another man, and yet he'd spoken with such conviction.

The words had haunted her, waking her up in the middle of the night in a cold sweat, along with memories of the way he'd looked at her, the way he'd dragged at her skirts as he'd forced his tongue inside her mouth. She'd wanted to tell her aunt, but then she'd had a feeling that the old woman wouldn't take such news lightly, and now that she knew what the Baronet was capable of, that he was violent as well as obsessed...

No, it was *her* secret, she'd decided, no matter how much she wanted a shoulder to cry on. She didn't want to involve her aunt any more than she wanted her new fiancé defending her honour. Despite rescuing her at the ball, Robert had made it clear that he wanted a business partner, not a damsel in distress, and he certainly wouldn't want to become embroiled in her family's sordid affairs. Besides, *she* was the one who'd gone to the castle alone and unchaperoned, something a sensible, respectable woman ought never to have dreamt of doing. As angry as he'd be at Sir Charles, he might not approve of *her* behaviour either, might use it as an excuse to call off the wedding.

Overall, she'd concluded, it was better for everyone that she stayed silent. Once she was married, she could put the whole nightmare behind her. Sir Charles would never dare to attack *Mrs Felstone* and then her dreams would finally stop. She could go back to being herself again—the new, respectable version of herself anyway… Just as long as Robert hadn't changed his mind.

It had felt like the longest three months of her life.

'You look troubled, dear.' Aunt Sophoria patted her knee sympathetically. 'Is there anything you'd like to ask me about?'

'No!' Ianthe answered hastily. Her aunt had already provided an embarrassing amount of detail about what to expect on her wedding night, making her doubly glad that it was only a business arrangement. She'd no desire to sit through that conversation again, though she *was* curious to know how her spinster aunt had come across quite so much detailed information.

'I keep telling you, Aunt, it's not like that.'

'If you say so, dear.'

'It's not! It's a business arrangement.'

'And I'm not supposed to tell anyone. Yes, dear, I remember.'

Ianthe rolled her eyes in frustration. No matter how many times she told her aunt that it wasn't a love match, she simply refused to believe it. Even Robert's lengthy absence hadn't dented her rose-tinted perspective. On the contrary, she'd taken the fact of their short engagement as evidence that he was eager to do more than just *see* her...

She glanced out of the window, relieved to find that they were already rolling into the station. At least that ought to stop her aunt from offering any more *advice*.

'So we're going straight to the ceremony?' Aunt Sophoria reached into her reticule, pulling out a large frilly handkerchief.

'Yes, Robert said he'd meet us under the clock with Kitty and Giles.'

'Is that everyone?'

'Yes, Aunt.' They'd been over this before as well. 'We wanted to keep it small. He doesn't have any family and I've only got you.'

'What about his business associates?'

'This is the way we want it. It would look strange if he had lots of guests on his side.'

'I suppose so.' Her aunt sighed dramatically. 'Though it's such a shame Percy couldn't be here.'

'He said he couldn't take any more time off work, but it's all right, Giles is going to give me away.'

'Well, in that case...' Aunt Sophoria waved her handkerchief in the air. 'I'd better keep this ready. Just the thought of a wedding makes me cry.'

'There's *nothing* to cry about! Honestly, Aunt, I just wish it were over.'

'I wouldn't let Mr Felstone hear you say that. What would he think?'

Ianthe grimaced. She'd no idea what her fiancé would think. Three months before, when they'd discussed terms in the ballroom, she'd thought that she had a reasonable sense of the man behind the stern, business-driven exterior. Now she felt as though she were on her way to marry a stranger.

'I don't care what he thinks.' She pushed the carriage door open angrily, looking back over her shoulder for one final outburst. 'And love has nothing to do with it!'

'I'm pleased to see you again, too, Ianthe.'

She froze, turning her head slowly towards the sound of Robert's deep, irony-laced voice. He was standing in the open doorway, regarding her with an impenetrable expression.

'I didn't mean…' She felt her cheeks turn a vivid shade of scarlet. 'That is… Good morning.'

'Good morning.' He lifted an eyebrow along with his top hat. 'Are you ready?'

'I… Yes.' She caught her breath unsteadily. So much for pleasantries. He looked both heart-stoppingly handsome and sternly forbidding at the same time, dressed impeccably in a suit of black superfine cloth with a quilted silk waistcoat beneath.

'Well, then.' He reached past her, helping her aunt down on to the platform first before offering a hand to her. 'Shall we?'

Ianthe swallowed, trying to maintain some

sense of composure. He didn't look particularly pleased to see her—though given what she'd just said she could hardly blame him—his all-black outfit giving him the look of a man attending a funeral rather than his own wedding. Was he angry with her, then? He'd no right to be. She hadn't said anything he wouldn't agree with.

'Is there a problem?' His eyes narrowed slightly when she didn't move.

'Not at all. I'm perfectly happy to proceed.' She gave him a meaningful look. 'If you are.'

'I am.'

'Oh...' His swift answer made her feel foolish even for asking. 'Because I thought we should talk first. It's been a while and—'

'We'll be late, Ianthe.' He sounded impatient. 'I prefer not to miss appointments. So if this is your way of telling me that you've changed your mind, I'd prefer it if you got straight to the point.'

'It's not!' She bristled indignantly. 'I just...'

'Then we're wasting time and *my* time is valuable. I have other things to do today besides this.'

This...? This...? She didn't know whether to feel relieved or furious at his response. He was talking about *this* as if it were simply a minor event, an irksome interruption in his busy workload. Clearly she'd overestimated his motives for not visiting her. Here she'd driven herself half-crazy with worry and self-recrimination when all he'd been thinking about was business! He hadn't been ignoring her because he'd changed his mind about marriage. He simply hadn't thought about her—or their kiss—at all!

She wasn't sure which was worse.

She pushed past him, ignoring his outstretched hand as she climbed out of the carriage. He responded by grasping her fingers instead, practically hauling her along the platform to where Aunt Sophoria was already waiting with Kitty and Giles.

She took a sharp intake of breath, almost running to keep up as a torrent of conflicting emotions raced through her body. On the one hand, she was still furious. On the other, it was impossible to ignore the heated, spine-tingling sensation that seemed to pass from his fingers into hers, making her stomach quiver with excitement. After three months, she'd hoped that the feeling, whatever it was, might have passed, but it was still there, as potent and unnerving as ever.

'Ianthe!' Kitty rushed forward to greet her, resplendent in a bright emerald-green gown that almost disguised a growing baby bump. 'You look lovely.'

'Thank you.' She glanced down self-consciously. Her home-made efforts had seemed perfectly suitable that morning, though next to her smartly dressed fiancé they felt decidedly shabby.

'We can talk about fashion later.' Robert's

step didn't falter. 'I want to get this settled this morning.'

This! She threw Kitty an apologetic look as he swept her onwards, out of the station and into a waiting carriage, walking so fast that Aunt Sophoria finally had to beg him to slow down.

It wasn't long before she realised why. Robert seemed to have organised everything to the exact minute, so that by the time she found herself on Giles's arm, waiting for the ceremony to start, it was too late to turn back. There was no opportunity to speak in private, no chance hardly to catch her breath. The arrangement was sealed with a ruthless, businesslike efficiency.

The rest of the morning seemed to pass in a haze. They moved from the ceremony to a wedding luncheon at the Royal Hotel, not that she felt very hungry. More than anything, she realised with surprise, she wanted to sleep. Funny how she'd dreaded going to bed of late, afraid of the dreams that might wake her again, but now she felt as though she could sleep for a week, as if all the tension of the past few months had finally caught up with her. Thankfully, with Kitty and Aunt Sophoria present there was no shortage of conversation, though after a while she stopped listening, too tired to offer anything more than monosyllabic replies.

What was her husband's excuse, then? she

wondered. He was barely talking either, seeming to become sterner and more taciturn every time he glanced in her direction, which was often, though contrary to his earlier statement, he seemed in no rush to hasten the meal, ordering three courses as well as champagne.

As a result, it was the middle of the afternoon before all the toasts had been said and they were able to leave their guests at the station, sitting alone in their carriage in a silence that seemed to grow heavier and stonier with each passing moment. Ianthe found herself holding her breath, uncomfortably aware of her new husband's proximity, beset by a combination of anxiety and unwanted excitement. Since saying 'I do' she doubted he'd spoken more than ten words to her directly. Was he displeased? Disappointed? Or was this just what he meant by a *practical arrangement*—one in which he could simply ignore her?

She opened her eyes as wide as she could, desperately trying to keep them open as a wave of exhaustion swept over her, though the effort seemed futile. Despite the cobblestone streets, the sway of the cab was actually lulling her to sleep. She could feel her head tipping to one side, searching for somewhere to rest…

'We're here.'

The soft tone of Robert's voice, strikingly at odds with his earlier manner of speaking, drew her gently back to consciousness. With a wide yawn she opened her eyes, dismayed to find her face pressed up against a smooth, black jacket.

'How long have I been asleep?' She jolted upright at once.

'Just a few minutes.'

'Oh.' She stifled another yawn. 'Sorry.'

'Still tired?' He sounded vaguely concerned, but his eyes were full of shadows, their expression unreadable in the dark carriage.

'A little.' She gave a dismissive shrug. *Little* was an understatement. She'd never felt so exhausted in her life.

'Then let's get you to bed, Mrs Felstone.'

She gave a small start. It wasn't the first time that she'd been called by her married name, but it sounded different coming from his lips, with a hint of possession that she found strangely exciting. On the other hand, the mention of bed was more than a little alarming. What did he mean, *get her to bed*? That definitely wasn't part of their agreement, especially after his earlier behaviour! Or did he think that their kiss had altered the terms somehow?

'On your own, of course.' His lips curled sardonically as if he'd just guessed what she was thinking. 'Love has nothing to do with it, remember?' He jumped down from the carriage before she could answer. 'In any case, I still have plenty of work to do today. You can get some rest as soon as I've introduced you to the staff.'

'Staff?' She followed him out on to the pavement and then stopped short, tilting her head up. And up. And up. '*This* is your house?'

'*Our* house, yes.'

Ianthe opened her mouth and then closed it again. The rain had finally stopped and the afternoon sun was glinting off the slate roof, five storeys above. She'd never thought to ask him where he lived, but she'd expected it to be near the shipyard, somewhere down in the harbour itself. Instead he'd brought her up to the Royal Crescent, a sweep of large terrace houses set high above the north cliff, their gleaming white frontages facing straight out to sea.

'Not what you expected?'

She shook her head, rendered speechless with amazement. Each house looked to be at least four times the size of the one where she'd grown up, even bigger and grander than her employer's in Bournemouth had been.

'Did you believe the gossipmongers, then?'

'What gossipmongers?' She glanced at him warily, but he looked amused rather than angry.

'The ones who say a man like me doesn't belong in a place like this.'

'Of course not! It's just more than I expected, that's all.'

'Then welcome home, Ianthe.'

She smiled hesitantly, following him up the steps and through the front door into a vast, tiled hall. There was so much to take in, but at least the hard part of the day was over. Their wedding might not have been a great success, but at least it was over and done with. Now perhaps she could finally lie down, have a long sleep and… She exclaimed in surprise, the sight of a dozen people standing in a reception line almost making her turn around again.

'This is Mrs Felstone.' As if sensing her reticence, Robert took hold of her elbow, propelling her forward. 'I hope you'll all help her to feel at home here.'

For a moment, Ianthe's heart misgave her. In her wildest imaginings she'd never pictured anything quite so intimidating. Kitty had said that Robert was rich, but she'd been too wrapped up in her worries to pay much attention to the other woman's chatter. This was grander than anything she'd ever seen before. Her parents had kept a cook and one housemaid. She'd no experience of running a household this size. Quite the contrary— a few months before she'd been one of the staff herself, standing in line to greet Albert when he'd come home from university. And now here she was, mistress of an even greater house in her own right. Her head was already fuzzy with exhaustion. Now the change in her circumstances made her feel dizzy, too.

'This is my housekeeper, Mrs Baxter.' Robert was all business again, ushering her along the line briskly. 'And my cook, Mrs Lughton.'

'How do you do, Mrs Baxter?' She resisted the tug of his arm, refusing to be moved on so quickly. No matter how overwhelmed she felt, she had to think of something to say.

'Mrs Felstone.' The housekeeper bobbed a small curtsy.

'Thank you so much for this lovely reception. It was very thoughtful of you.'

'Not at all, ma'am.'

'And, Mrs Lughton, I'm delighted to meet you, too.'

'Pleased to meet you, ma'am. May I introduce our kitchen maids, Peggy and Hannah?'

'Peggy. Hannah.' She shook each of the girls' hands in turn. 'Thank you for coming to greet me.'

She moved along the line slowly, trying to memorise names as she talked to every footman and housemaid in turn. At the end she breathed a sigh of relief, turning to find Robert watching her with a look of approval.

'Thank you, everyone, that will do for now.' He kept his eyes on her as he spoke, waiting until the others had filed away before gesturing towards the staircase. 'I'll show you to your room.'

'Thank you.'

She crossed the hall eagerly. *Her room.* She

hadn't had a room that was truly *hers* since she'd left home after her father's funeral. To have a place of her own again, a place to feel safe and protected...that was all she wanted now. She could hardly believe that she was so close to finding it again.

Excitedly, she followed him up the staircase and along a wide corridor, legs trembling with anticipation as he opened a door near the end and then stood aside to let her pass. Tentatively, she peered around the door frame, closing her eyes in disbelief and then opening them wide with a gasp of delight. It was beautiful. Large and airy, bathed in a soft golden glow as rays of sunlight streamed in through an expanse of bright white-net curtains, making the whole room seem to radiate light and warmth.

She wandered inside slowly, hardly daring to breathe in case it broke the spell, twirling around on the spot with a sense of wonderment. This was more, far more than she'd ever expected. Definitely more than she deserved...

She pushed the thought away, refusing to let it spoil the joy of the moment, trailing a hand over the elegant furniture—a large four-poster bed, a chest of drawers, a vanity table with a three-sided mirror and a large mahogany wardrobe, standing open to reveal her dresses already hanging inside. The modest chest of belongings she'd brought with her on the train must have been sent ahead and unpacked, though her sensible grey cloth-ing looked somewhat incongruous in their new environment.

'It's wonderful.' She found her voice at last, looking back over her shoulder to where Robert was still standing in the doorway, one shoulder propped against the frame. 'I don't know what to say.'

'I'm glad you like it.' His expression was as inscrutable as ever.

'How could I not?' Her gaze fell on a door in the corner. 'What's through there?'

'That leads to my room, though they're quite separate, I assure you. You can lock the door from your side if you wish.'

'I'm sure there's no need.' Her cheeks flushed self-consciously. Whilst that thought was com-forting, she didn't want to offend him by doing so, still less to cause gossip amongst the servants.

'There isn't. This is your room, Ianthe, I won't bother you in here.'

'Oh.' She cast her eyes downwards. *Bother her?* She didn't know how to respond to that.

'You did well before—meeting everyone, I mean. They liked you.'

'Do you think so?'

'I wouldn't say it otherwise.' He pushed him-self up off the door frame, prowling slowly to-wards her. 'Though I'm afraid there might still be gossip.'

'What do you mean?'

'About how quickly we were married.'

She frowned. 'But I thought you told people we had a long-distance courtship?'

'I did, but my staff know more about my business than most people. They know my plans altered. Fortunately, they're also discreet.'

'Then I don't understand. What would they talk about?'

Pale eyes flashed with something like amusement. 'Generally, when couples rush into marriage, it's because they don't wish the reason to be *too* obvious.'

'What reason?'

He stopped an arm's length away. 'There's usually a baby involved.'

'You mean your staff think I'm *pregnant*?' She drew a shocked intake of breath.

'It's a natural assumption, I'm afraid, given the circumstances. You can't really blame them.'

'I most certainly can!'

'Well, we can put that rumour to rest soon enough. Your appearance today might have done it already. You're too thin, Ianthe. Have you been ill?'

'No.' She crossed her arms defensively. Admittedly she'd lost a little weight over the past few months, but she hadn't thought it was noticeable. Now Robert looked as if he were determined to find out the reason why.

She changed the subject adroitly. 'Speaking of children, I thought your ward would be at the ceremony?'

His face seemed to shut down at once. 'I'm afraid ten-year-old boys aren't particularly interested in weddings. I told him it wasn't necessary to attend.'

'Will I see him at dinner, then? I'd like to meet my new pupil. He was the one subject Kitty didn't seem to know anything about.'

'Kitty hasn't met him. What do you want to know?'

She blinked, taken aback by the sudden hard edge to his voice. 'His name, for a start.'

'Matthew.'

'Oh.' She waited, but he didn't volunteer any more information. 'Well then, I look forward to meeting him tonight.'

Robert nodded, though his expression remained tense. 'There's just one more thing. I need to go to London in the morning.'

'So soon?'

'I have some business that can't wait.'

'Oh.' She forced herself to smile placidly. After all, this was what he wanted, a sensible wife who wouldn't interfere with his business affairs. Even if they *were* only just married. 'How long will you be gone?'

'Three days at the most. I'd invite you to come

with me, but there won't be much time for sight-seeing.'

'No, of course.' She battled an unexpected feeling of hurt. Not that she wanted to go with him, but apparently *he* didn't want her to go either, not even for a brief pretence of a honeymoon. 'Then I'll see you at dinner.'

'Very well.' He nodded with a look of satisfaction before walking back towards the door. 'Dinner's at eight.'

He left the room, and she flung herself backwards, sprawling across the bed in a confused state of relief and resentment. But at least she was in her *own* room, in her *own* home. Whatever else she felt, she was finally safe. Safe from Sir Charles and her past—sensible, respectable and married. For the first time in as long as she could remember, she could finally relax. Now all she needed was a nap, a brief rest before she went downstairs and introduced herself properly to Mrs Baxter.

She could feel herself drifting off to sleep already.

Just a nap…

Chapter Ten

Robert stood by the drawing-room fireplace, swilling a tumbler of whisky in one hand as he waited for Ianthe to come down to dinner.

All in all, he felt satisfied with the events of the day. Despite a rocky start, everything had proceeded almost exactly as he'd planned. After he'd brought his new bride home, he'd walked down to the shipyard and made an announcement to his stunned workforce, before giving them the rest of the day off as a holiday. Then he'd done some paperwork, made a tour of the workshops, inspected the hull of his new vessel and finally come home to change. Not bad for a day's work. So why was he so anxious about seeing her again?

He tossed his head back, swallowing the contents of his glass in one gulp.

Love has nothing to do with it!

Strange how much those words had bothered him. It wasn't the first time he'd overheard her say something indiscreet on a train, but this time he really wished that he hadn't. He ought to have applauded the sentiment, ought to have been pleased by her businesslike approach, but instead he'd felt an inexplicable feeling of hurt. Not that he expected her love. He neither wanted nor needed it. He wasn't accustomed to the emotion, had never heard the words, not even from his own mother, yet to hear the truth expressed so bluntly, so unexpectedly when he'd actually been eager—eager!—to see her again, had made his chest ache in a way that he hadn't anticipated.

He'd reacted sternly, half-expecting her to call off the wedding there and then, though she'd actually seemed more concerned that *he* might have changed his mind. Clearly she'd taken his lack of attention over the past three months to signal an equal lack of interest, though in fact the very opposite was true. Much as he hated to admit it, he'd done little *but* think of her.

The way she'd accepted his proposal had bothered him ever since he'd left her on her aunt's doorstep. He'd thought about it at length—during meetings, on journeys, in the middle of the night—though he still hadn't been able to fathom the motive behind it. The more he'd thought of it, however, the more convinced he'd become that it hadn't simply been wedding jitters, that something had happened to *make* her say yes.

Once again, his suspicions had fallen on Sir

Charles, though discreet enquiries had revealed that he hadn't been seen in Pickering since the night of the ball, had in fact left for London soon after. Other enquiries had drawn an equal blank. There seemed to be no obvious reason for her bizarre behaviour, but he'd kept away precisely to avoid asking questions. If he'd seen her, he would have been tempted to pry and he'd had a feeling that pushing her was the very worst thing he could do.

So he'd been deliberately neglectful instead, wanting to give her time to recover from whatever it was that had panicked her, time to calm down and reconsider if necessary. If she changed her mind, he'd told her she had only to write to him. No matter what his ambitions for the shipyard, he wanted a willing wife, not a frightened one.

Ironic, then, that he'd actually wanted to see her. To kiss her again, too, though his mind shied away from the implications of that. More than once, he'd considered boarding the train to Pickering, but common sense had prevailed. As bad as it might appear, staying away for so long, he hadn't wanted to mislead her. Their kiss had been the result of a passing physical attraction, plain and simple. It hadn't meant—and it certainly didn't promise—anything more. The longer he left her alone, the better they'd both understand that.

Even so, her appearance that morning had come as a shock, her pallid skin and red-rimmed eyes giving her the appearance of someone who'd been sick, not eagerly anticipating her wedding. She *definitely* wasn't pregnant. He didn't think he'd ever seen a tinier waist. In retrospect, he concluded, perhaps keeping away for three months hadn't been one of his better ideas. What the hell had happened?

On the other hand, she'd seemed overjoyed by the sight of her new bedroom that afternoon. At least he'd managed to do one thing right...

He glanced up as the scamper of running feet in the hall provided a welcome distraction.

'Matthew?'

'Yes, sir?' A small, mischievous-looking face peered around the door.

'Where were you this morning?' He beckoned the boy inside. 'You were supposed to be here when Mrs Felstone arrived.'

'At the stables with Joe. Mrs Lughton said it was all right.'

'Didn't she tell you to be back by noon?'

'Yes, sir.' The boy shuffled his feet with a shame-faced expression. 'She did.'

'So?'

'I forgot, sir.'

'You forgot that I was getting married?'

The boy curled his small hands into fists. 'Joe says that women are the root of all evil!'

'Did he?' Robert fought the temptation to laugh. That sounded like something his curmudgeonly old groom would say. 'Though I hope that statement doesn't extend to my wife.'

'He says she must have got her claws into you right quick.'

'Indeed?' His expression hardened. 'Did he say that to *you*?'

'No, to Nate when he brought the carriage back. Nate said she seemed nice, though.'

'She is.' Robert unclenched his jaw. He'd have to deal with Joe later. At the very least, tell him to keep his thoughts to himself when the boy was around. 'She's your new governess, too.'

'I don't want a governess.' Matthew scowled ferociously. 'Why can't I just come with you to the yard?'

'Because there's more to learning than how to build ships.'

'Not if I'm going to be like you. *You* never even went to school. Joe told me.'

Robert rolled his eyes, resolving to confront his groom first thing in the morning. 'You'll be glad of it one day. You can still spend your afternoons with me, provided that you let her tutor you first. Understand?'

'Yes, sir.' Matthew folded his arms sulkily. 'Do I have to eat in the dining room tonight?'

Robert pondered for a moment. He'd intended to introduce Ianthe to Matthew as soon as possible, if only to get the meeting over with, but after the tense atmosphere that day he was reluctant to do so now. Perhaps it could wait until the morning and he could let the lad eat in the kitchens tonight instead...

He'd just opened his mouth to answer when he heard the rapid tread of footsteps descending the stairs. Damn. It was too late to send the boy away now. They'd have to get the scene—and he'd no doubt it *would* be a scene—over with tonight after all.

He took a step towards the door, bracing himself as Ianthe came hurtling through it.

'Oh!' She almost skidded to a halt when she saw him. 'I lost track of time.'

'So I see.' Judging by the crumpled state of her wedding dress, not to mention the pillow imprint on her cheek, she'd only just woken up. He glanced at the clock. Had she really been asleep since he'd left? That had been four hours ago.

'There's no need to rush. I'm happy to wait if you wish to change.'

'No.' She shook her head breathlessly, reaching a hand up to smooth her hair out of her face. 'Unless you want me to?'

'Not at all. There's only the two of us, after all. And Matthew here.' He stepped aside to reveal the boy, half-hidden behind his legs.

'Oh!' Her smile of enthusiasm froze instantly. 'H-hello, Matthew.'

'How do you do?' The boy's voice was sullen.

'Very well, thank you. I'm so glad to meet you. Your…guardian has told me such nice things.'

Robert grimaced. This was what he'd been afraid of. That momentary hesitation told him everything about what she was thinking. It was the same thing everyone thought when they saw him and Matthew together. Over time, he'd hoped that the resemblance between them might have lessened, but if anything it had only become more pronounced.

To give his wife credit, however, at least she was trying to hide her shock from the boy himself. Most people weren't so thoughtful. That was the real reason he hadn't brought Matthew to the wedding. That, and to avoid Kitty. He'd managed to keep him out of her line of sight for five years, ever since he'd first brought him home, not wanting to deal with people's assumptions *then* any more than he wanted to deal with them *now*. Even if the person making the assumption was his wife.

'Can I eat downstairs, then?'

'If you want to.' Robert gritted his teeth at the boy's manners. 'Just do as you're told.'

'I will!' The boy scurried away, remembering at the last moment to turn and give a brief, formal bow. 'Good evening, Mrs Felstone.'

'Good evening, Matthew.' Ianthe gave what looked like a genuine smile. 'I'm looking forward to starting our lessons tomorrow.'

'Tomorrow?' The boy threw him a look of appeal.

'Tomorrow.' Robert jerked his head, struggling to conceal his own sense of surprise. He'd assumed that Ianthe would want to settle in before starting the boy's schooling, but apparently the role of governess was more appealing than that of wife.

'You might have your hands full with him.' He cleared his throat as the door closed behind Matthew. 'I'm afraid I've allowed him too much freedom. He needs structure, but he's not used to a classroom.'

'Children need freedom, too.' Her face was still turned towards the door, as if she were reluctant to look at him. 'But I'll do my best.'

'I'm sure you will.' Robert clasped his hands firmly behind his back, waiting for the accusation to follow, but she didn't make so much as a murmur. Somehow that felt even more unnerving. If she were going to accuse him, then he wished that she'd just go ahead and do it. How could he refute the words if she wouldn't say them?

'Is there a problem?' At last he couldn't stand the silence any longer.

'Not at all.' She turned at last, her face the very picture of innocence. 'He seems like a nice boy.'

'He is.' Robert drew his brows together, uncertain about how to proceed. 'Shall we go in to dinner, then?'

She nodded, and he led the way out of the parlour and across the hall into the dining room. It was one of his favourite rooms in the house, painted a pale duck-egg green, with white cornice mouldings and a white plaster rose on a high ceiling, gleaming exposed floorboards and a large bay window facing out to sea.

'I hope you're hungry.' He helped her into a chair at one end of a long table before taking his own opposite. 'I think Mrs Lughton wants to impress you.'

'I could eat a horse.'

'Good. You didn't eat much at the hotel, I noticed.'

Her smile wavered slightly. 'It was a big day. You can't blame me for being nervous.'

'Didn't your aunt feed you either?'

She dropped her eyes to the tablecloth. 'She's been very kind, but…I haven't had much of an appetite lately.'

'Or much sleep either, I think.'

'No-o. I'm afraid I haven't been sleeping well. Until today, that is.'

Robert's frown eased slightly. That fact was encouraging at least. Doubtless he was overthinking things and she'd simply been worried about taking such a big step. Now that the wedding was over, perhaps she'd start to relax. Perhaps they both would.

The arrival of a maid carrying a tureen of

soup prevented him from asking any more questions. Instead, he watched in surprise as Ianthe fell upon the liquid with gusto, swallowing each mouthful with a relish that suggested she hadn't eaten anything for days. The contrast with their wedding luncheon could hardly have been any greater. She certainly didn't look anxious now. She was already scooping up her last spoonful, licking her lips with satisfaction.

He tore his gaze away from her mouth quickly.

'That was delicious.' She patted a napkin to her lips. 'Your Mrs Lughton is an excellent cook.'

'I'll be sure to tell her you enjoyed it.'

'She seemed very pleasant. Everyone did. And it's a beautiful house, what I've seen of it anyway. Although I think this is only the third room I've been in.'

'Then I'll give you a proper tour after dinner. I wouldn't want you to get lost on your way to bed.'

'I'd like that. Though it doesn't seem like a fair exchange.'

'What's that?'

'All of this for me.'

'Perhaps you underestimate yourself.'

A shadow flitted across her face. 'I don't think so.'

She dropped her gaze to the table again, staring at it in silence as the maid returned with a tray, clearing away the bowls and replacing them with plates of roast beef, potatoes, carrots and steaming hot gravy.

'About your ward…' She looked up again once the maid had gone.

'What about him?' He tensed immediately.

'You should know that my former pupils were both girls.'

'So?' He wasn't sure what she was getting at.

'I'm not used to teaching boys.'

'Weren't there any in the family you worked for?'

She started as if he'd just said something shocking, fork suspended halfway to her mouth.

'Ianthe?'

'There was.' Her voice sounded oddly tremulous. 'But he was older. You know, most boys are sent away to school.'

'So I've heard, but I prefer to keep Matthew with me.'

'It might be better for his education.'

Robert knit his brows together suspiciously. 'Do you *want* me to send him away?'

'No! Of course not.'

'Good. He's had enough upheaval in his life.'

'Then I'll do my best. I just thought you should know that my experience is…limited.'

He relaxed slightly. 'I'm sure you'll do a good job, Ianthe. Better than anything I could do anyway. I've had one of the bedrooms on the first floor turned into a schoolroom. It faces east with a view of the sea. It should be very pleasant there in the mornings.'

'That was very thoughtful. Is there anything in particular you want me to teach him?'

Robert shrugged. 'I haven't thought too much about it. I've been teaching him reading and numbers at the yard, but I'd like you to round out his education with the things I can't teach.'

'Languages?'

'Do you know any?'

'German and Italian, and I can read Latin. A little Greek, too.'

'Just a little?' He lifted his eyebrows, impressed.

'I like words, whatever the language.' She smiled shyly. 'Even when they're not poetry.'

'I had no idea of your talents. Perhaps we should forget about Matthew and have you come to work at the yard instead.'

'What do you mean?'

'I deal with traders from all over Europe. It might be useful to have a translator.'

Her face brightened enthusiastically. 'Then I'd be happy to help. I'd like to see your shipyard anyway.'

'Really?'

'Of course. It was the reason we got married, wasn't it? I'd like to see what I'm helping to build.'

'Then I'll arrange it.'

'Thank you.'

Robert smiled across the table with a new sense of appreciation. Things were definitely looking up. Apparently there was more to his wife than he'd first given her credit for. She might prove an asset to his business in more ways than one. The soup clearly hadn't satiated her appetite either. She was eating even more heartily now than before.

'Did you go to school?' She paused briefly between mouthfuls.

'Me?' He almost dropped his fork in surprise. 'No. We hardly had money for food, let alone schooling.'

'Oh, I'm sorry. I didn't think...'

'I'm not offended, Ianthe, but I thought you knew about my background. Surely Kitty told you.'

'She's been distracted with plans for the baby, I think. Aunt Sophoria told me your mother raised you, but if you taught Matthew to read and write then you must have learnt those skills somewhere?'

'I was always good with numbers.' He speared a potato, feeling a vague sense of discomfort. He wasn't accustomed to talking about himself or his past, but then, she was his wife. She had a right to ask a few questions about him. As long as it was only a few...

'I couldn't read or write when we moved to

Whitby, but I could turn my hand to most things and I was a quick learner. When I was twelve, I got a job at Masham's Shipyard as an apprentice. Mr Masham saw something in me and took me under his wing.'

'So he taught you?'

'After I'd finished my regular work, yes. Then, when I was good enough, he made me a clerk in his office. It turned out I had a talent for business. Old Masham had come up from nothing himself and we made a good team. By the time he died, we were partners. He left me the rest of the yard in his will.'

'Didn't he have any family?'

'No, he loved his work, practically lived at the yard. He didn't want any distractions...' He winced at his tactlessness. 'Not that marriage is a distraction necessarily.'

She gave a placatory smile. 'You don't have to defend yourself. Our marriage is a business arrangement, after all. Mr Masham might have approved.'

'Probably. Not that he ever cared about being respectable.'

'He might have been right.' She sounded thoughtful. 'Why *is* respectability so important after all?'

'Only a person who's never had to worry about it would ask that question.' His voice hardened dangerously.

'You just said that Mr Masham didn't care.'

'His mother was never called a whore in the street.'

Robert clenched his jaw, regretting the words the instant they were out of his mouth. Damn it, *this* was the reason he didn't answer questions about himself. He could keep his temper on almost every other subject.

'They called her *that*?' Ianthe was staring at him with a frankly appalled expression.

'Amongst other things.'

'Because of your father?'

'In part.' He put his cutlery down, losing his appetite suddenly. 'There were other rumours, too, not that there was any truth to them. Some people just prefer to see the worst. They think that when a woman makes a mistake once, she'll make it again.'

'But that's not fair!'

He gave a bitter laugh. 'No, but that's how it works.'

'So that's why being respectable is so important to you? It's not just to convince Mr Harper to sell?'

He heaved a sigh. 'It's important because I've heard enough insults in my life, Ianthe. I've had my fill of rumour and gossip. I won't give anyone the chance to spread any more about me. *That's* why respectability matters.'

'But…' Her voice trailed away as if she were about to burst into tears.

'What is it?' Robert frowned across the table. Why was she so shocked? She knew that he was illegitimate. Surely she might have guessed how his mother had been treated, too—the names she'd been called. Or was she so horrified by the connection?

'I thought you only wanted a respectable wife to impress Mr Harper.'

Her voice was so faint that he had to strain to hear it.

'I do.'

'Someone to teach your ward and make calls— that was what you said.'

'It was. It is.'

'You didn't say anything about gossip.'

His frown deepened. 'That's all in the past, Ianthe.'

She pushed her chair back abruptly. 'I think I've had enough to eat. Everything was delicious, but I'm tired. I'd like to go to bed.'

'Again?' He looked at her sceptically, but she was already heading for the door.

'I'm sorry.' She turned slightly in the doorway, though she seemed reluctant to look him in the eye. 'Will I see you in the morning?'

'No.' He reached for the crystal decanter in the middle of the table, pouring himself a large glass of wine. He *had* intended to breakfast with her, but now an extra hour at the shipyard seemed a far more appealing idea. 'Mrs Baxter will help you with anything you need while I'm away.'

'Then have a good journey.' She was already halfway through the door. 'Goodnight.'

He didn't bother to answer, waiting until the door had closed completely before draining his glass and hurling it violently into the fireplace.

What had gone wrong? One minute they'd been talking about the shipyard and the next she was running away! Because of his mother? He balled his hands into fists at the thought. He'd told her that he had no intention of discussing his past, that it was somewhat less than salubrious, but he'd assumed that she'd find out the details on her own. She'd had three months to do so! The short engagement that *she'd* wanted! Why hadn't Kitty told her? Typical if this was the one time Giles's wife had actually managed to be discreet!

He glowered at the door as if she were still standing in front of it. So much for respectability. His own wife seemed mortified at the thought of being married to him. It was just like Louisa had said. No *respectable* woman would want to be associated with a man with his past. Somehow he'd thought better of Ianthe, but she was just like everyone else, assuming the worst, first about Matthew, then his mother, too!

Well, if she didn't like her situation, it wasn't

his fault. He'd told her to make enquiries. Too bad if she hadn't followed his advice.

From now on their marriage would be what it was supposed to be in the first place. A business arrangement.

Chapter Eleven

'What about geography? Do you like that?'

Ianthe gestured towards a large globe by the window, repressing a sigh as Matthew shrugged for what seemed like the hundredth time that morning.

She gritted her teeth, glancing around the room for any other sources of inspiration. After two days, all she'd managed to learn about her new pupil was that whilst he was adequate at reading and writing, he was ambivalent about art, literature and almost every other subject she could think of, with no enthusiasm for anything—least of all her.

She was only relieved that her new husband wasn't there to witness her failure. His absence was a respite in more ways than one. After what he'd told her about his mother and the importance of respectability, she'd needed space to decide what to do next. She'd known that running out of the dining room had offended him, but if she'd stayed she might have blurted the truth out there and then.

Why hadn't he told her before? He'd said that he wanted a respectable bride, not some paragon of virtue! She could never live up to that! If she'd known *why* being respectable meant so much to him, she would never have married him, Sir Charles or not! She'd thought that the worst that might happen was that Harper would refuse to sell his shipyard. Now she felt as though she were living with a sword over her head. If the truth about her past ever came out, there'd be more gossip than he knew what to do with!

Not that it was entirely her fault. If he'd only visited her during their engagement then they might have discussed it. She could have called off the wedding. Whereas now... She heaved a sigh. Even if she told him about Albert now, what good would it do? The truth would only drive a further wedge between them. No, it was too late either to tell him or to back out...

'Are we finished?' Matthew's voice broke through her reverie.

'No.' She straightened up with a snap. Even if she'd already failed as a wife, she'd no intention of failing as a teacher as well. 'Wouldn't you like to learn where all the ships in the harbour travel to? All the ones that your...guardian builds?'

As usual, she hesitated over the word guardian,

though surely Robert didn't think her so naive as not to guess the real relationship between him and the boy. Matthew could hardly have looked any more like him. So why on earth hadn't he told her he had a son? Apparently, maintaining an appearance of respectability was even more important to him than she'd thought. The things they *weren't* telling each other would fill a book at this rate.

'S'pose.' Matthew rested his head on his arms.

'Good.' She tapped the wooden desk with her knuckles, making him spring up again. 'Come to the window.'

'Why?'

She didn't answer, gesturing towards the horizon. 'Now, if you were to sail in a straight line directly from here, you'd get to Denmark. This is us…' she trailed her fingers across the globe '…and this is Denmark. It's part of Scandinavia, where the Vikings came from.'

'The ones with horns on their helmets?'

'That's them. They came here a long time ago and destroyed the whole town.'

'Here?'

'Then a few of them decided to stay. They were the ones who named it Whitby. The word means "white settlement" in old Norse.'

Matthew gave a begrudging look of interest before remembering to frown again. 'Are you going to be teaching me every day?'

'In the mornings, yes.'

'Does it have to be here?' He peered wistfully out of the window. 'Only it's been raining for weeks. Now it's finally sunny again.'

'And you'd rather be outside?'

He nodded vigorously. 'We could go down to the shore. You could tell me some more about Vikings on the way.'

Ianthe glanced outside, torn between the desire to make friends and a sudden rush of panic. The day was bright and inviting, the sunshine bouncing off the water just over the cliff's edge, making the air itself seem to sparkle, and yet even the thought of venturing outside made her hands start to sweat and her stomach to churn alarmingly. After three months of staying mostly indoors, the outside world felt dangerous somehow.

'It's a high tide, isn't it?' She tried to sound discouraging.

'It's going out again now.'

'Trying to get out of class already?'

They both swung around at the sound of Robert's voice. He was standing only a few paces behind them, pale eyes glinting with amusement.

'You're back!' Matthew charged across the room, flinging himself enthusiastically against Robert's legs.

'So I am.' He wrapped an arm around the boy's shoulders. 'A good thing, too, I suspect. Are you trying avoid lessons?'

'Not at all.' Ianthe leapt to Matthew's defence, trying to ignore the sudden thumping sensation in her chest, as if her heart were actually jumping around inside there. 'We were just talking about Vikings.'

'Whitby means white settlement,' the boy announced proudly.

'Is that so? Then I stand corrected.' Robert winked at Matthew before turning to her with a look of polite, guarded enquiry. 'Have you been researching local history?'

'A little.' She tried to smile, but her features seemed frozen into place. 'I thought I ought to learn something about my new home.'

'I'm pleased to hear it.'

Ianthe reached behind her, grasping hold of the window ledge for support. She'd replayed their last conversation in her head so many times that seeing him again seemed almost unreal. Now he was there she had no idea what to say, no idea how to pick up the pieces left by her running away.

'We were about to go down to the harbour.' Matthew sounded as if he were trying to convince both of them.

'Really?' Robert quirked an eyebrow.

'Yes.' Matthew jutted his chin out determinedly. 'I'm going to show her around. Mrs Lughton says she hasn't been anywhere yet.'

Ianthe blinked in surprise. She hadn't realised

that her movements, or lack of them, had been the subject of conversation in the house. Fortunately, Robert didn't appear to find anything strange about it.

'Then perhaps you might permit me to join you? If you don't mind my spending some time with your new governess, that is?'

'Can we still go to the beach?'

'We'll go along the pier. Now go and fetch a coat.'

Ianthe's pulse quickened as Matthew charged out of the room, leaving them alone together. With him gone, the room seemed smaller somehow, stifling almost, as if there wasn't enough air to breath.

'What about you, Ianthe?' Robert's voice sounded different now, too, quieter and more sombre. 'Do *you* object to me accompanying you?'

'I... No.' She wavered uncertainly. His unexpected arrival was making her feel flustered enough. The thought of going outside with him as well made her feel positively faint. She hadn't even *agreed* to Matthew's plan! But if she refused now, it might make the situation between them even worse. She pursed her lips anxiously. How could she explain that it wasn't *him* she objected to so much as the thought of going outdoors at all? She felt crazy even admitting the fear to herself.

A muscle twitched in his jaw. 'Are you certain?'

She took a deep breath, forcing the fear away. 'Of course. A walk sounds very pleasant.'

'Good.' The tension in his face seemed to ease slightly. 'How are you, Ianthe?'

'I'm well.' She swallowed, trying to think of something else to say. 'I thought you weren't due back until Saturday?'

'My business didn't take as long as I expected.'

'Oh.'

Silence.

'Have you settled in?'

'Yes. Mrs Baxter showed me around.' She gestured towards the household keys hanging in a loop from her belt. 'I still might need a map, though. I can't remember where any of these go.'

'Ah.' He didn't return her smile. 'I was going to give you a tour, wasn't I?'

'It doesn't matter. I think she enjoyed it.'

'Probably.' He paced around the room, still keeping the desk between them. 'How's Matthew doing?'

'I think we're starting to make progress.'

'Let me know if he isn't paying attention.'

'He's a good boy.' She picked up a small blackboard. 'Here's his work from this morning if you'd like to check.'

Robert's brow creased. 'I'm not here to inspect you, Ianthe.'

'Oh.' She let her hand fall again. 'My old employer always wanted to look.'

'I'm not your employer. I just wondered if there was anything you might need?'

'Not that I can think of—but thank you.'

He gave a curt nod, hesitating for a moment before speaking again. 'We may not have a conventional marriage, but I'd like for us to be friends.'

'Friends?' Her voice sounded strangely high pitched.

'Since we're married... Unless you'd prefer that I leave you alone?'

'No!' She shook her head quickly. 'That sounds... good.'

'Good.' His lips twitched slightly as he echoed the word. 'Then I'll meet you in the hall in five minutes.'

Ianthe nodded mutely, waiting until he'd gone before putting her hands over her face with mortification. What was the matter with her? *Good?* As if she couldn't think of anything more intelligent to say! The shock of seeing him again seemed to have scattered her wits along with her senses.

Not that she had much time to recover. Now that she'd tacitly agreed to go down to the pier, she had to hurry and get ready. On top of everything else, she didn't want to be late, too!

Quickly, she ran along to her room, donning her most respectable-looking woollen cloak and a plain poke bonnet, regarding herself in the mirror with satisfaction. Surely it would be impossible to look any *more* respectable. Percy would be horrified.

'It's not cold.' Matthew gave her an inquisitorial look as she descended the stairs. 'You'll be too hot in that.'

'Matthew,' Robert admonished the boy with a stern look, coming to meet her as she reached the last step. 'Though he might be right. It's quite warm today.'

He himself was dressed lightly, she noticed, having discarded his formal waistcoat and cravat in favour of a simple white shirt and black jacket. If he was right about the temperature, then it would make sense for her to go and change, too, but she was reluctant to put aside her respectable attire so soon. A three-quarter-length cloak was what a respectable woman would wear.

'I'm not used to a sea climate.' She smiled indifferently, wrapping the cloak tightly around her shoulders. 'There might be a breeze.'

'There's no wind.'

'Matthew!'

'But there isn't!' the boy protested. 'And it's a long way down to the harbour. You'll need sensible boots.'

'For pity's sake, boy…'

'I always wear sensible boots.' She laughed as Robert ground his teeth in frustration. 'It was one of the first things your guardian noticed about me, wasn't it, Robert?'

'One of them.' He gave a bemused smile, gesturing towards the front door. 'Shall we?'

She took a few steps forward, hoping that her movements didn't look as unsteady as they felt, pausing on the threshold with a feeling of trepidation. The wide expanse of the crescent seemed to make the outside world look even more intimidating. The last thing she wanted to do was go out there, but if she turned back now, she didn't know when she'd have the nerve to try again. She had to go through with it, had to conquer the fear for her own sake. Besides, what would Robert think if she ran away again? She could feel his eyes watching her, probably wondering why she was hesitating.

She took a deep breath and stepped outside, keeping her head down and her gaze fixed on the ground as they followed the curve of the pavement, before crossing the road that led to the promenade.

'Matthew's right about the distance.' Robert's tone was solicitous. 'I can call for a carriage if you wish.'

'There's no need.' She shook her head obstinately. 'I'm perfectly capable of walking.'

'As you wish.'

She glanced towards him, suddenly regretting her brusqueness. After all, he was only trying to help.

'I'm looking forward to seeing the view,' she offered.

'You haven't been out at all, then?'

He sounded surprised, and she could have bitten her own tongue out. 'No. I thought I'd learn my way around the house first. Mrs Baxter had a lot to tell me.'

That was true, she told herself, if not entirely convincing. Mrs Baxter had been exhaustive in her description of how to manage the household. It had felt like two days at any rate.

'Have you been into town?'

'Not yet.' She shrugged, trying to make it seem as if there were nothing odd about such reclusive behaviour. 'I'm glad to be out now, though.'

He stopped all of a sudden and swept an arm out, gesturing over the edge of the cliff. 'In that case, this is Whitby.'

Ianthe caught her breath, rendered momentarily speechless by the view of the immense harbour below. The shimmering water was dotted with at least fifty different ships—fishing boats, schooners, merchant vessels, barques, even a couple of naval frigates—while the harbour walls were a throng of activity, too, with fishermen, merchants and sailors intermingling with tourists promenading along the pier.

'It's quite impressive the first time you see it.' Robert's voice held a hint of pride.

'I think it must be impressive at any time.'

She felt mesmerised by the sight. 'How do we get down?'

He gestured towards a narrow flight of steps. 'Don't say we didn't warn you. It's still not too late for a carriage.'

Ianthe lifted her chin rebelliously, starting down the long, winding steps as Matthew scampered on ahead. The boy *had* been right, the temperature was far warmer than she'd expected and getting hotter every moment. The extra exertion was making her heavy clothes feel itchy as well, though at least it distracted her mind from its fear of the outdoors. How many steps could there possibly be? She must have counted a hundred already.

'Can I play on the beach?' Matthew was already at the bottom, hopping from foot to foot impatiently.

'Stay where we can see you.' Robert took her arm as they finally reached the pavement. 'And no swimming!'

Ianthe averted her face as they walked along the harbourside, trying to hide her flaming cheeks. She was so hot she felt faint. If only she could take off her cloak, but that wouldn't be respectable...

'He's not my son.'

'What?' She spun towards him in surprise, temperature suddenly forgotten. 'I didn't say...'

'But you thought it.'

'Ye-es.' She had a feeling he'd know if she was lying. 'You're just so alike.'

'I know, but he's not mine. You should know that.'

They stepped on to the pier, and she glanced towards the beach on the west side of the harbour wall, to where Matthew was already playing with a group of other boys. He was throwing stones into the sea, his black hair gleaming with blue lights in the sunshine. Even from a distance the resemblance was almost uncanny. Surely Robert knew how obvious their relation was? Still, if he wanted her to believe it, who was she to argue? She had her own pretence to maintain after all.

'All right.'

'I should have explained the other night, but I find certain subjects difficult to talk about.'

'I understand. It's none of my business.'

'It is. You're my wife. You have a right to know some things. Matthew isn't my son, but I'm raising him as one. I've given him a home and my name. It was his mother's last request and I intend to honour it. That's all I can tell you.'

'Oh.' She didn't know how else to answer. He seemed genuine, but surely he knew how far-fetched his denial sounded. Why didn't he just admit the truth? It wasn't as if it would bother her. Or did he think she was too respectable to hear it?

'As for my mother...' He sounded tense again.

'We weren't close, but I wouldn't want you to think ill of her.'

'Why would I think ill of her?' She looked up at him in surprise.

'Because the other night you seemed upset by what I told you. Given the circumstances, I'd understand if you were bothered by the connection, though I would have preferred it if you'd mentioned it sooner.'

'I thought no such thing!' She wrenched her arm out of his indignantly.

'You left in a hurry.'

'Not because of that!'

His severe expression seemed to ease slightly. 'Then I'm sorry. I've been told before that my past makes me a less-than-desirable match. Perhaps I misinterpreted your behaviour.'

'If you thought that, then, yes, you did! If I was upset it was because I was sorry for bringing the subject up. Sorry for your mother, too. It must have very hard for her.' Despite her anger, she found herself regarding him sympathetically. 'For both of you.'

'It was. Most people only insulted her behind her back, but there were others who spread gossip openly.'

'Some people don't understand how much words can hurt.'

'Most don't care.'

She took his arm again, trying to lighten the

mood as they headed towards the eighty-foot lighthouse at the far end of the pier. 'Why stay here, then? If what people say bothers you, why not start again somewhere else?'

'Because I'm not ashamed of my mother. If I left it would be like admitting everyone was right about her. And because the truth has a way of catching up with people. When I was a boy we were always moving, running from town to town, trying to escape the rumours. They always found us. Eventually my mother got tired of running. She was from Whitby and wanted to come back. Once we arrived, she told me she'd never run away again, no matter what.' Pale eyes flashed defiantly. 'I won't run away either, Ianthe, but I will prove everyone wrong. They said I wouldn't amount to anything and I have. They said I'd never be respectable...'

'So you married me.'

She stared out to sea, clasping the metal railings that ran along the edge of the pier for support. *The truth has a way of catching up with people.* But that wasn't always true...was it?

'Besides...' he leaned over the railing beside her, looking out to where Matthew was playing on the sand '...this is my home. I wouldn't want to live anywhere else.'

'I can see why. It's beautiful.'

'Even more so at sunset. You know the harbour mouth faces north. This is one of the few places in England where you can see the sun rise and set directly over the sea.'

'I'd like to see that. It seems to have been raining ever since I got here.'

'The sun's shining now.'

'Yes.' She smiled wistfully. 'Maybe tonight then.'

He looked at her seriously. 'Not feeling homesick, then?'

'No.' She felt oddly touched by the question. 'I don't have a home in London any more. It was never the same after my parents died and at least here I'm close to my aunt.'

'You should invite her to stay.'

'Aunt Sophoria?' She tilted her head in surprise.

'Why not?'

'Because...' She hesitated, wondering how to be tactful. 'She's a little eccentric.'

'So I've noticed.' A black eyebrow quirked upwards ironically. 'I might not want her to dress you again, Ianthe, but I enjoy her company.'

She felt the corners of her mouth twitch before bursting into a peal of laughter. 'I did look ridiculous that first morning, didn't I?'

'And yet I still proposed.' He laughed too. 'Speaking of clothes, didn't you buy any new gowns? I see that you're still wearing grey.'

'I thought you liked me in grey.' She glanced down self-consciously.

'You can wear whatever colour you like, but it would make me happy to buy you a few new dresses. Perhaps something a bit cooler for the summer.'

'But I thought this was…'

'If you say respectable one more time, I'll throw that cloak into the harbour myself.'

'All right.' She put her hands on her hips. 'Then I thought you wanted me to dress a certain way?'

'I do, but I'd prefer you not to collapse from heatstroke while doing it. I don't think respectable means wearing wool on a hot day.' He looked at her indignant stance and grinned. 'Half an hour at the harbour and she turns into a fishwife. Here.'

He caught hold of the corners of her cloak suddenly, tugging her towards him as he unwrapped it gently from around her shoulders.

'How's that?'

'Better,' she admitted, voice quavering slightly. When he'd pulled her towards him, she'd had the brief, startling impression that he'd been about to kiss her again. 'But what if one of your acquaintances sees me?'

'You're wearing a morning gown, Ianthe, not a petticoat.' He tugged at the bow beneath her chin, letting the ribbon unravel before lifting her bonnet carefully away from her head.

'Besides…' he leant down, bringing his lips

close to her ear '...if I see anyone coming, I can always stand in front of you.'

She threw him a scathing look and turned her face towards the sea, letting the air cool her cheeks. That *was* better, even if she felt more confused now than ever. He was the one who'd said he wanted her to be respectable and yet now he seemed to find the whole idea amusing, half-undressing her in broad daylight! He seemed a tangle of contradictions. A man who craved re-spectability and yet stayed in the one place he could never achieve it—who gave his name and a home to a boy he refused to acknowledge as his son! She couldn't make sense of him at all, but at least the tension between them seemed to have passed. He seemed altogether mellower now, the way he'd been at the ball. She felt as though she were getting to know him again.

'So...friends?' His shoulder brushed against hers as he stood beside her.

She took a deep breath and exhaled. In his company, her fear of the outdoors seemed to have receded somewhat, at least for the moment. For the first time since the ball, she was aware of her old self again; that buried self she'd almost forgotten—happy, relaxed and carefree. That wasn't the Ianthe Robert wanted, but she didn't want him to push her away again, not just yet. She wanted to enjoy the view, the moment, the start of her new life...

She tilted her face up towards him, unable to hide a sudden burst of happiness.

'Friends.'

Robert regarded his wife in amazement. He'd returned to Whitby that morning with a heavy heart, braced for another argument, and yet now arguing was the very last thing on his mind.

What *was* on his mind was something he ought not to think about, but it was impossible not to. The way she was looking at him—smiling as if she were genuinely happy—made him wish that theirs wasn't such a straightforward business arrangement after all. The urge to kiss her was almost overpowering.

Clearly, he must be losing his senses along with his sanity, he decided. He'd just invited her aunt to visit *and* offered to take her shopping! If he wasn't careful he'd be propositioning her next.

'Which one is yours?'

'Hmm?' He cleared his throat huskily.

'Which one is your shipyard?' She leaned back against the railings, facing into the harbour. 'Can we see it from here?'

'No.' He brought his face alongside hers, checking the angle. 'See where the River Esk curves out of sight? It's just around the bend, on the west bank next to the mudflats.'

'Oh.' Her voice sounded breathless suddenly. 'How many yards are there altogether?'

'Now? Only about a dozen, though there used to be a lot more. A hundred years ago, we were the second-biggest shipbuilding town in the country. Two of Captain Cook's ships, the *Endeavour* and the *Resolution*, were built here. Back then we made twenty full-size ships a years. Now we're lucky if we make half that number.'

'What happened?'

'London and Newcastle expanded, started building in iron, too. That's what we need to do. In a few years, no one will be building wooden ships any more, but some of my colleagues don't want to accept that.'

'Including Mr Harper?'

'He's the worst of all. Deep down, he knows that if he doesn't adapt then he'll go bankrupt, but he refuses to admit it. He's an old man, he's not well and he doesn't like change, but he can't stand still any longer.'

'Is he ailing?'

'He's been ailing for a few years, but I'm not taking advantage of a sick old man if that's what you're thinking. He's a cantankerous, judgemental old bigot who'd rather run his business into the ground than sell to a low-born bastard like me.' He made a face. 'Excuse me, but the only reason he's considering it is because of you.'

'You must really want his yard.'

'I do. The biggest and the best, remember?' He smiled at the thought. 'I'm offering him a better price than he deserves *and* easing his scruples about me into the bargain. He can't ask for much more than that.'

'So it all comes down to whether or not he ap-approves of me?'

'Essentially, yes. He was pleased to hear we were married. Now we just need to show him how eminently respectable you are.'

She dropped her gaze abruptly. 'So what next? Should I call on him?'

'I've already arranged it. We're visiting him and his daughter next week.'

'His *daughter*?' Her eyes flew back to his. 'You never said he had a daughter.'

'I didn't think it mattered. Her name's Violet.'

'How old is she?'

'About the same as you, I should think.'

'Do you like her?'

'*Like* her?' He frowned, wondering what she was getting at. 'She's pleasant enough, I suppose. A bit timid, though that's no surprise living with her father. Why?'

'Isn't it obvious?' Ianthe was staring at him with a flabbergasted expression. 'Why didn't you just marry *her*?'

Robert knit his brows together, taken aback by the question. It was a good one. Marrying Violet would have made good business sense, yet the idea had never occurred to him. In all likelihood, Harper would never have approved of him as a suitor, but that wasn't the point. He *ought* to have thought of it. So why hadn't he? Perhaps because since meeting Ianthe, he hadn't thought of any other woman at all.

'And I thought you were a man of business.' Brown eyes sparkled with laughter. 'He'd definitely have sold you his yard then. He might even have given it to you.'

'You might be right.' He shook his head, vaguely unnerved by the exchange. 'But I'm afraid it's time we were going. I ought to get back to work.'

She fell into step beside him, swinging her bonnet loosely in one hand as they made their way back along the pier towards the cliff steps. Exposed to the elements, her hair now seemed determined to escape the confines of its bun, billowing around her face in wispy tendrils that she made no effort to brush away. Oddly enough, he seemed to prefer her dishevelled.

'I'm sorry to drag you away so soon.' He waved a summons to Matthew, stepped aside for a man in a brown jacket to pass by. 'You can stay longer if you wish.'

'On my own?' Her voice sounded panicky all of a sudden.

'With Matthew. I'm sure he'd enjoy showing you around.'

'I'd rather go back.'

He glanced at her surreptitiously. All that he'd

said was that she could stay there with Matthew and yet her whole manner had suddenly changed. She seemed to have retreated inside herself again, just as she'd done when they'd first left the house, though he'd put that down to nerves about their newly established truce. Just as she'd done the other night, too, when she'd fled from the dining room. The happy, carefree woman seemed to have been replaced by a pale, frightened wraith.

What on earth was there to be frightened of?

'As you wish.' He kept his tone even, trying not to alarm her any further.

'Will you still escort us home?'

'Of course.' He drew to a halt as they reached the bottom of the steps, waiting for Matthew to catch up. 'Though we can go through the town if you prefer? It's a longer route, but not quite as steep. We could do some shopping now, too.'

'No.' She swept past him so quickly that for a moment he thought she intended to run up the steps.

'Can't we stay any longer?' Matthew scampered up and tugged at his sleeve. 'We've hardly been here an hour.'

'Not today. Mrs Felstone needs to get home.' He took one look at the boy's crestfallen expression and relented. 'You can come with me to the yard instead.'

'Yes!' Matthew gave an enthusiastic leap. 'I said she'd be too hot.'

'She's indisposed.'

'Indis—what?'

'Concerned about something, but don't mention it to anyone, lad. I'll find out what's the matter later.'

He narrowed his eyes as he mounted the steps, following Ianthe's retreating back with a look of grim determination. Whatever had happened to make her panic, this time he wasn't going to let her tell him she was tired or hot or any other excuse. This time he was going to find out exactly what was going on.

Chapter Twelve

'So…' Ianthe twirled around in the doorway. 'What do you think?'

'You look fine.' Robert barely glanced up from the game of chess he was playing with Matthew.

''S all right.' His ward sounded even less impressed.

Ianthe gave an underwhelmed sigh. *Fine* and *all right* weren't quite the responses she'd been hoping for. Given that Robert had helped to choose her new wardrobe, she'd expected him to be slightly more enthusiastic about the results. The gown she'd selected for their visit to Mr Harper was, in her opinion, both beautiful *and* respectable, a pale cerulean blue with a high-buttoned neck, long sleeves and medium-sized skirts that extended backwards in the new fashion.

'I thought we were going to learn about Romans today.' Matthew pouted.

'We still will. Your guardian and I just need to make a call first.'

She smiled, secretly pleased by his petulant expression. Since their trip to the harbour, he'd become a whole different boy, positively eager for her time and attention. In striking contrast to his guardian. The atmosphere between *them* had been strained ever since.

So far Robert hadn't said anything directly about her behaviour at the harbour, though she'd caught him watching her occasionally with a speculative expression, as if trying to work something out. Even during their trip to the dressmaker's, she'd had the uneasy feeling that she'd been under surveillance. She'd done her best to avoid being alone with him, trying to avoid questions, not that she could have given him any answers anyway. The sudden, vivid sensation of panic when he'd suggested that she stay at the harbour had surprised even her. In that moment, even his presence by her side hadn't helped. All she'd wanted was to get back to the house as quickly as possible.

Once there, she'd pleaded a headache and retreated to her room, aware of how bizarre her behaviour must seem, but unable to do anything about it. Ever since, she'd done her best not to give him any further cause for suspicion, though she still hadn't been able to bring herself to go outside.

'Will you be long?'

'A couple of hours, maybe.' Robert answered for them. 'Now run along. We'll finish the game later.'

He stood up, adopting a stern expression as Matthew bolted away to the kitchens. 'You don't have to make up for his lesson later. You can have a day off when you want one.'

'I know, but I enjoy teaching him. He seems to like history.'

'The kind with blood and battles, I presume?'

'Ye-es. But I think he's coming along.' She pulled on her bonnet, arranging the veil neatly. 'Ready?'

He gave her an intense look and she forced herself to smile, resting a hand on his arm and trying not to grip too tightly as they walked down the front steps and on to the street.

'I thought that we'd walk.' He sounded suspiciously nonchalant. 'It's not far and the weather's fine.'

She gave a murmur of assent, not trusting herself to speak as they walked along a succession of side streets, keeping her head up and trying to concentrate on the loveliness of her surroundings and not the sudden feeling of exposure. Truly, it was a beautiful town, the Georgian architecture perfectly in keeping with the cliff face below, as if the town itself had somehow grown out of the rock.

She liked it here, she reminded herself. This was her new home. She was safe. And Robert was right beside her. Surely no one would hurt her when he was there.

'Here we are.' They were at Harper's in a matter of minutes.

'Here?' She gulped, shuddering at the sight of at least twenty gargoyles peering down at them from the red-stone turrets and crenellations of a large Gothic villa.

'It suits its owner, I'm afraid.' Robert pressed her hand reassuringly. 'But don't worry. This is just a formality. The last piece of the puzzle, that's all.'

'The last piece...' she murmured, adopting her most respectable demeanour. 'All right, I'm ready.'

'There's no need to scowl.'

'I didn't know I was.' She felt vaguely offended. 'I'm just trying to do what you want.'

'Just be yourself.'

Herself? She lifted her eyebrows incredulously. That wasn't what they'd agreed. They'd agreed that she be sensible and respectable. He'd never said anything about being herself before. Though of course, she realised with a sinking feeling, that was who he thought she *really* was...

And it *was* who she was! She gave a start, alarmed to have drifted so far from the new, respectable Ianthe. Ever since their walk on the pier and that moment when she'd allowed her old self to escape for a few moments, she'd found it harder and harder to put her back in her cage. Now she felt as if her old and new identities were at war with each other, each struggling for dominance. She wasn't sure *who* she was any more, but she knew who she was supposed to be.

She straightened her shoulders, pursing her lips as she put the respectable mask back on again. Now she wished that she'd worn one of her old grey dresses instead. They would have reminded her how the new Ianthe ought to behave…

A maid opened the door, and she felt her stomach lurch as they stepped inside. The gloomy interior seemed the perfect accompaniment to her anxiety. This was it, the real test, the whole reason that Robert had married her. She felt sick.

'Mrs Felstone?' A young woman with white-blonde hair emerged from a side door almost at once, smiling a welcome. 'I'm so pleased to meet you finally. I'm Violet Harper.'

'Miss Harper.' Ianthe held out a hand, starting to relax slightly. The woman was unusually small, almost tiny, with striking blue eyes that gave her an almost waif-like appearance, but she seemed friendly. 'Please call me Ianthe.'

'What a beautiful name.' The woman's voice was soft and breathless-sounding. 'It's from a poem by Shelley, isn't it? Did your parents admire the Romantics?'

'Why, yes.' She smiled appreciatively. 'Do you like poetry, too?'

'I adore it.' Violet threw a surreptitious glance over her shoulder. 'Father says it's all foolishness, but I just love the Romantics, especially Byron.'

'Have you read *Don Juan*?' Ianthe bit her tongue instantly. That was definitely the old her talking. A truly respectable woman wouldn't talk about anything so frivolous as poetry, especially not Byron or *Don Juan*, and absolutely not with young, unmarried daughters. Fortunately Violet didn't seem to find anything untoward about it.

'I'm afraid not.' Violet sighed wistfully. 'Father likes to check everything I read and there are some subjects he doesn't approve of. He only allowed Byron at first because he was a baron.'

'Oh.' Ianthe struggled to keep a straight face. 'You know they call him the wicked lord.'

'I know.' Violet giggled. 'Father was quite upset when he found out. But to have lived as much as Byron did, to have seen Italy and Greece…' She sighed again. 'How I'd love to visit them. But you're from London, Mr Felstone tells us. I'd like to go there, too.'

'You haven't been?'

'I haven't been anywhere.' Violet looked almost apologetic. 'Except in my imagination, of course. Father worries about me. It's partly due to my size, I think.' She gave a self-deprecating smile. 'He's afraid I might get stepped on. But it would be nice to see a little of the world outside Whitby for a change.'

'Then perhaps we'll make a trip one day.'

'Truly?' Violet clasped her hand with a look of sheer delight. 'Oh, I should love to. Father doesn't approve of many women, but I feel sure he'll like you. It would be so nice to have a friend of my own age to talk to.'

'I'd like that, too.' Ianthe felt her spirits lift. If the father were anything at all like his daughter then Robert was worrying unnecessarily. Violet already felt like a kindred spirit.

'Then I'm so glad we've met.' The other woman blushed suddenly. 'But you must forgive me for talking so much. I know you're here to see my father. Please do come this way.'

She led them into a dark, oak-panelled parlour hung with a series of increasingly severe-looking portraits, before gesturing towards a large armchair set beside a blazing fireplace.

'Mr and Mrs Felstone are here to see you, Papa.'

'How do you do, Mr Harper?' Ianthe took a step forward, bowing her head modestly.

'So he's brought you to see me at last then, has he?'

She looked up into a pair of unblinking, cold eyes, regarding her dispassionately from the depths of the armchair. 'I'm glad to be here, Mr Harper.'

'Take a seat, then.'

'Thank you.' She sat down opposite, perching on the edge of a particularly uncomfortable-looking chair as Violet moved to stand beside him. 'You have a very interesting house, sir.'

'Do I?' The old man's brows twitched in what might have been a frown, though his face was so craggy it was impossible to tell. The furrows were so deeply set it was impossible to imagine him ever smiling.

'Yes, it's ve—'

'What do you want from me, madam?'

She blinked at the interruption. 'Nothing *from* you, sir. I simply wanted to meet you and your daughter. I've no acquaintances in Whitby and my husband's told me so much about you.'

'About my shipyard, you mean?' The old man gave a snort of derision. 'You're here to persuade me to sell up, I suppose?'

'Not at all. It's yours to do with as you wish.'

'I'm glad to hear it. I make up my own mind, don't I, Violet?'

'Yes, Fa—'

'Are you a sensible woman?' He didn't wait for his daughter to finish. 'This one fills her head with stories and other such nonsense. I hope you're not so foolish.'

Ianthe pursed her lips, torn between the impulse to take Violet's side and the need to impress her father. 'I have a high regard for education, sir.'

'For women, too?'

She faltered, glancing at Robert for support. He was standing a small distance away, looking out of the window as if he weren't part of the conversation at all. How was she supposed to answer such a question? He might offer her some clue… Did he expect her to betray her real opinions and lie?

'I believe that everyone has the right to an education, sir.' She tried to keep her tone as respectful as possible.

'Ha! Now you *do* sound like my daughter. She wants to start a school for the children who work in my yard.'

'But that sounds like an excellent idea!'

'Not a proper school,' Violet explained hastily. 'Just a room where they can come for an hour every day to learn how to read and write.'

'Don't let Felstone hear you say so!' Harper gave a rasping laugh. 'If he buys the yard those are *his* workers you'll be taking away from their duties.'

'Oh… I'm sorry, Mr Felstone.' Violet seemed to diminish visibly.

'Not at all, Miss Harper.' Robert turned towards them at last, though his expression was unreadable. 'It sounds like a laudable idea.'

'Laudable?' Harper barked. 'So you wouldn't mind losing a third of your workforce every day?'

'I'd mind very much, but there are ways that it could be done. I've no objection in principle.'

'No, I suppose *you* wouldn't.'

Ianthe bristled indignantly, answering back without thinking. 'I think that my husband's done very well to achieve what he has without a formal education.'

'Indeed he has.' Harper regarded her sternly. 'Though there are some things a man can't learn by himself. Birth and breeding will out, Mrs Felstone.'

'Of course.' She swallowed a further retort. 'And believe me, Mr Harper, I know how much my husband values good breeding. He was very keen to impress that upon me when we first met.'

'Mmm.' Harper looked slightly mollified. 'And of course, marriage is a reforming influence. Just as long as it's to the right woman. Who were *your* parents?'

'My mother was a gentleman's daughter from Pickering and my father was a gentleman himself.' She had a feeling that describing him as an artist wasn't going to raise the old man's opinion. 'Though he painted a little, too.'

'Indeed? I thought he must have been in business. How else did you two meet?'

'How?' She baulked at the question. Robert

had mentioned something about saying they'd had a long-distance courtship, though she hadn't thought to discuss the details. Now she wasn't sure what to say, but she had to say something!

'We met through my brother,' she ventured at last. 'I lived with him after my parents died. He works as a clerk in an insurance company and, as you know, my husband does a great deal of business in London.'

There. She felt a rush of satisfaction. That was true, sort of. They *had* met through Percy, even if not in the way she implied.

'You're an orphan, then?' The old man reached out a hand suddenly, grasping his daughter's in a surprisingly firm-looking grip. 'My Violet lost her mother when she was born. That's why there's only the two of us. Now she takes care of me.'

Ianthe smiled politely, feeling a spontaneous rush of sympathy for the other woman. Somehow she doubted that Violet had ever been given a choice about that.

'Very well then, Mrs Felstone.' Mr Harper gave an approving nod. 'You may stay for tea. See to it, Violet.'

'I know how much my husband values good breeding?' Robert grabbed Ianthe's waist, swinging her up and around in a circle the moment they were out of sight of the house. 'It was all I could do to keep a straight face.'

'Really?' Ianthe looked surprised. 'I'd never have known. I wasn't even sure you were listening.'

'Do you blame me?' He lowered her back down to the ground, marvelling at how light she felt in his arms. 'If I hadn't kept out of it then I might have told him what I really thought of his *breeding*.'

'So I was respectable enough for you?'

'Above and beyond. You're full of surprises, Mrs Felstone.' He let go of her reluctantly, moving away as a man in a strangely familiar brown jacket rounded the corner of the street. 'Now shall we take a walk down to the shore? I'd like to blow the cobwebs away. That house always makes me think of a graveyard.'

'All right.' She peeped up at him from under her lashes, her doe eyes alarmingly enticing. 'As long as you don't tell Matthew. He'll be furious if he finds out we've been to the beach without him.'

'That boy's starting to behave like your lapdog.'

She laughed gleefully as they made their way towards the promenade. 'He even wants to be walked. He's always trying to persuade me to hold our lessons outside.'

'And have you?'

'Not yet.'

He threw a quick glance towards her, trying to

keep his tone casual as he tested a theory. 'I've heard that some people are scared of the sea.'

'I'm not.' Her expression became wary at once.

'Good. Though if there was something that did frighten you, I hope that you'd tell me. I might be able to help.'

She looked pensive, pursing her lips in that familiar way of hers as they started down the winding path that led to the west beach. 'I'm not sure I can explain it. It's not something I understand myself. Sometimes I just…panic.'

'Have you always done so?'

'No.' She spoke hesitantly, as if choosing her words with care. 'Something happened a little while ago. Something that upset me. It's over and done with, but I haven't wanted to go outside ever since. All the space…it just feels overwhelming.'

'Do you feel overwhelmed now?'

'No.' She shook her head. 'Now I feel normal.'

He clenched his jaw, head whirling with possibilities. 'The thing that happened…was it on the day after the ball?'

She was silent long enough to confirm it.

'And was that what convinced you to marry me?'

'Yes.' Her voice sounded small and unsteady.

'Will you tell me what happened?'

'No.'

'Were you hurt?'

'No.'

He let out a breath of relief. 'Then will you tell me if there's anything I can do about it?'

'Yes, but it won't happen again.' She glanced towards him nervously. 'Does it bother you?'

'It bothers me that something happened and that you're still scared because of it. But I'm glad that you told me.' They reached the deserted sea wall, and he jumped down, reaching his hands up to help her. 'Here.'

'I can't go down there.' She gestured at her new dress. 'I'll get all sandy.'

'We're done being respectable today, Ianthe.'

'We're *done*?'

'Yes.' He grinned, trying to put her at ease again. 'There's only so much a man without breeding can take.'

She gave him an arch look as she put her hands on his shoulders and jumped.

'There.' He kept his hands on her waist, holding her tight in the circle of his arms. 'Now it's your turn.'

'To do what?'

'To ask me a question. I know that telling me that can't have been easy for you, Ianthe. It only seems fair that you get to ask me something in return.'

'No.'

'*No?*'

'We're having a pleasant afternoon.' She pulled away from him gently. 'I don't want to spoil it.'

'Am I that moody?' He felt mildly aggrieved. 'What if I promise that it won't?'

'No.' She tilted her chin up stubbornly. 'I don't want to pry. Why don't you just tell me something I don't know?'

'All right.' He wandered down towards the water's edge. 'Most people want to know about my father.' He bent down and picked up a stone, turning it over in his hand. 'You know who he was?'

'Yes, my aunt told me.'

'Ah. I always knew who he was. Even as a boy, I was used to the gossip, but my mother never spoke of him, not once in twenty-one years.'

'Didn't you ever ask her about him?'

'No. I thought the stories about my father upset her. Whenever she spoke of the past she looked so unhappy. I didn't want to make her look like that so I never asked.' He flung his hand back and then quickly forward again, flicking the stone across the water, watching as it bounced five, six, seven times. 'Then after she died I got a letter from him saying he wanted to meet. I thought that perhaps he cared for me after all, that he'd been watching and waiting all those years, keeping away out of respect for her. I thought that I must have proved myself—that he wanted to acknowledge me.'

He stooped to pick up another stone and then changed his mind, sitting down on the sand instead. Why was he telling her all this—bringing up the pain of the past as if it would change anything? And yet, oddly enough, it did change things. Even if he didn't feel better, he felt strangely relieved. After only a few days in her company, he'd told her more than he'd *ever* told anyone else, as if he'd known her for years.

He turned in surprise as she sat down beside him.

'What about your dress?'

'It's just a bit of sand.'

'People will wonder what we've been doing.'

He gave a sly smile, but she ignored the comment. 'Will you tell me what happened with your father?'

'I thought you weren't going to ask any questions?'

'I changed my mind.'

He shook his head ruefully. 'It's a common enough story. You can probably guess the rest. He wanted money.'

'Money?' She gave an audible gasp.

'He was a gambler and he had debts. He thought it might be convenient to have a businessman in the family. He thought that I'd pay just for the honour of calling him my father.'

'Did you?'

'I gave him a choice between me or the money. Guess which he chose.'

'Oh, Robert.' She let out a soft sigh. 'I'm so sorry.'

'So am I. A year later he contacted me again, though this time he didn't bother with the pretence of a reconciliation. I tore his letter up.'

'I don't blame you.'

'I do. If it had been a business decision then I could have lived with it, but it wasn't. I made the decision in anger. He died a few months later.'

'I still don't blame you.' She sounded defiant, and he leaned back on his elbows to look at her.

'Are you defending me?'

'Yes. He treated you badly.'

'I ought to be glad of it really. If he'd been clever enough to pretend then he could have had me *and* the money, but it probably never occurred to him that I might actually *want* him to care for me. I doubt he was capable of love. He only wanted a business arrangement.' He winced at the irony. 'I must get it from somewhere.'

Ianthe's voice turned sombre. 'If you really weren't capable of love, then you wouldn't have cared how he felt about you.'

'Defending me again?' He lifted an eyebrow sardonically. 'Maybe it was just hurt pride.'

'You loved your mother, didn't you?'

'I suppose so.' He swallowed against the sudden lump in his throat. 'But she wasn't what you would call a warm-hearted woman. She tried her best, I think, but part of her always resented me for ruining her life. In her mind, if she hadn't fallen pregnant then she'd never have lost her position, never been separated from my father.' He clenched his jaw. 'She loved him, you see. Worthless as he was, she loved him to the end.'

'How do you know?'

'Because she told me. When she was dying, she looked up at me and said the words. It was the only time in her life she ever told me she loved me and she thought I was him.' He twisted towards her, unable to keep the anguish out of his eyes. 'She wasted her life on a man who forgot her a long time before. I told you, I've seen what love does to people. Love is for artists and fools.'

'You might be right.'

He blinked, surprised by the bitterness in her voice. 'I thought you were close to your parents?'

'I was, but they were artists. They raised me to believe in love, to expect everyone else to believe in it, too... It's not like that in the real world.'

He frowned. It was one thing for him to be cynical. When she said something similar, he felt a strange urge to contradict her. Never mind that the wistful note in her voice made it sound as if she were speaking from experience. Had she had love affairs in the past, then? The very idea made his chest constrict with jealousy.

'What's the matter?' She gave him a quizzical look.

'Nothing.' He stretched himself out in the sand, throwing one arm casually behind his head.

'It just seems we've more in common than we first thought.'

'What are you doing?' She sounded scandalised.

'Lying down.'

'Well, you shouldn't. What will people say if they see you?'

'They'll say they always knew I wasn't a gentleman.'

'I'm serious!'

'So am I. Lying on a beach in broad daylight next to my own wife. Tsk-tsk. It's just the kind of reprehensible behaviour they would expect.'

'I don't understand you.' She sounded exasperated.

'What don't you understand?'

He raised a hand, shielding his eyes from the sun to study her. She was shaking her head reprovingly, though the twinkle in her eyes gave her away.

'I can't decide if you really care about what people think of you or not.'

'Sometimes I do. Other times I want to tell everyone to mind their own damned business.'

'Then make up your mind.' She laughed and lay down on the sand beside him, propping her head up on her hand. 'You can't be a respectable gentleman *and* a rebel, so which is it? What do you really want?'

He moved so fast he hardly knew what he intended to do until he did it. Only the answer to her question was so clearly, blindingly obvious that he wasn't able to stop himself, seizing her lips with a fervour that took them both by surprise.

For a moment, he kept completely still, waiting for her to push him away, but she didn't. Instead, she gave a low murmur, opening her mouth slightly so he could taste the sweet tang of her lips. Slowly, he smoothed a hand over her waist, gathering her towards him as she put a hand on his chest to steady herself. Then there was nothing else, no other sight or sound, just the feeling of her in his arms and the warm, silky smoothness of her mouth against his.

He didn't know how long he held her, only that she was the first to break the embrace. She pulled away with a gasp, glancing around nervously as if to make sure no one had seen them.

'Robert...' she sounded out of breath '...our agreement...'

The agreement. His blood cooled instantly at the reminder. For an intoxicating moment, he'd forgotten all about it—had thought she had, too. Apparently not. But after everything he'd just told her about his past, he didn't feel up to discussing their arrangement just then. He certainly didn't know how to explain what had just happened.

'I'd like to swim.'

'What?'

'You asked me what I wanted. I want to swim.'

'Now?'

He looked out to sea, trying to distract himself so that he wasn't tempted to haul her back into his arms, agreement or not. They felt altogether too empty without her.

'When I was a boy, I swam here all the time. Nobody cared. Then I got older, took on more responsibilities, became Robert Felstone Esquire, and people expected me to behave a certain way. But I still want to swim.'

She sat up, brushing the sand off her skirts. 'I'd like to learn one day.'

He looked at her incredulously. 'You can't swim?'

'I've never tried.'

'You can't live by the sea and not swim. It's dangerous.'

'Why?' She sounded defensive. 'It's not as though I'm going to jump in.'

'That's not the point. I'm not taking you to the shipyard until you learn.'

'But you promised!'

'I didn't know you'd be a liability.'

'Then I wish I hadn't told you.' She scowled down at him. 'Are you saying that everyone who works for you can swim?'

'I make certain of it. Safety's important.'

'Oh.' She was quiet for a moment. 'So how would you go about teaching me?'

'You can rent bathing huts further down the beach.'

'It's autumn!'

'It's the warmest October I can remember.'

'Won't people on the promenade be able to see?'

He shrugged. 'A horse pulls the hut out into the water, but it's perfectly respectable, I assure you. Ridiculous, but respectable.'

'All right.' She sounded circumspect. 'I'll let you teach me to swim, but only on one condition.'

'Which is…?'

'You have to recite a poem.'

'What?'

'Find one you like and recite it to Matthew.'

'I thought we just agreed that poetry was for fools?'

'No. We agreed that poetry wasn't real life. It's not poetry's fault that people let it down.'

'So you want me to learn a poem because…?'

'Because Matthew looks up to you. If he hears you recite one, he might not be so closed-minded about it.'

Robert arched an eyebrow. 'Is that your way of saying you think *I'm* closed-minded?'

She didn't answer. 'You might enjoy it.'

'So you want another agreement…' He took a

deep breath, already regretting his next words. 'Shall we shake on this one?'

He held out a hand and she took it tentatively. 'You have a deal, Mr Felstone.'

'Good.' He closed his fingers around hers. 'We'll start tomorrow.'

Chapter Thirteen

'I'm having second thoughts!' Ianthe shouted through the wall of the bathing hut, trying to pluck up the courage to open the door.

'You're not backing out now!' Robert's voice outside was muffled.

She glanced down at her costume, the only one she'd been able to find at short notice, a short belted jacket over a pair of long bloomers, wondering whether so many clothes were strictly necessary. The flannel fabric wasn't uncomfortable, but for a dip in the sea she felt ridiculously overdressed. Even worse, the bright pink-and-white stripes looked like something Aunt Sophoria might have chosen.

'All right.' She pulled on the matching mob cap before twisting the door handle. 'Here I am.'

'You look…' Robert stood in front of her, hand on his hips, looking suspiciously like a man trying very hard not to laugh. 'I'm lost for words.'

She made a face. 'I think the hat finishes it off, don't you?'

'It's my favourite part.' White teeth flashed in a grin. 'You should get a few more like that.'

'Be careful or I just might.'

He laughed and strode out into the sea, beckoning for her to follow. 'Shall we get started then?'

Ianthe looked at the water with trepidation. The hut had been pulled out into the shallows so that she was far enough away from the promenade not to feel completely exposed, but now she was there, she was a long way from certain that she actually wanted to learn at all. Robert was dressed in a full-length white flannel costume and the resemblance to male undergarments was distinctly unnerving.

'It looks cold.'

'It is.' He was already waist-deep in the water. 'But it's a warm day, you won't freeze. Look.'

He dived under the surface, coming up again after a few moments wearing a broad grin and shaking his head like a dog. Ianthe caught her breath. He looked completely happy and at ease in the water, the waves lapping gently around his body and sculpting his costume to his chest in a way that accentuated every bulging muscle. She'd had no idea that he was so…solid.

She dropped her eyes, gingerly sticking a toe in the water before retracting it again quickly. It *was* cold, though the sight of his athletic body made her feel red hot all over. Her imagination was running riot as she imagined what he looked like beneath his costume.

'I think I've changed my mind.'

'We made a deal, Ianthe.'

'I'm reneging.'

'Too late.' He folded his arms, though the action seemed to make his muscles bulge even more. 'I've already learnt a poem.'

'Already?'

'Yes. So come here.'

She pursed her lips. A deal was a deal, but now that she was there, she wasn't sure she could go through with it. What if he touched her? If he was going to teach her to swim, he'd need to be close to her. If she started to sink, he'd surely *have* to touch her! She might have to touch *him*! She was confused enough after what had happened between them on the beach. Touching him definitely wasn't going to help clarify matters!

She gasped, the memory of their kiss still making her pulse quicken alarmingly. Even after they'd agreed that love was folly, she'd fallen into the old trap of letting emotion get the better of her, kissing him as if it were natural to do so, as if she weren't hiding the shameful truth about herself. She'd felt so close to him, closer than she'd ever felt to Albert, drawn towards him like a butterfly to sunshine.

When he'd told her about his upbringing she'd

seen the hurt in his face, that of a young boy, then a young man, craving love from his parents and finding no comfort from either. She'd finally understood why he said he wasn't capable of love. He had had no experience of it. No wonder he felt such a strong urge to prove himself and his respectability to the world, channelling all his energies into business as if that was the only way he had any value, as if he didn't truly believe in his own worth.

The old Ianthe had wanted to comfort him, but the new Ianthe had known better. She couldn't comfort and deceive him at the same time. If her secret ever came out then it could destroy everything he'd worked for, making whatever comfort she offered him now seem like just another lie. She'd gone to bed that night with guilt gnawing a hole in her stomach.

'The deal was that you read a poem to Matthew. You haven't done that yet, so I can still call it off.'

There! She swung on her heel, heading back inside the hut. He'd just have to be angry with her. There was no way she was going into the water with him looking like that. She wasn't going to let herself be tempted again.

No sooner had the thought crossed her mind than she felt his hands around her waist, scooping her up and over his shoulder.

'Put me down!' She pounded her fists against

his back, but he ignored her, wading out into deeper water as she wriggled against him.

'We had an agreement, Ianthe.'

'I've changed my mind!'

'That's not allowed.' His hands tightened around her legs. 'Not without both parties' consent.'

'Don't you dare!'

The cold water knocked the air from her lungs, sending shock waves cascading through every limb as she splashed around frantically, waving her arms in a panic before she finally found her feet on the seabed.

'How…could…you!' She stood up, spluttering like a landed fish.

'You don't renege on a deal.' His expression was distinctly unsympathetic.

'It's…so…cold.' She wrapped her arms around her body, rubbing herself for warmth, not that it made much difference.

'Then let's try this again. Here.' He uncurled her arms and reached for her waist. 'We'll work on your feet first.'

'What are you doing?' She leapt away from him with a startled squeak, almost losing her footing again.

'Teaching you to swim. I'll hold on to your waist, then you kick your legs out behind and move them up and down like this.' He made a gesture with his arms.

'Oh.' She tensed as he placed a hand on either side of her body.

'There. Now lean forward, over my arms.'

She did as he instructed, lying flat in the water, suddenly glad of the cold that disguised her trembling as shivering.

'Good. Now move your feet. Small, steady movements. There's no need to splash.'

She kicked her feet out behind her, trying to concentrate on the action and not the feeling of his biceps pressed against her stomach.

'Now stretch your arms out in front of you.'

After a while she found herself starting to relax, almost to enjoy herself. Robert was a surprisingly patient teacher, and she *did* want to learn after all. The other bathers, mostly young boys splashing around, made it look so easy and natural. She wanted to be able to swim like that.

'You're doing well.' His voice was reassuring. 'I'm going to let go now.'

'What?' She twisted her head around in alarm.

'Just keep doing what you're doing. You won't get it the first time, but I'll catch you, I promise.'

'What...?'

He let go abruptly, and she yelped in panic, opening her mouth and swallowing a mouthful of seawater. Instantly, she scrambled for her feet, but the ground wasn't there. She was sinking!

In another moment, she felt hands on her shoulders, pulling her back to the surface.

'Don't panic.' Robert laid her flat on her stomach again. 'Remember, nice smooth movements.'

'I need a rest.'

'Not until you've swum a few feet.'

He pushed her off again and she moved her arms and feet as he'd shown her, propelling herself through the water with ungainly, but apparently successful strokes. She was doing it! Not very well, perhaps, but she was swimming!

A wave swept towards her, and she thrashed her way through it, losing her rhythm again, but Robert was back at her side instantly, catching her as she started to flounder.

'I did it!' She flung her arms around his neck triumphantly.

'I saw.' He grinned, tugging her back towards the shallows. 'Not bad for a beginner.'

'I swam!' She tossed her head back, laughing with glee. Her heart was still pounding with fear and excitement, but in a good way. She felt more intensely alive and vital than she had in a long time.

She could feel the pulse of another heartbeat, too. She gasped, coming back to her senses, belatedly realising where she was and what she was doing. The water was shallow enough for her to stand up in now, but her arms were still coiled around Robert's neck, her chest still pressed against his, her face only inches away as the waves lapped softly around them. She was pressed up against her husband on a public beach—and she seemed incapable of moving away.

Instead, she held her breath, waiting for the moment to pass, but it only stretched out, every second deepening the tension between them. She looked into his eyes and felt her insides quiver. Every look he'd given her before seemed to pale in comparison to the one he was giving her now, his grey eyes blazing with an intensity she'd never seen there before.

'You did well, Ianthe.' His voice was even deeper than usual.

Another wave, higher and stronger than the rest, swept towards them, and she tightened her hold instinctively. He did so, too, pulling her closer as if afraid she might slip from his grasp, so close that she could feel every hard line and contour of his body. She heaved in a breath, all of her stomach muscles seeming to contract at once. There was no space between them now, not so much as a sliver of air. She could feel every bit of him, even the part pushing between her legs, a hot hard pressure that was obvious even through both their bathing suits.

'Ianthe?' His voice sounded ragged, as if he were asking some kind of question.

Somehow she forced herself to breathe. This— whatever *this* was—couldn't happen. It wasn't part of the agreement. It wasn't the way she ought to behave…

He took hold of the mob cap and pulled it gently away from her head, fingers stroking her hair as he did so. She inhaled sharply, fighting the urge to purr. Some of her pins must have come loose because her bun started to unravel at once, falling in a ponytail down her back. Instinctively, she tipped her head up, arching her throat like the wanton she clearly was, but unable to control herself…

A shout from the beach made them both start in surprise.

'Matthew!' Robert recovered first, raising one hand to wave even as the other kept a tight hold of her waist below the water line.

She twisted her head towards the shore. The boy was running along the sand towards them, accompanied by two men carrying a picnic basket and someone else… She screwed up her eyes to make sure they weren't deceiving her…a woman dressed entirely in pink, brandishing a large frilly parasol.

'Aunt Sophoria!'

'I thought it would be a nice surprise.' Robert's voice was a combination of frustration and apology.

'It is.' It *was*—everything except for the timing. She leaned away, trying to extract herself from his grasp before Aunt Sophoria saw them. 'I should go and get dressed.'

His hold slackened at last and she waded back towards the hut, trying to escape before any of the new arrivals came close enough to see her flaming cheeks. Once inside, she tore off her wet things, standing naked and dripping in a futile attempt to cool down. Her body seemed to have gone from one extreme of temperature to another. What was wrong with her? All her hard-won self-control seemed to vanish whenever Robert touched her. If Matthew and her aunt hadn't come along... She took a deep breath. She didn't know what would have happened, but it was probably best *not* to think about it.

She dressed and fixed her hair quickly, hurrying outside to find her husband and aunt sprawled in a pair of deckchairs.

'Ianthe, my dear!' Aunt Sophoria tossed her parasol to one side. 'Come and hug an old woman!'

'Aunt Sophoria.' Ianthe bent down to embrace her. 'It's lovely to see you again. I'd no idea you were coming to stay.'

'Just for tonight, dear. Your husband tried to persuade me to stay longer, but you know I like to be amongst my own things. And it's not as if Pickering's very far away. We can visit each other as often as we like.'

'We can. It's still a nice surprise, though. Thank you, Robert.'

She smiled shyly at her husband, but his expression was unreadable as he lounged in the chair watching them, a towel draped casually around his broad shoulders.

'I'm glad it worked out.' He heaved himself to his feet. 'Now if you'll excuse me, I have a ten-year-old boy to play with. Apparently the picnic can wait.'

Ianthe watched as he strode away, admiring the way his shoulder muscles rippled beneath his damp costume, before dragging her eyes away quickly as she realised her aunt was watching her.

'I told the footmen to come back in an hour. I hope you don't mind, but I think we can manage a picnic on our own. It gives us a chance to talk in private.' Aunt Sophoria settled back in her chair with a wicked grin. 'So...enjoying married life?'

'Hmmm.' Ianthe made a vague affirmative sound, sitting down on the blanket and tucking her legs primly beneath her.

'Still just a business arrangement?'

'Yes.'

'Is that why you had your arms around his neck just now?'

She froze with her hand halfway towards the hamper. 'He's teaching me to swim.'

'Swim? Is that what you call it?' Aunt Sophoria chuckled. 'Now you'd better tell me everything before he comes back.'

'There's nothing to tell.'

Her aunt heaved a languishing sigh. 'You know, he reminds me of my Horace. A little taller perhaps, but just as handsome.'

'Who's Horace?'

'My husband, dear.'

'Your *what*?'

'Husband.' Aunt Sophoria looked nonplussed. 'Didn't your mother ever tell you I'd been married?'

'No.' Ianthe shook her head in bewilderment. She'd always assumed that her aunt was a spinster. No one had ever mentioned a husband anyway. 'But aren't you still called Gibbs?'

'Oh, yes, dear, my parents insisted. When I came back home after a year, they made me tell everyone I'd been staying with relatives. No one in Pickering knows I've been married.'

'But why don't *I* know about him?'

'I suppose your mother thought it was better kept secret. I haven't been the best role model, I suppose.'

'So what happened?'

Aunt Sophoria leaned backwards, her face taking on a dreamy expression. 'He was a soldier, the handsomest man I ever saw. Black hair, long moustache, dazzling green eyes. We met at a regimental ball and I'd agreed to run away with him by the end of the week.'

'You *eloped*?' The very word made her stiffen with panic.

'It was the only way. Neither of us had any money and our families would never have approved.'

Ianthe gaped open-mouthed, shock giving way to a strange sense of relief. All this time, she'd been afraid of telling her aunt about Albert, yet it seemed that she was the one person who might understand. *She'd* made the same mistake. If she'd come home after a year, her alliance must have ended badly, too.

'So what made you come home again?'

'He died, dear.'

'Oh!' She put a hand to her mouth.

'He was posted to Burma. I wanted to go with him, but he said it was too dangerous. Quite rightly, as it turned out. There was an outbreak of cholera in his camp.'

'Oh, Aunt.' Ianthe wiped at her eyes, brushing away tears. 'I'm so sorry.'

'So am I, dear. Even forty years later, it still hurts.'

'Did you love him so very much?'

'We loved each other very much. We weren't romantic like your parents. Their love was based on words and ideas. Ours was somewhat earthier, but just as real.'

'Earthier?' She frowned in puzzlement. 'What do you mean?'

Her aunt's eyes flashed with amusement. 'Your mother would never forgive me for telling you. Though I've a feeling you might find out on your own.'

Ianthe looked away quickly, to where Robert and Matthew were splashing about in the shallows. She had a feeling she might have found out already.

'Just like Horace.' Aunt Sophoria smiled dreamily.

'So you never regretted eloping?'

'Not for a moment.'

'Then you don't think… That is… Elopements themselves…' She took a deep breath, the words escaping in a rush. 'You wouldn't judge somebody else for doing the same thing?'

'Ah.' Her aunt's expression softened with understanding. 'No, dear, I wouldn't judge. Is that what happened last year?'

Ianthe hung her head, shame-faced. 'We didn't get far before his family caught up with us. They convinced him that it was a mistake—that *I* was a mistake. He didn't really love me, Aunt.'

'Then he wasn't the right man.'

She blinked, taken aback by her aunt's matter-of-fact tone. 'But it's so shameful. I was wicked!'

'I don't see why. Did you pursue him?'

'No.'

'Was it your idea to elope?'

'No.'

'Did you do anything your mother might have disapproved of?'

'No!' She felt her cheeks start to burn again. 'But if people found out they might think that I... That we... That is...'

'Oh, my dear, if you can't even say it, then you really have nothing to be ashamed of.' Aunt Sophoria screwed her mouth up thoughtfully. 'That explains it then.'

'What?'

'All the grey. I knew it wasn't you.'

'But I wanted it to be!' Ianthe almost wailed. 'I wanted to be sensible and respectable, so nothing like it would ever happen again. I thought I was different, that I'd changed. That's why I agreed to marry Robert. And now...'

'Now you're the young woman I remember.' Aunt Sophoria reached down and patted her cheek. 'I'm glad to see her again.'

'But you don't understand, Aunt. I married him under false pretences. He thinks I'm still *her*, the woman in grey. I haven't told him any of this. I know I should have, but I couldn't. I thought that if I could be the respectable wife that he wanted...'

'Then what he didn't know wouldn't hurt him? You might be right. Though I think he'd understand more than most.'

'No!' Ianthe shook her head adamantly. 'You don't know how important respectability is to him. I didn't realise how much until after we were married. Just look at the way he is with Matthew!'

'What do you mean?'

'He won't even acknowledge his own son!'

Aunt Sophoria tilted her head to one side quizzically. 'But he's not his son, dear. Who on earth told you that?'

'It's obvious, isn't it?'

'It's obvious that they're related, but not like that. They both take after their father, that's all.'

'*Their* father?'

'Yes, dear, they're half-brothers.'

'Brothers?' Ianthe's mouth dropped open. 'How do you know?'

'Oh, there were always rumours. Old Theakston wasn't known for being discreet. Matthew's mother was another poor housemaid. She came to Pickering after she was dismissed, but she fell ill when the boy was still young. I've no idea how your Robert found out about it, but he just turned up one day with a doctor. From what I gather, she asked him to take the boy if anything happened to her.'

'Why didn't you tell me any of this before?'

'You said he'd mentioned his ward. I assumed he'd told you the rest. Though I'd no idea they looked so similar. It's quite incredible really.'

Ianthe felt the knot of guilt in her stomach tighten painfully. She hadn't believed Robert when he'd denied that the boy was his son. She'd wronged him instead, condemning him as a hypocrite when in fact the very opposite was true. He was prepared to let most people think the worst just to keep his promise to a dying woman.

'I thought respectability was the most important thing to him,' she murmured.

'If it was, I don't suppose he'd keep the boy so close. Most people will think the same thing as you did. Understandably, I might add.'

Ianthe sat back on her heels, trying to adjust her version of reality. She ought to be pleased. If respectability wasn't so important to Robert after all, then maybe there was a chance she could tell him the truth about her past and he might forgive her. Except that now her deceit seemed even worse in comparison to his honourable behaviour.

'He doesn't care for me, Aunt.' She shook her head stubbornly. 'He says he's not capable of love.'

Aunt Sophoria looked thoughtful. 'If he took after his father then I'd agree that might be the case, but from what I've seen, he's only inherited the looks. The more important question is, do you care for him?'

Ianthe bit her lip, unable at that moment to frame an answer. *Did* she care for him? She shouldn't. It was madness to even consider it. And yet, after their kiss on the beach, her emotions were so tangled that she couldn't deny it either. But how could she open up her heart and risk being hurt again, especially with a man who'd openly said he couldn't love her? And even if he *could*, he was already damaged enough. She couldn't risk hurting him any more. If she truly cared for him, she'd have to tell him about Albert—then see the horror on his face when he realised the sort of woman he'd married.

No. She couldn't bear the thought of it. She had to bury her feelings, whatever they were, before it was too late. She couldn't risk that kind of pain for either of them. They had to keep to the terms of the original agreement for their own good. Even if she wasn't sure that she could...

She forced her features into a smile as Robert and Matthew emerged from the water at last, running up the beach and throwing themselves in the sand at their feet.

'You look like a pair of wet dogs.' Aunt Sophoria chuckled.

'Hungry ones, too.' Robert grinned. 'So what do we have to eat?'

Ianthe peered into the hamper, listing each sandwich in turn. 'Beef and Worcestershire sauce, chicken and celery, cress and cucumber, ginger preserve, cheese...'

'Beef, please.'

'There are some pies, too. As well as crackers

and sardines, cold salmon, grapes and a strawberry tart each. We're not going to starve.'

'Perfect.' Robert propped himself on one elbow with a contented sigh.

'Aren't you going to get dressed?' She threw a swift glance towards him, trying not to be distracted by the way his swimming costume was clinging to his muscular torso.

'Not yet. It's too hot for layers. Your aunt doesn't mind, do you, Miss Gibbs?'

'Not at all. You provide quite a charming vista, if I might say so.'

'Aunt!'

'I'll have a ginger sandwich please, Ianthe.' Aunt Sophoria's eyes twinkled mischievously. 'So, Mr Felstone, I understand that you've been giving my niece swimming lessons?'

'Yes.' Robert looked unperturbed. 'We made a deal.'

'Indeed?'

'Swimming in exchange for poetry. I said that she couldn't live in Whitby and not swim. She said I couldn't criticise poetry until I'd actually read some. So...' He finished the last bite of his sandwich and then sat up, brushing his hands together as he turned towards her. 'Ready for my side of the bargain?'

'Now?' She regarded him with astonishment. 'Where's your book?'

'I don't need one.' He tapped his forehead.

'You *memorised* it?'

'It's not very long, but it's my favourite. Pay attention, Matthew. It's time for some poetry.'

'Poetry?' Matthew shoved the last crumbs of a pie into his mouth. 'Why?'

'Because it's important to learn new things.'

He gave her a wink and then fixed his eyes on the horizon, clearing his throat before reciting the verse in a strong, clear voice. Ianthe held her breath in amazement. It was *her* poem. 'To Ianthe', Shelley's sonnet to his newborn daughter, words that perfectly described the awakening of new love. Not that she ought to read too much into that, she warned herself.

'That was wonderful.' Aunt Sophoria was the first to congratulate him. 'You ought to have been an actor, Mr Felstone. Such wonderful enunciation.'

'That's my poem.' She couldn't keep the smile off her face. 'The one I was named after. You found it.'

'You told Violet Harper it was by Shelley.'

'But you remembered.' Her cheeks flushed self-consciously. 'My parents said it expressed how they felt when they had me.'

'I think it suits you very well.'

His gaze held on to hers for a few moments before Matthew interrupted. 'Can you help me build a sandcastle now?'

'Philistine.' Robert sighed and heaved himself to his feet. 'Save me some food, ladies.'

'We can't promise.' Aunt Sophoria gave a knowing chuckle once they were out of hearing. 'Still think he's not capable of love?'

Ianthe looked away, resisting the temptation to hope. 'It's just a poem, Aunt. It doesn't mean anything. And besides, the truth behind it wasn't so beautiful.'

'What do you mean?'

'Shelley left Ianthe's mother for another woman before she was even born.' Her mouth twisted slightly. 'So much for words.'

'Your parents still liked it.'

'They were too romantic for their own good, remember?'

'I didn't mean it like that, dear. Their romantic sensibilities worked for them, but there are lots of different types of love. One for everyone, I like to think.'

Ianthe looked down at her fingers, twisting them together anxiously. 'He married me because he thought I was respectable, Aunt. What if I tell him the truth and he doesn't want me any more?'

'It's a risk, dear, but you can't live your life pretending to be someone else. And it seems to me that he rather likes the real you. You ought to give him the chance to really know her.'

Ianthe stared out to sea, watching a flock

of seagulls swoop down to land on the water. Maybe it was possible. Maybe he could care for her. Maybe she would tell him the truth.

Just as soon as the deal with Harper was over.

Chapter Fourteen

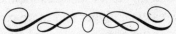

Robert peered out of his office window and frowned at the lowering sky. The morning had been bright and golden, but now mid-afternoon looked like twilight. A bank of clouds was already building to the west, piling up in a ridge to block out the sunshine, turning the sky a drab, monochrome grey. It might all come to nothing, but he'd have to keep one eye on the horizon. A sea storm could blow up in minutes and, if it did, they'd need to work quickly to cover the dry docks and batten down the workshops.

He glanced towards the gates, distracted by the arrival of a carriage. *His* carriage. Damn. He swore softly under his breath, torn between conflicting emotions of frustration and excitement, wondering what strange impulse had possessed him to invite Ianthe to visit the shipyard that day. He'd been under no obligation to do so. She hadn't learnt to swim properly yet and there was no rush to show her around, yet he'd heard himself issue the invitation at breakfast as if his brain weren't in charge of his mouth. It hadn't helped that she'd been wearing her new blue-and-white striped dress, his favourite of their recent purchases, with her hair scooped up in a loose chignon that made her features look softer and her doe eyes even bigger and more captivating, like pools of rich toffee gazing at him across the table. She seemed to have gained weight in the past week as well, her cheeks filling out and taking on a healthy glow he hadn't seen there before. Somehow the thought of spending a whole day away from her had seemed far too long to contemplate.

He moved away from the window and rolled down his shirt sleeves, vaguely discomforted by his own eagerness. She was becoming a distraction. There were a thousand things he ought to have been doing that past week, and yet he'd spent his time organising picnics and swimming lessons instead. He *ought* to have been drawing up legal papers and visiting the bank, but he'd felt strangely unfocussed, unable to concentrate, thinking about his wife far too often for comfort. He *ought* to have been closing the deal with Harper and yet he'd had to remind himself even to think about it. He wasn't sick—he wished he could explain such uncharacteristic behaviour so easily—but whatever the matter with him was, it seemed to have started on the beach, in that moment when she'd asked what he wanted and he'd realised he wanted to kiss her.

He'd found himself asking the same question repeatedly over the past couple of days, telling himself that the answer was obvious—Harper's shipyard. *That* was what he wanted, what he was working towards, what he knew how to get—it was the whole reason he'd married her, for pity's sake! She was a means to an end, not an end in herself. And yet on its own, somehow the shipyard didn't seem like enough any more. As if there was something else he wanted as well. Something he wanted more.

No. He pushed open the front door, dodging around some barrels as he strode purposefully across the yard. He wasn't going to think about that. He was probably just nervous about the dinner he'd arranged for the following night. Harper was ready to sign the deed of sale, he could sense it. A good dinner, arranged by his respectable wife, with Giles and Kitty there for support, and the yard would be his. That was surely all he was worried about. He certainly wasn't fool enough to fall in love with a woman he'd married for business reasons. Love was for fools. Love caused pain. It had brought his mother nothing but suffering. He didn't, *couldn't* care for her. Even if he couldn't stop thinking about her.

'Ianthe!' He raised a hand in greeting, resenting the tightening sensation in his chest as she turned to smile at him.

'Oh, Robert. Your driver was just telling me there might be a storm coming.'

'He might be right.' He took another look at the sky. It seemed even darker than it had a few minutes ago.

'It was sunny when I left.'

'Sea climates are unpredictable, especially when the weather's been warm like this.'

'Is it a bad time to visit? I can always come back another time.'

'No,' he heard himself answer incredulously. It would make a *lot* more sense for her to visit another time, but now she was there he felt strangely reluctant to let her go again.

'If you're sure.' She looked around the yard, craning her neck with curiosity. 'Are all these buildings yours?'

'These four workshops and the two dry docks over there. We have our own loft for sail-making as well, but when I buy Harper's it'll be twice the size.'

'Very impressive.'

'Thank you.' He smiled, suddenly unable to contain his enthusiasm. 'Come on, I'll show you around.'

Eagerly, he led her across the yard and into the largest, barn-like workshop, stopping beneath a giant grey hulk.

'What is it?' Ianthe looked between him and the hulk uncertainly.

'You tell me.'

'It's metal. Is it a ship's hull?'

'Exactly, but made entirely of iron. When it's finished it'll be the first full steam ship we've ever built. One of the first in Whitby.'

'It's huge! How long until it's ready?'

'Four months maybe.'

She looked impressed. 'So won't you build any more wooden ships at all?'

'A few smaller ones, perhaps.' He led her outside, past a group of surprised-looking metalworkers, to one of the dry docks. 'Here's where we still work in wood. This cat's almost finished.'

'Cat?'

'It stands for coal-and-timber ship. Most people call them colliers, but Whitby cats are famous. They're shallow with wide beams, easy to pull on to the shore.'

'What are they doing?' She gestured to where two men were working on the deck with mallets and chisels.

'They're caulking the planks, driving oakum into the seams to make them watertight. It's a skilled job. Too much or too little pressure and the planks leak.'

'And will you still need caulkers once you switch to metal ships?'

He grimaced. 'The decks will still be made of wood, but it won't be the same. We'll have to retrain as many people as we can.'

'So such skills might be lost? That seems a shame.'

'It does. It's one of the reasons why men like Harper don't want to see it happen. I sympathise, but the alternative is that we all go bankrupt.'

She let out a long breath, gazing around with an expression of admiration. 'It's incredible. How do you organise it all?'

'Practice.' He frowned suddenly, feeling a rush of salty air on his skin. That was it—all the warning he needed.

'What's the matter?' She followed his gaze out to sea. 'Is it the storm?'

'The start of it. Come on.' He took a firm hold of her hand, pulling her behind him. 'You need to get inside.'

'What about you?'

'I need to shut everything down.'

He flung open the door to the offices, almost dragging her along the corridor to his room at the back. It wasn't much—a spartan, wooden-floored office with a paper-strewn desk in the middle—

but it had the benefit of large windows along two sides, perfectly positioned to see everything that went on in the shipyard.

'You'll be safe here.' He strode across to his desk and pulled out a red leather chair for her to sit down. 'Don't move. I won't be long.'

He was gone so quickly that Ianthe didn't have a chance to answer.

She glanced briefly at the chair he'd pulled out for her and then crossed to the window instead, watching as he strode back out into the yard. A group of serious-looking men approached him at once and they all huddled together, talking intently for a few moments before marching off in different directions.

There was a low rumble of thunder, and she looked up at the sky. The clouds were definitely gathering now, lining up like a battalion of grey soldiers, ready to charge at the harbour. She looked back to where Robert had been standing, but he wasn't there any longer. Anxiously, her eyes searched the yard, skimming over the caulkers and joiners and ropers who were all rushing to close the workshop doors and take shelter. *Where was he?*

She gave a cry of relief as she found him at last, out on the mudflats, though how he'd reached them so quickly she had no idea. He was working alongside his men, hauling giant tarpaulins over the mud before hoisting them up and over the boats on the shore, trying to provide the half-built vessels with some protection from the elements.

She tightened her grip on the windowpane as it started to rattle ominously, wishing she could do something to help. The wind seemed to be gaining in strength every second. What had started as a gentle breeze now had the power to almost wrench the tarpaulin out of their hands. Robert's shirt was billowing around his chest like a sail, while the boats in the river were pitching from side to side so violently it looked as though they might never come upright again.

Then the rain started. There was no drizzle, no light warning shower, just a sudden sheet of water falling straight from the sky, drenching the men in seconds. There were only a few of them left outside now, Robert amongst them, hammering pegs into the mud as he lashed the tarpaulins to the ground. She fought the urge to call out to him, hardly daring to breathe until he finally got up, waving at the others to take shelter as he ran back towards the office.

'Robert!' She hurtled out of the room and down the corridor.

'I'm all right.' He slammed the door shut, running a hand through his hair as a puddle started to form around him. 'Where are the clerks?'

'Who?'

He gestured towards another door. 'My clerks work in there. Are they still here?'

'I haven't seen anyone. Oh!' A vague memory came back to her. 'The door banged a little while ago. I saw some men run across to the workshop. That must have been them.'

'They were probably going to help.' He nodded with satisfaction. 'They'll be safe over there.'

'What should *we* do?'

'Keep away from windows for a start. The storm's worse than I expected.'

'Will the boats be all right?'

'We'll have to wait and see. There's nothing we can do about it now.'

'What about the ships out in the harbour?'

His expression turned sober. 'Those aren't the ones to worry about.'

'You mean the ones at sea?' She gasped at such a terrible thought.

'This type of storm rises up out of nowhere. I don't know of any ships due in port today, but if there are any out there and they don't reach the harbour in time... It wouldn't be a good place to be.'

She shuddered, and he put an arm around her before pulling away quickly again.

'I'm soaking.'

'It's all right.' She leaned back into his embrace. 'I don't care.'

'Wait.' He reached down and pulled his shirt over his head. 'I don't want you catching a chill.'

'Me? What about you? Your trousers are soaking wet, too.' She clamped a hand over her mouth as she realised what she'd just said. Bad enough that he was standing half-naked in front of her already. She oughtn't to encourage him to remove anything else! 'Not that you should take them off. I didn't mean that.'

He arched an eyebrow sardonically as he pulled her towards him, resting his chin on the top of her head. 'Tempting as that sounds, this may not be the best time.'

'No.' She bit her lip, listening to the howl of the storm outside and trying not to think about the feel of his skin against her cheek. His body felt warm and solid and surprisingly smooth. What did *that* mean, not the best time? The words implied there might be other occasions...

'How long do these storms usually last?' she asked the question to distract herself.

'It depends. Sometimes twenty minutes, sometimes hours.'

'Hours?'

'Scared of being alone with me?'

She opened her mouth to retort, before practically leaping into his arms at the sound of a heavy pounding on the door.

Robert reacted at once, setting her gently to one

side as he heaved it open to reveal a man in sailor's clothes, soaking wet and wild-eyed, looking as if he were being pursued by some kind of monster.

'Steady!' Robert grasped the man's arms as he stumbled inside. 'What's the matter?'

'Wreck… Saltwick Bay.'

'What?' Robert's jaw tightened at once. 'There's a shipwreck?'

'Aye.' The man hauled in a deep breath, gasping between words. 'I was up…on the cliffs. Saw it…hit sandbank.'

'What kind of ship?'

'Merchant vessel.'

'How many crew?'

'About a dozen.'

'Is it damaged?'

'The mast…doesn't look good.' He'd regained some of his breath now. 'But it's still salvageable. I ran down the cliff, went to the first yard I found. They told me to come here and find you.'

'Why?' Ianthe heard the quaver in her own voice.

Robert paused for a moment before answering. 'I'm on the lifeboat crew.'

'But you said it was dangerous out there!' She whirled on the sailor in panic. 'You can't ask men to go out in this!'

'I know that, ma'am.' He looked faintly guilty. 'But I had to do something.'

'It's our job.' Robert's voice sounded stern.

'But…' She felt the blood drain from her face as the full horror of the situation dawned on her. Without Robert and the lifeboat, the crew of the stricken vessel would be doomed. But if he went, he'd be risking his own life. She felt appalled by the impossibility of the choice.

'It might not be possible anyways.' The sailor seemed to be trying to comfort her. 'In this weather, they'll have a job getting the lifeboat past the harbour wall. And even if they manage that, they'll be fighting the current just to get round the cliff.'

'But isn't there some other way to help?' She didn't know which side she was on now.

Robert met her gaze, holding it sombrely for a few seconds before his expression cleared abruptly.

'There is. We won't go around the cliff. We'll go over it.'

'You mean carry the boat over?' The sailor nodded appreciatively.

'It's been done before. Then we can launch from the other side.'

He strode back into his office, re-emerging a few seconds later wearing a large oilskin overcoat. 'It'll take a few hours, but it's the safest option. There's no lightning, only rain and wind.' He rested a hand on the sailor's shoulder. 'Go over to the workshop and ask for my foreman, George. Tell him I need volunteers. Then you have a rest. I'll be there in a few minutes.'

He advanced towards her as the other man ran outside, grasping her shoulders as he stared down into her face.

'I'll take you across to the workshop, too. You can stay there until the storm passes and then…'

'No.'

He frowned. 'Ianthe…'

'I'm coming with you.' She jutted her chin out determinedly. 'You said you needed volunteers.'

'You can't carry a boat!'

'No, but you'll need someone to look after the crew you bring back to shore. I can do that.'

'I'll have enough to do without worrying about you, too.'

'But you'll leave me here to worry about you? No!' She stamped her foot angrily. 'You said you wouldn't stop me from doing anything I wanted!'

'What?'

'When you proposed. You said I could do whatever I wanted.'

'Within reason!'

'*This* is a good reason. The crew on that ship need help. I want to help them and you said you needed volunteers.'

'That's not what I meant and you know it! Dammit, Ianthe, see sense!'

'I *am* seeing sense. And you're wasting time! Now are you going to let me come or not?'

'Fine.' He swore violently before kicking open the door of the other office, wrenching another oilskin off a peg by the entrance. 'Put this on and stay close to me. It won't be easy, but once we get going, you can't change your mind.'

'I know that.' She pulled the coat over her shoulders. It was several sizes too big and smelt of oil and tar, but it felt reassuringly thick, enough to keep out the worst of the elements. 'I'll keep up, I promise.'

'All right.' He looked her up and down approvingly before taking hold of her hand. 'If you're sure about this then let's go.'

He opened the door, and she staggered backwards at once, caught off guard by the force of the wind. Fortunately, Robert seemed not to notice, pulling her on towards the workshop as she clutched the hood of her coat tightly around her face.

'Mr Felstone.' George met them at the door. 'He says you're planning to go over the cliff?'

'Aye.' Robert's expression was grim. 'Any volunteers?'

'Ten men here. I've sent some lads round t'other yards as well so we should get a few more.'

'It's a long way and the storm's not over yet. No one's under any obligation.'

'We know that, sir.'

'Good. Then we'll meet at the lifeboat station in twenty minutes.' He glanced down at her for a moment, as if he were on the verge of saying something, before changing his mind. 'The sooner we get started, the better.'

Chapter Fifteen

Robert kept a tight hold of Ianthe's hand, muttering under his breath as they hurried along the edge of the harbour wall towards the lifeboat station, a large wooden shed with a steep slipway into the water.

'The boat's in here!' he shouted over the tempest, pulling her into the shelter.

'Phew!' Ianthe pushed back her hood once they were inside, revealing red cheeks and glittering eyes.

'Changed your mind?' he asked hopefully.

'Not at all.'

He glowered, knowing it was useless to argue. Insane as it was, he didn't have a good enough argument to stop her from helping. Just as long as she didn't do anything crazy like want to go out on the lifeboat itself—which he absolutely would *not* allow—she ought to be safe enough.

'There are blankets and medical supplies in

that cupboard. We won't be able to take a cart in this weather so you'll have to carry everything you need. Hopefully you'll have some help, but I'll need some people to carry oars, too. Just remember to wrap up the blankets so they don't get wet. And walk on the leeward side of the boat for shelter.'

She nodded, rifling through the cupboard and making a pile by the door as men started to arrive. Robert watched for a moment, nodding in approval before turning his attention to the volunteers.

'Ready?' He pushed open the doors of the shed with an effort, then shouted directions to the others as they lifted the boat up and carried it backwards out on to the harbourside. Once there, they rested it precariously on its side, before flipping it over so that the hull was pointing upwards, making it easier to carry. *Slightly* easier anyway, he thought ironically, counting the number of volunteers. There were twenty-four altogether, himself included, twenty for the boat, another four for equipment. That would have to be enough.

'All right, lads? Nice evening for a stroll, eh?' There was a cheer as he took his place at the head of the lifeboat and they lifted it up on to their shoulders, setting off at a crawl.

He twisted his head, trying to catch sight of Ianthe. There was no risk of her not keeping up at such a slow pace. The biggest danger was in the fierce gusts of wind trying to blow them into the harbour. As they reached the bridge, however, he caught sight of her, walking exactly where he'd instructed, holding a huge tarpaulin bundle in her arms. There were a couple of other women with her, too, also carrying bundles. He gave a reluctant smile. Unpredictable and skittish as she was, there was something indomitable about his wife, too. He doubted he'd have been able to stop her from helping even if he'd tried.

They reached the eastern side of the harbour and turned right, away from the steep cliff steps and towards the road that ran along the side of the Esk before curving gently up the hillside. It was a longer route, but they had no choice. The storm was showing no sign of abating and the stone steps were streaming with water. If even one man slipped and fell, the rest might go down with him, dragging the boat down on top of them. He couldn't risk that.

Instead, they trudged on for what felt like hours, stopping every so often, though not for long. Rest brought no relief, only an increase in anxiety as he looked out at the turbulent sea, thinking of the stricken ship. At least when they were moving, they were doing *something*. When they stopped, he could feel precious seconds slipping away, seconds that might be needed later. There were only a couple of hours of daylight left and they had to make the most of them.

At last they came within sight of the bay, a secluded cove with a sweeping expanse of sand and rock. At any other time, the view might have been beautiful, but now his gaze was drawn inexorably towards the vessel on the sandbank. It was still in one piece, though barely. Towering waves were pounding the sides as if determined to break them apart, enveloping the rigging in a raging torrent of froth and foam, while the mast was broken already, hanging uselessly over one side as if admitting defeat, though he could see men clinging to it, too, their desperation obvious even from a distance.

The sight seemed to give his own men fresh impetus as they accelerated their pace down the narrow path that led to the beach, going so fast that he had to warn them to be careful. At long last, however, they made it, dropping the boat on to the sand before flipping it over again.

'Ianthe?' He hurried over to her as the men distributed oars, needing to make sure she was all right before doing anything else.

She smiled, though her exhaustion was obvious. 'Aren't you glad I wear sensible boots now?'

'Extremely.' He managed an answering grin.

'Be careful, Robert. Please.'

He didn't need any other encouragement, sweeping her into his arms and kissing her with an ardour he hadn't known he possessed, savouring the taste and feel of her lips until they were both breathless.

'I will.'

He released her just as abruptly, striding back down the beach and jumping aboard the lifeboat as it launched into the water.

Ianthe watched the lifeboat bounce up and down on the roaring waves, half-terrified, half-enthralled by the sight. It didn't seem possible that something so small could attempt something so daunting, but it was ploughing through the water like a teetering arrow seeking its target.

She turned away, unable to bear the sight any longer, searching instead for a sheltered spot on the hillside, somewhere to take the crew once they were rescued, but there was nothing, no-where, not so much as a dip where they could build a fire. There'd be nowhere to warm them whilst they waited for the carts Robert had arranged to collect them once the storm was over.

'They've reached them!' one of the other women called out.

'What's happening?' She didn't dare to turn her head.

'They're throwing a line. It'll take a couple of trips to get them all, I reckon.'

Two trips! Her heart stalled. She could barely stand the tension of one.

'Is the line holding?'

'Can't tell. Wait…'

'What?' She whirled around just in time to see a particularly huge wave hit the side of the merchant ship, sending the rigging teetering over precariously. Instinctively, she gripped the other woman's arm for support.

'They'll be swept away!'

'No.' The other woman shook her head with an air of authority. 'That ship's stuck fast on the sandbank, don't you worry. Your husband'll get them back. Look, he's pulling some of them in now!'

Ianthe watched in agitation as the lifeboat came about, heading back towards the shore with five members of the shipwrecked crew aboard. Once it reached the shallows, she ran with the other women to help, splashing out into the water to help the weary sailors back on to dry land, wrapping blankets around their shoulders as they sank to the ground in weary relief.

'Does anyone need bandaging?' She moved between them, passing around a bottle of gin as she tried not to notice the lifeboat bobbing away again.

'Thank you, miss.' One of the crewmen grabbed her hand, squeezing it in gratitude. 'We thought we were done for.'

'You're safe now.' She smiled reassuringly. 'We'll get you back to Whitby soon.'

Though exactly *how* they were going to manage such a feat, she thought anxiously, was a whole other matter. The rescued sailors were exhausted, shivering and probably starving, too, lying immobile on the sand as they watched their sinking ship with expressions of morbid fascination. Some of them looked half-unconscious already. None of them were in any fit state to walk, though if they stayed where they were they'd freeze for certain. Not to mention that the lifeboat crew would be wet and exhausted, too. It was already obvious that the few supplies she and the other women had managed to carry weren't going to be anywhere near enough. They needed more help and quickly.

'They're coming back!' a sailor called out and she looked up at once. He was right. The lifeboat was swinging around a second time. *Just* in time, too. The ship looked as though it were about to be snapped in two by the force of the waves. Urgently, she counted the number of heads in the lifeboat, shoulders slumping with relief as she caught sight of black hair.

That was it. She couldn't just stand there and watch any longer. If they didn't find help or shelter then all of this would have been for nothing. They'd freeze before the carts ever came for them.

'I'm going for help!' she shouted over the wind to the woman standing beside her.

'It's almost dark!' The woman looked at her as if she'd run mad.

'That's why I have to go now!'

She grasped her skirts in one hand and made

her way determinedly back up the cliff path, walking as fast as she dared. The sky was a mottled dark grey, though the rain had eased slightly, allowing occasional moonbeams to break through the cloud and illuminate the path ahead of her. Her feet felt like lead, but she refused to stop and turn back. There had to be somewhere she could go, someone to turn to for help, even if she had to walk the whole way back to Whitby and demand that the carts follow her at once!

She reached the top of the cliff at last and sat down, straining to get her breath back. Strange how being outside now didn't bother her. She wasn't afraid of the open space or the sky or even the wildness of the elements any more. Instead, she let out a sob of relief as she made out the faint shadowy outline of the lifeboat below, finally returning to shore. Robert was safe. Until that moment, she hadn't truly realised how much she cared, but now she knew the full, terrifying extent of her feelings. She hadn't come to rescue the crewmen, though she'd truly wanted to help. She'd come because the thought of being away from him, of his being in danger without her there to help, had been too much to bear.

She heaved herself back to her feet, turning in the direction of Whitby before spinning around again abruptly, hoping her eyes weren't deceiving her and she wasn't simply imagining what she wanted to see—a cluster of lights in the dis-

tance, just below her in the next bay. Lights—
which meant houses! She started towards them
at once, slipping and sliding her way unsteadily
down another path as she made her way towards
a row of fishermen's cottages.

'Help!' She pounded frantically on the first
door.

'What on earth?' The door swung open almost
at once, revealing a middle-aged woman with a
friendly face and curly hair tied up in a scarf.
'What are you doing out in this weather, miss?
Come inside.'

'There's a shipwreck!' Ianthe grasped the
woman's hand desperately. 'The crew have been
rescued, but they need shelter. Help me…please!'

A man emerged out of the darkness of the cottage, already pulling on a coat and hat. 'I'll get
the others.'

'There you go, miss.' The woman smiled reassuringly. 'The lads'll go and fetch them. Why
don't you come in and rest? I'm Nancy.'

'No.' Ianthe shook her head. She'd no intention of resting, not until Robert was there beside
her. 'I have to go with them.'

'All right then.' The woman moved away from
the door for a moment, before returning with a
mug of tea. 'But drink this first. You look like
you need something.'

'Thank you.' She gulped the liquid down gratefully, feeling a deep sense of relief as a group

of fishermen started to gather behind her with lanterns.

'Now then, miss.' The man at the head gave her a terse nod. 'Let's go.'

Robert was the last man out of the lifeboat, relishing the feeling of wet sand beneath his feet as he threw off his cork life jacket and staggered back up the beach. It had been one of the worst rescues they'd ever attempted, the currents even more treacherous than he'd anticipated, but amazingly they'd succeeded without any losses. That fact alone made him feel buoyant despite the freezing conditions. The dangerous part was behind them. Now they just had to get the hell out of there.

He looked up at the cliffs with a fresh sense of dread. He'd left instructions for carts to follow and collect them once the storm had abated, but it would be slow going at night, and the horses wouldn't be able to get down the cliff path, which meant that the exhausted men would have to climb up and on to the exposed clifftop. He didn't relish the thought of telling them so, but it was the only way. They had to wait for another rescue now.

Before he did anything else though, he had to find Ianthe and make sure she was safe. No—more than that—he wanted, *needed* to pull her into his arms again and kiss her with even more thoroughness than before. Her willingness to help that evening, not to mention the way she'd kept up without so much as a murmur of complaint, had shown yet another side to her character. She'd surprised him again. She seemed to surprise him every day. Somehow he felt as though just seeing her again would give him the strength to get back up the cliff side.

He re-joined the others and came to an abrupt halt. 'Where's my wife?'

'She went for help,' one of the women answered, though she seemed reluctant to look him in the eye.

'What?' He felt a thud like a fist punching him hard in the chest.

'I warned her not to.'

'You let her go on her *own*?'

'I tried to tell her.'

He let loose a volley of oaths, hardly able to believe what he was hearing. Was she mad? Did he really have to warn her not to go climbing cliffs in the dark? He felt sick to his stomach, picturing everything that might have happened to her. If she'd fallen then he'd never forgive himself.

'Which way?'

'She took the path.'

He sprinted towards it, panic giving him a fresh burst of energy, relieved that she'd at least had the sense not to branch off on her own. With any luck, he'd catch up with her before she got too far.

He heard a noise and halted abruptly, eyes narrowing towards a cluster of yellow dots glowing through the darkness, getting bigger and brighter as they bobbed closer towards him. He felt the knot of panic in his chest start to ease. If they were lanterns then they must belong to a rescue party, which meant that there was a good chance that Ianthe was with them, that she'd found help after all, that she was alive…

'Robert!'

He heard her voice before he saw her, a small figure hurtling out of the darkness and into his arms, flinging herself against him almost before he had a chance to make her out.

'Are you all right?' She squeezed him tightly, as if trying to make sure he was really there. 'I've been so worried!'

'*You've* been worried?' He jerked away, seized with a sudden fury, wrenching her arms away and holding them tightly at her sides. '*You?*'

'What?' She looked surprised by his reaction.

He glowered at her, so full of conflicting emotions that he couldn't speak, stunned by the intensity of his feelings. She was alive. Which meant that he could breathe again, that his heart could beat again—that same heart he'd thought didn't function like other men's, that he'd assumed was incapable of love. He felt as though it had just stopped and restarted.

Not that he was going to let her off the hook so easily. She'd just scared the life out of him, even more so than the rescue had done. Fighting the storm hadn't frightened him half as much as the thought of losing her, but the realisation that had struck him the moment he'd seen her again had been almost as terrifying. He hadn't just been worried. He'd been frantic, distraught even. And now he was beyond furious, beyond rational thought, because now he recognised the feeling for what it was. He was in love with his wife and there wasn't a damn thing he could do about it.

Chapter Sixteen

Ianthe awoke to darkness. She didn't know how long she'd slept, but the storm outside seemed to have quietened slightly, the fierce howl dulled to a murmur, though judging by the pitter-patter of rain on the slate roof it was still a long way from over.

She vaguely remembered the long trudge back up the cliff side, their weary and bedraggled group splintering apart as they finally reached the cottages. Nancy had led her away, giving her a bowl of soup to eat and a nightgown to sleep in, before she'd crawled wearily into bed, unable to keep her eyes open a moment longer. Then something had woken her, not a touch or a noise, but a nagging feeling that something wasn't quite right… Where was Robert?

She forced her eyelids open, looking around the cottage in the flickering firelight, but the one big room seemed deserted. Was she alone then?

Robert had kept a vice-like grip on her arm the whole way back up the cliff side, though he hadn't said a word, his brows set in a heavy black line as he'd simply handed her over to Nancy. Seeing his expression, she hadn't argued, though she'd wondered what had been wrong. What could possibly have made him so angry? The rescue had been a success and everyone was safe. What was there to be angry about? He ought to be celebrating, not acting as if she'd somehow caused the whole shipwreck!

The door opened suddenly, letting in a gust of cold air as a tall figure paused on the threshold to remove its overcoat.

'Robert?' She squinted, trying to make out his face in the darkness.

'You're awake?' There was no mistaking his deep voice, though it sounded oddly distant.

'Yes.'

He hesitated, as if trying to decide whether or not to come inside, before the draught from the door made the fire splutter and he seemed to make up his mind, closing it firmly behind him.

'You should get warm.'

She swung her legs off the bed and hurried across to the fire, moving aside the rack where her clothes were drying. 'I don't know where Nancy is.'

'She's sleeping elsewhere.' He followed her

to the fireplace. 'She says the cottage is ours for tonight.'

'Just ours?' She swung around and almost collided with his chest, breath hitching as her lips pressed inadvertently against his bare skin. She'd forgotten that he'd been shirtless beneath his overcoat. Now the smooth contours of his body looked even more rugged in the firelight, glistening with a combination of rain and sweat, tasting vaguely of salt.

He seemed to stiffen, though the severity of his expression didn't waver. 'Just ours.'

'Oh.' She tried to move away and found that she couldn't. Between his body and the fireplace she was effectively trapped. 'Would you like something to eat?' She cleared her throat nervously. 'There's some bread somewhere...'

'I've eaten.' He took another step closer, resting his hands on either side of the fireplace behind her. 'We need to talk, Ianthe.'

She backed up against the chimney breast, vaguely alarmed by his sudden close proximity. What was the matter with him? He was probably just tired from the rescue, but his stern voice and even sterner expression reminded her of the first time they'd met. They were the look and tone of a man about to lose his temper.

'What about?' She inched her chin up defiantly. After all, she was tired, too! Whatever was causing his bad temper, if he thought he could take it out on her then he could think again. How dare he corner her as if she'd done something wrong?

'What about?' He looked incredulous. 'Are you seriously telling me you don't know?'

'I don't know why you're so angry, no! We're all all right, aren't we? I don't know why you're acting like we're not.'

'Because you shouldn't have gone off on your own!' His voice rose to a shout. 'Do you have any idea how dangerous that was? What might have happened?'

'What?' She blinked in shock. She'd gone to get help—had actually *found* help—and this was the way he reacted? This was her thanks?

'You went off on your own in the dark!'

'To get help!'

'You could have been hurt!'

She caught her breath at the unfamiliar note of anguish in his voice. Was that why he was angry then, because he'd been worried about her? Because he cared about her enough to be worried? The thought made her pulse start to flutter excitedly.

'But I wasn't hurt.' She placed a placatory hand on his arm. 'I'm all right.'

'It was still a bloody stupid thing to do. If you'd fallen then we'd have had to spend the rest of the night looking for you. You could have endangered more lives!'

Her pulse faltered again. So much for caring. He was angry at her for not being sensible enough!

'You should have waited for me, Ianthe.'

'It was almost dark!' she shouted back at him furiously, raising her voice to meet his. Even if it *had* been a reckless thing to do, he had no right to attack her for doing what she'd thought was right—what had *turned out* to be right.

'That's not the point.' He seemed in no mood to back down. 'You don't know these cliffs.'

'Somebody had to go and find help!'

'Not you!'

'Nobody else offered.'

'You were irresponsible!'

'Well, I'm sorry if I wasn't sensible or *respectable* enough for you, but I wanted to save your life!'

She tried to push past him, but he grabbed her arm, hauling her back again.

'You scared me, Ianthe.'

She froze at once. His voice sounded different again now, huskier somehow, sending a quivering sensation all through her body.

'Do you think I *wasn't* scared when you were out on the lifeboat?'

'You don't understand.' He closed his eyes briefly, his anger seeming to abate all of a sudden. 'I'm not just angry because you went off on your own. I'm angry because of how much it scared me. I couldn't bear the thought of losing you.' He raised a hand to her cheek, brushing the backs of his fingers against it before moving them around to cup the back of her neck.

She closed her eyes, tilting her head back into his hand. There was only her nightgown between them, only a thin slip of material between their two bodies, so close that she could feel his heartbeat thudding almost as quickly as hers. He cared for her. He hadn't said so exactly, but the implication was there in his words. He cared for her in the same way she cared for him. Not because she was part of a business deal, but because of who she was…who she was pretending to be anyway. The thought made her stiffen at once.

'Promise me you won't do anything like that again.' Robert seemed not to notice, his lips grazing her throat, pressing kisses in a line along her jaw.

'I promise.' She didn't know what else to say.

'I need you, Ianthe.'

His voice was almost a growl, making her knees almost give way beneath her. She raised her hands to his chest, trying to summon the strength to push away and finding her hands curling their way around his neck instead. He couldn't mean that! It wasn't part of their agreement. She was supposed to be sensible and respectable. While he…he clearly wasn't thinking straight. He was exhausted. So was she, for that matter, even if the last thing she wanted was to go back to sleep.

She opened her lips, but there were no words. His lips on her skin felt so good that she didn't want him to stop. She felt as though something in her body were loosening, as if all the fear and anxiety of the previous evening were oozing away beneath his touch. She wanted more of him, not less. Even if it were wrong, even if he thought she was a different woman, she couldn't stop, not unless he stopped first.

'Ianthe?' His mouth hovered over hers, making her name into a question.

'Yes,' she answered even before she had a chance to consider what the question might be, lifting her lips to his with a gasp of surrender.

For the space of heartbeat, they stayed that way, held together in a tender, almost poignant embrace, before a surge of feeling seemed to overtake them both at the same moment. Then hands and lips were everywhere, touching and caressing, exploring each other in a frenzy of anticipation.

Eagerly she ran her hands over his chest, revelling in the sensation of corded muscle beneath her fingertips. His skin was warm and yet delectably soft, like a pillow she wanted to rest her head against. In return, his fingers trailed over the curve of her back and down to her bottom, cupping her cheeks in both hands as his tongue delved deeper into her mouth, becoming fiercer and more insistent as if he wanted to taste every part of her. Instinctively, she pushed towards him, nipples tightening beneath her thin covering as if her body itself were straining to escape.

As if he could sense it, he reached down and grabbed the ends of her nightgown, pulling the whole garment up and over her head before she realised what he was doing.

'Wait!' She tried to grab it back, but it was already in a heap on the floor.

'Wait?' His face looked guarded suddenly.

She lifted her arms, covering her swollen breasts with embarrassment, and he gave a slow smile of understanding.

'You're right, it isn't fair that only one of us is naked.'

'Oh.' Her mouth was so dry that she could hardly speak. Not that she could look away either, her gaze drawn irresistibly downwards as he unlaced the ties of his trousers and let them fall to the floor, the evidence of his desire presenting itself to her stunned eyes.

She opened her mouth and then closed it again soundlessly, cheeks flushing scarlet as she looked back at his face in amazement.

'I want you, Ianthe,' he repeated, his gaze sweeping over her so heatedly that every part of her body seemed to contract. 'But if you don't…'

his voice cracked slightly as if he were forcing the words out '…tell me now.'

'I…' She hesitated, hardly able to hear herself think over the sound of her own pounding heartbeat. Of course she wanted him, she wanted to scream. She wanted him so badly it almost hurt. But not as the new Ianthe he'd married. As the old her—the *real* her, she now realised—the woman who was pounding so violently against the door of her prison that she could feel every wall, every barrier she'd built up over the last year, start to crumble.

But if she surrendered to him now then it would be as good as admitting the truth—that she was as bad as Albert's mother had said she was. If she succumbed to desire then she wouldn't be able to hide or deny her true nature any longer, not from him or from herself either. He'd know who she really was, not the sensible and respectable bride he thought he'd married, but a shameless, brazen wanton. There'd be no way back for them. It was probably too late already. She could feel the last bolt on the prison door sliding open and her old self breaking free…

'Tell me, Ianthe,' he almost groaned.

She couldn't restrain herself any longer. She was in his arms before he'd finished speaking, abandoning herself to the surge of desire coursing through every vein. Even if it was just for one night—one night before he woke up and realised what kind of woman he'd married—she wanted to be as close to him as she could be, to share herself and discover everything there was to know about love before it was too late.

She threw her hands around his neck and he clasped his arms around her, lifting her up and carrying her towards the bed as she wrapped her legs around his waist, pressing kisses against his neck and shoulders as they tumbled headlong on to the mattress.

Quickly, he shifted to one side, stretching out alongside her as their tongues touched again, twining together hungrily as his fingers caressed her breasts, teasing each nipple in turn until she bucked beneath him, straining for more.

'Robert?' she gasped against his mouth.

He gave a soft laugh and released her, shifting his weight downwards to brush his lips over her stomach and down between her legs.

'Robert!' she almost shouted his name this time, instinctively trying to jerk away, but his hands held her steady, his lips continuing their slow progression downwards to kiss her in a place she'd never imagined could be kissed.

She inhaled sharply, trying to understand what was happening. Not that her brain seemed to be working. Her body seemed to have taken charge of her senses, drowning out everything except the irresistible, undeniable impulse to start moving.

'I want you, too.' She panted the words. There

was no point in denying it. Even if she kept silent, her treacherous body would only betray her. It was already writhing indecently as his fingers sought the space between her legs, drawing her apart and teasing her in her most private of areas. She didn't know what he was doing, but she didn't want him to stop. Whatever it was, she wanted more. She wanted him. Now.

She squirmed beneath him, letting her fingertips trail a path over his shoulders. He stopped moving at once and she felt a sudden rush of panic. Had she hurt him somehow? Was he in pain? Even worse, had he changed his mind? If he had, she thought the ground would open up and swallow her.

'Ianthe?' He moved back up the bed, positioning himself over her with a look that was part query, part need. 'Are you ready?'

She smiled with relief, finding his mouth and letting her lips answer for her. He gave an answering moan, lowering his body gently and pushing himself slowly inside her. She felt a tearing sensation, a sudden searing pain as her body parted beneath him, biting her lip to stop herself from crying out as he plunged deep inside her. She could scarcely move from the pain. Whatever she'd expected, it hadn't been this. How could she have wanted something so badly that now hurt so much? Surely kissing was infinitely preferable to this?

'Am I hurting you?' He looked down at her with concern and she shook her head, forcing herself to lie.

'It's all right.'

'If you want me to stop…'

'No.' She reached a hand up to his face, gently smoothing his cheek. 'I want this.'

'I don't want to hurt you.'

He didn't move so she shifted for him, wriggling her hips and feeling the pain start to diminish. More than that, she could feel a fluttering sensation in her stomach, a tantalising warmth that was starting to spread out through her body. This was better, definitely better.

'Ianthe.' His arms and legs pinioned hers, pressing her down into the mattress. 'Tell me the truth.'

'Don't stop.' She bucked beneath him, trying to demonstrate her point. It didn't hurt, not any more. Now she wanted him to move. She reached her hands down to his waist to encourage him and saw the fleeting look of surprise on his face before he started to pull away.

'No!' She made a grab to stop him and he pushed downwards again, smiling wickedly as he thrust back inside her.

'Better?'

'I thought you were stopping.' She pouted up at him.

'Not yet.' He gave another heart-stopping grin. 'Trust me, Ianthe.'

'I do.' She smiled, not wanting to talk any longer, arching her body as he moved over her with strong, rhythmic movements. The fluttering sensation in her stomach felt different now, more vital and thrilling, as if it were building in intensity, filling the whole lower part of her abdomen. Instinctively, she wrapped her legs around him, tilting her hips up as she echoed each movement with her own.

'Wait.' His voice sounded strained now, but she kept going, unable and unwilling to stop herself. The tingling sensation seemed to be reaching a peak. Just a bit more and… She tipped her head back and let out a cry. All she needed was a few more seconds. Just a few more and…

She jerked suddenly, her body erupting spontaneously as her numbed mind watched from a distance. She was vaguely aware of Robert calling out, too, of his body shuddering with release as he fell down on top of her, but she couldn't respond, couldn't do anything but wait for the spinning, whirling, spiralling sensation to slow down and gradually fade away, leading her back to a deep and exhausted sleep.

It was cold when she woke up the second time. The fire in the grate was lower and she could feel the prickle of goosebumps over her arms. Robert was still lying face down beside her, one arm draped possessively across her body as if he couldn't bear to let go, though he appeared to be sleeping deeply.

Carefully, she reached for the quilt, pulling it up to cover them. What had she done? Her body was aching in ways she hadn't thought possible. The climb up and down the cliff side had been bad enough on her legs, but the space between them was sore, too. Her cheeks glowed at the memory. Nothing in her experience had prepared her for their lovemaking. Not a single poem or novel or piece of music had even come close. What she'd felt had been beyond words, as if her body had sprung back to life again, her old self returning with a vengeance, breaking out of its prison with the full force of all the pent-up emotion she'd held back for months.

But it shouldn't have happened. She raised a hand to her eyes as a feeling of shame swept over her. Somehow, whilst she'd kept to the letter of their agreement, she'd been able to bury the fact of her deceit. Now she'd given up any pretence of respectability, that deceit seemed even worse. Last night Robert had seemed to care for her, but that was before he'd found out what kind of woman she really was. When he woke up and remembered the way she'd behaved—a way no decent woman ought to behave—he'd be disgusted.

She reached out, tentatively smoothing a lock of dark hair away from his cheek. How could she have fallen in love so quickly and hopelessly?

For a few brief happy moments, she'd revelled in the possibility that he might love her, too, but now she had to set such dreams aside. Last night she'd shown him how very far from respectable she really was. Once his deal with Harper was signed, she owed him the truth about Albert, too. And once she did that, she'd offer him a divorce. It wouldn't be very respectable, but he'd have his new, bigger shipyard to console himself for that. He'd probably jump at the chance to set her aside.

In the meantime, she had to put her mask back on, get the dinner party over with and try not to show him how much she cared. There was no doubt in her mind. Once she told him the truth it would be over.

Chapter Seventeen

Robert yawned, stretched and rolled over, opening his eyes with a smile that faded the moment he found the space beside him empty.

He rubbed a hand over his face, memories of the night before flooding back in a torrent. The storm, the long climb over the cliffs, the rescue, the fishermen's cottages…the argument with Ianthe and what it had led to. *That* was the most vivid memory of all, though if it hadn't been for the fact that he was lying in a strange bed completely naked with only her scent on his pillow for company, he might have thought it had all been a dream.

He heaved himself upright, groaning as his sore muscles protested. His whole body felt as if it had been thoroughly and violently pummelled. There wasn't a single part of him that didn't ache. Not that he could regret the evening completely. He'd just woken up from a particularly pleasant dream in which he'd been reliving the latter events of the night and imagining a few more things he'd like to do with his wife. Things he'd *still* like to do, just as soon as he found her. Bruised and battered he might be, but he'd no intention of letting a bit of physical discomfort deter him. If one thing was clear to him this morning, it was that they'd wasted enough time. There were parts of her he was more than eager to explore in more detail. The very thought was arousing.

'Did I wake you?'

'Ianthe?' He twisted his head too quickly in the direction of her voice and let out an oath.

'Are you all right?' She crossed the room in two seconds, leaning over him with a look of concern.

'Just a bit sore.' He rubbed a hand over the back of his neck. 'Nothing that won't mend.'

'Oh… Good.'

She stepped back from the bed, folding her hands primly in front of her. He frowned at the familiar gesture. It was the way she'd behaved when they'd first met, though he hadn't seen her do it for a while. She was already dressed, too, though he must have interrupted her because her hair was still loose, flowing in dark blonde tendrils over her shoulders to just below her breasts.

His heart seemed to skip a beat. Funny, but he'd never seen her hair completely loose before. Even last night, she'd kept it tied in a knot at the back of her head. The style seemed almost as much a part of her as her high collars and ridiculously sensible boots. Now it was gone, he felt as though he were looking at a whole different woman.

'You look beautiful.'

'What?' She looked genuinely stunned. 'You don't mean that.'

'I don't think I've ever meant anything more.' He reached across and grabbed one of her hands, tugging her back towards the bed. 'Though I preferred what you weren't wearing last night. Come back to bed.'

'Robert.' She cast her eyes down as she pulled away from him. 'The carts are here. The ones you told to follow us last night. The men are preparing to leave.'

'Let them.' He released her hand and leaned back against the wall, throwing one arm behind his head as he studied her. What had happened? Last night, she'd made love to him with wild, sensual, thrilling abandon. This morning, she looked as if she wanted to get as far away from him as possible. She seemed to be retreating before his very eyes. Why? Surely she wasn't ashamed of what had happened between them? He'd heard it said that ladies were told they shouldn't enjoy physical relations with their husbands. In which case, he'd just have to convince her otherwise...

'I'd rather you came back to bed.'

'It's after seven. People will talk.'

'I don't care.'

'Well, I do! I have a reputation to maintain.'

He tipped his head to one side, detecting the faint tremor in her voice. 'What's the matter, Ianthe?'

'Nothing. I'd like to go home, that's all. I still have a lot of preparation to do for tonight.'

'Tonight?'

'The dinner party.' She sounded shocked. 'With Mr Harper.'

'Oh.' He sighed wearily. 'That.'

'Yes, that. You said it was important.'

'Did I?'

'Yes!'

He felt vaguely surprised by his own lack of interest. 'I suppose it was.'

'It still is. You said he was ready to sign the papers. We can't fail now. We just need to get through tonight and then...'

'And then?' He raised an eyebrow as her voice trailed away.

'Then we'll both have fulfilled the terms of our agreement.'

He clenched his jaw. She was speaking as if the agreement was all that existed between them, as if their marriage were still just a business arrangement. Then again, with their relationship in such uncharted territory, he wasn't quite sure how to proceed either. Not to mention that it wasn't the only new experience she was dealing with. The faint stain of blood on the bedsheets was a reminder of that. Perhaps, after everything else that had happened the previous day, she was simply feeling overwhelmed. Or perhaps he'd been too rough. Perhaps he'd hurt or frightened her... The very idea made his heart clench.

He threw back the covers, reaching out to embrace her. 'About last night...'

She took a definite step backwards. 'I think it would be best if we don't talk about it. We were tired and...distressed.'

'*Distressed?*'

'Yes.' Her eyes flashed accusingly. 'And you said that you didn't want an heir!'

He stared at her in disbelief. Is that what she thought he'd been doing? 'I wasn't trying to get an heir, Ianthe.'

'Oh.' She bit her lip, twisting away from him evasively. 'In that case, there's no reason for us to be...together. It wasn't part of the agreement.'

'Forget the agreement! I don't care about the blasted agreement!'

She shook her head, still refusing to look at him. 'I can't.'

'Why not? I love you!'

He thought he heard a small sob as her body seemed to go completely rigid for a moment.

'Ianthe?'

She didn't answer, and he grasped her shoulders, wrenching her back round to face him.

'What's changed since last night?'

'Nothing.' She lifted her eyes up at that, her voice almost unnaturally calm suddenly. 'Nothing's changed.'

'Then why…?'

'Because you don't know me. Not really. You haven't had time to get to know me. It's ridiculous to think that we…' She pursed her lips as if she were trying to control herself. 'It was a mistake. We should forget that it ever happened.'

'I don't want to forget it.'

'Well, I do!' She wrenched herself free from his arms with a sudden burst of anger. 'We had— *have*—an agreement. If you're really a gentleman then you ought to honour the original terms!'

'But I'm not a gentleman, am I?' He folded his arms, feeling as though she'd just driven a knife into his chest. 'Maybe you don't know me so well either.'

'Maybe I don't.' She held his gaze unwaveringly before gesturing towards a neat pile of clothes on a chair. 'Your things are dry and ready. I'll meet you outside.'

She whirled around then, sprinting for the door without looking back, leaving him to simply stare after her, unable to move, scarcely able to breathe as a painful sense of rejection assailed him, just as vivid as it had been six years before when his mother had pushed him away for the last time.

He sank down on to the bed and put his head in his hands. How could he have been so stupid, walking headlong into the one trap he'd striven so hard to avoid? Somewhere between the moment she'd arrived at the shipyard yesterday and the moment he'd carried her to the bed, he'd fallen in love, or at least realised he had. As much as he'd claimed he wasn't capable of love, deep down he'd known that the opposite was true. He wasn't incapable, he was afraid. Afraid of the potential pain it could bring, the gut-wrenching pain of caring for someone who couldn't, or wouldn't, care for him back. And now what he'd always feared and expected would happen, had happened. Just like his parents, the woman he loved had rejected him, too. Because she preferred a business agreement—*his* agreement—to a real marriage with him. If the irony hadn't been so horrible, he might have laughed.

He'd never regretted a business deal more in his life.

Two hours later, Robert stood on the mudflats, listening with one ear to a report of damage to the yard. The roof of the sail loft had been partially blown away, and four of the smaller colliers on the flats had tipped over, needing minor repairs, but overall they'd got away comparatively lightly. If only he could have said the same for himself.

They'd passed the painfully slow journey back to Whitby in silence. He'd taken a seat beside her in the cart for form's sake, though they hadn't exchanged so much as a word, keeping their bodies studiously apart as they'd bumped their way back over the cliff tops.

He'd jumped down the moment they'd reached the outskirts of town, unable to bear the feeling of being so close and yet so far from her at the same time. He'd made the excuse of going to the shipyard, though in truth the thought of walking back into the house at her side had been too painful to contemplate. He preferred to get straight back to work instead. If he did that, he reasoned, then perhaps he could get back to a sense of normalcy, too. If only...

'Should I order some roof tiles then, sir?'

'What? Oh.' He ran a hand wearily over his face. 'Yes. I'll leave the repairs in your hands. Engage whomever we need.'

'You're going?' His foreman could hardly have looked any more surprised.

'I need a drink.'

'It's ten o'clock in the morning, sir.'

'Well, it feels later.' He gave a terse smile. 'Time for whisky, I think.'

He strode back towards the yard, glancing across at Harper's as he went. If everything went well tonight, he'd own both by tomorrow. He'd have what he'd always wanted—a position of standing with wealth, respectability and influence. One where no one could tell him he wasn't good enough, where people like Louisa Allendon and Charles Lester couldn't call him an upstart without looking up to him as well. Except that he didn't give a damn about any of it any more. He couldn't even bring himself to be interested in his own repairs.

He dragged a hand through his hair as a wave of desolation swept over him. Last night, he'd felt as though he'd finally overcome the painful legacy of his past, but now the old feelings were back, more powerful and destructive than ever. He felt as though he'd been fighting them his whole life, trying to pretend they weren't there by filling his life with other accomplishments instead. Now it was too late: he could see all his ambitions, all his achievements, for what they were—futile attempts to stave off the emptiness inside.

Deep down, he'd always suspected that his parents had been right and that there was something wrong, something fundamentally unlovable about him, as if he weren't worthy of love or affection, and now his own wife had proved it, turning everything he'd accomplished to rubble in a few short minutes. Only this time, the feeling of rejection had been even worse because he'd thought, hoped, *believed* that she'd loved him back. But she didn't. Their night together hadn't meant anything to her. She preferred a business deal, saying that nothing between them had changed.

He stopped mid-stride. How could she say that? Since they'd first met everything about her had changed! The longer he'd known her, the more he'd come to realise that she was nothing at all like the uptight and severe woman he'd met on the train. Until that morning, he'd almost forgotten that she'd ever existed.

And she had the nerve to tell *him* to go back to the original terms of the agreement! *She* was the one who'd altered the terms, forcing him to see the emptiness he'd spent so long trying to avoid. *He'd* wanted a sensible, respectable wife, one to help him build his business, not one who lured him away and then simply discarded him.

He threw a savage look up the road towards the crescent, wondering whether he ought to go and confront her, but what was there left to say? Nothing that would make him feel any better.

As for what *would* make him feel better... He glanced speculatively towards a tavern on the harbourside. He ought to go home and get some rest before the dinner party that evening. That was what Mr Felstone, respectable shipyard owner and husband, would do. But at that moment, all he really wanted was a drink.

* * *

Ianthe descended the stairs nervously, stomach fluttering with butterflies so huge they felt like bats. This was it. The moment to prove herself, the evening when Mr Harper would judge and hopefully not find her wanting, when he would finally sign the deed of sale.

She reached the hall and smoothed her hands over her sober, mauve evening gown, one of her own rather than one of Robert's choices, making sure there were no wrinkles, before patting her hair to make sure the pins were still neatly in place. Then she walked across to the dining room and peered around the door, sighing with a deep sense of satisfaction. Everything was ready—the settings laid, the cutlery polished, the crystal glasses sparkling under the low-hanging chandelier. She'd spent the whole day working alongside Mrs Baxter, ignoring the housekeeper's insistence that she take a rest, knowing that sleep would be impossible and preferring to keep busy rather than allow herself any time to think.

If she *did* stop to think, she had the unsettling conviction that she might simply collapse in a heap on the floor and start crying. Once she started to think, she might remember the look on Robert's face when she'd told him that their night together had been a mistake, the look of hurt that had tugged on her heartstrings so painfully that she'd almost changed her mind and flung herself into his arms right there and then. The look that suggested he'd meant what he said—that he loved her. Even despite the way she'd behaved, the wanton abandon she'd shown in his arms— he loved her.

Not that it mattered. She hardened her heart against the memory. Once she told him about her past, that look would be gone for ever. She'd pushed him away despite the pain it had cost her, knowing that she was acting for the best. She had to remember that now, had to stay strong for one more night so that when she told him about her elopement with Albert, she could still look him in the eye and say that at least she'd fulfilled her side of their bargain. Once Mr Harper signed the deed of sale she would have met the basic terms of the agreement. No matter how angry he might be at her deceit, he couldn't say she'd failed in that.

She pushed diffidently on the drawing room door, surprised to find the room inside empty. She'd assumed that Robert had come home at some point when she'd been busy in the kitchens, that she'd simply missed him going upstairs to bathe and change. She'd expected to find him there waiting when she came down, but there was no sign of anyone. The whole house seemed un- naturally quiet and empty, as if it were taking a deep breath, bracing itself for another big storm.

She shook her head to dispel the thought. It was drizzling outside, but there were no storm clouds tonight. She was simply being paranoid, jumping at shadows, letting her anxiety about the evening ahead get the better of her. There was no need to be worried. Robert might not have come down yet, but he wanted Harper's yard too much to do anything that might hinder the sale. He wouldn't let anyone else see there was anything amiss between them, she was sure of it. Once the evening got started, everything would be all right. It had to be.

'Mrs Felstone?'

'Oh!' She put a hand to her chest, startled and yet relieved to see another person. 'Sorry, Hannah. Is Mr Felstone in his office? I can't seem to find him.'

'No, ma'am. He's not here.'

'What?'

'He hasn't come home yet.'

'Not at all?' She felt a momentary disquiet. Robert had told her once that he was never late for an appointment. Why would he start now with one that was so important?

'Mrs Baxter sent someone to the yard an hour ago to remind him about dinner, but they said he wasn't there.'

Disquiet turned to a definite flutter of panic. 'But where else would he be?'

'I don't know, ma'am, but there's another gentleman here to see you.'

'Do you mean Mr Harper?' Ianthe glanced at

the carriage clock on the mantelpiece. It was only seven o'clock, a full half hour before their guests were due to arrive, but perhaps they'd come early by mistake. 'Please show him in.'

'It's not Mr Harper, ma'am. He says his name is Lester. Sir Charles Lester.'

'Lester?' She felt a jolt, as if the name itself were a weapon being hurled across the room at her. 'Are you sure?'

'Yes, ma'am. Shouldn't I have let him in?'

Ianthe grabbed hold of a chair, steadying herself as the room started to spin around her. Surely it couldn't be him, not now, not here, not *him*, not tonight! Surely it was too horrible a coincidence to be true—had to be some kind of mistake! What could he want with her tonight?

'It's all right, Hannah, it's not your fault.' She pulled herself up stiffly. 'Please tell him I'm not at home.'

The maid shifted uncomfortably from one foot to the other. 'He said you'd say that, ma'am. Then he said I should give you this.' She held out a small piece of folded paper.

'What's that?' She eyed the paper nervously.

'I don't know, ma'am.'

'Oh…no…of course not.' She reached out and unfolded the note quickly. There was only one word, the name of a place, but it made her stomach plummet to the floor.

Bournemouth.

'What should I tell him, ma'am?'

'I don't know.' Ianthe put a hand to her mouth, feeling as though she were about to be sick. How could he know about Bournemouth? *What* did he know? Whatever it was, he apparently felt confident enough to come to her house and demand entry.

'Mrs Felstone?'

'Show him in.' She clasped her hands together unsteadily. What *could* she do except see him? The threat in his note was obvious. If she refused to see him, there was no telling what he might say or do. Though, on the other hand, there was no telling what he might say or do if she did…

'Very good, ma'am. Would you like me to stay?'

She gave a faint smile, touched by the maid's offer. 'Thank you, Hannah, but it's all right. If the Harpers or Lovedays arrive, please show them into the small parlour and tell them I'll be there in a moment.'

'Yes, ma'am.'

'And, Hannah…?' She hesitated over her next words, knowing how bad they sounded, but needing to say them all the same. 'If Mr Felstone returns, please don't mention Sir Charles to him.'

Then she stood in the middle of the room, a prickling sensation running up and down the length of her spine as she waited for the Baronet to arrive. After what had happened in Pickering, she'd tried to convince herself that she'd never have to see him again, that he'd never dare show his face in Whitby, but here he was, proving that her irrational fears hadn't been quite so irrational after all. Well, whatever he wanted, she'd just have to deal with it and send him on his way as quickly as possible. She still had half an hour to salvage the evening.

'Ianthe.' The Baronet appeared in the doorway almost at once, looking just as poised and elegant as she remembered, surveying her with an expression that could only be described as gloating. 'It's been too long.'

'What do you want?' She didn't bother with pleasantries, pulling her shoulders back and facing up to him squarely. Whatever he'd come for, she wasn't going to be intimidated, not again. This was her house. He couldn't touch her here. One scream would bring everyone in hearing distance rushing to her aid.

'What, no greeting?' He feigned surprise. 'You disappoint me, my dear. We used to be such good friends.'

'We were never friends.'

'A situation I intend to remedy now.' He sat down in a chair as if making himself at home, eyes shining with the triumphant gleam of a predator who knows he has his prey cornered.

Well, she wasn't cornered, not yet.

'You've come to make *friends*?'

'In a manner of speaking, yes. I think we ought to get on very well from now on. You know, your little performance had me quite fooled.'

'What do you mean, performance?'

'All this.' He waved a hand in her general direction. 'Little Miss Prim and Proper. But you can stop pretending to be quite so innocent, my dear. I know all about what happened in Bournemouth.'

'I don't know what you're talking about.'

'That's what your former fiancé said too at first. Fortunately, he was persuaded to talk.'

'Albert?' She gasped in horror. 'What did you do to him?'

'Oh, nothing violent, I assure you. There was no need to resort to such measures. He sold you out quite cheaply, I'm afraid. Foolishly, too. I was prepared to pay a lot more for the information.'

'He's a liar.'

'I don't think so.' He gave her a vaguely pitying look. 'He wasn't the only one I spoke to. His mother was most forthcoming, too. I have all the facts. Now I just have to decide what to do with them. Which brings me to why I'm here.'

Ianthe swallowed painfully. After all these months, she'd thought that he'd given up on pursuing her, but now she realised the truth was far more chilling. He'd been using the time to find out about her, plotting blackmail behind her back, returning just when she'd thought she was safe from him.

'I wonder what your husband would say if he knew?' He said the words lightly, as if he were making a simple query, not a threat.

'He already knows,' she tried bluffing. 'I told him before we got married.'

'I think not. The upright and honourable Mr Felstone married to a woman with *your* background? I can't see it somehow. If he knew the truth, I doubt you'd be taking seaside strolls together.'

'Seasi—!' She inhaled sharply. 'Have you been watching me?'

'Not personally, but I have associates. They tell me the two of you make quite a charming couple.' He stood up and stalked slowly towards her, smiling wolfishly. 'Of course, even if your husband *did* know the truth, it wouldn't matter. The rest of Whitby doesn't. And somehow I doubt he'd want the story getting around. As to whether it does or not...that's up to you.'

'What do you want?' She felt nauseated.

'What I've always wanted. I thought that would be obvious.'

'You want me to be your mistress? I'm married!'

He placed a finger under her chin, tilting it upwards. 'An inconvenience, my dear, not an obstacle.'

'You're despicable!' She jerked her chin away in disgust. 'What if Robert found out?'

'I should imagine he'd be somewhat displeased. Though perhaps not as much as he'd be at having the rest of Yorkshire know the truth about you. In any case, I want more than that. You're leaving with me, Ianthe. Tonight.'

'I'll do no such thing!'

He ignored her protest. 'You can write a note if you like, informing your husband of the transfer of your affections. That should be enough.'

'Never!'

'Then we'll wait here for him together. I'm even prepared to let you do the honours and tell him everything yourself. It should be amusing to watch.' His expression hardened. 'You might be glad to come with me after he throws you out.'

'I'll never come to you.'

'We'll see about that.'

Ianthe gritted her teeth, about to retort when she heard the chime of the front doorbell. The Harpers! She felt a surge of panic. It had to be them—Kitty was never so punctual!

'Tomorrow, then.' She grasped at the only idea she could think of. 'I'll come to you tomorrow.'

'I'm not so gullible, Ianthe. Do you think I don't know about your husband's business plans? When I mentioned the rest of the world knowing the truth, naturally I included Mr Harper.'

'You wouldn't!'

He laughed pitilessly. 'Of course I would.'

She dragged in a breath, glancing anxiously

towards the door. She could hear voices out in the hall now, Mr Harper's and Violet's. She ought to go out and greet them. The lack of a proper reception would look bad enough already. But if she went now, then Sir Charles would surely follow. He'd tell them everything... And that was the only way that she could think of to stop him.

'I promise I'll leave with you tomorrow. Just give me a chance to persuade Mr Harper to sign the papers tonight. Then I'll tell Robert everything. He'll cast me off, you're right, but there'll be no risk of him stopping us. He won't care where I go.'

'You outwitted me once before, Ianthe.' The Baronet looked contemptuous. 'Why would I give you the chance to do it again?'

'Because if you insist on me leaving tonight then I'll never forgive you. I'll fight you every moment we're together and then I'll run away. I'll never be yours.'

'And if I let you wait until tomorrow?'

'Then I won't fight. I'll come willingly.' Somehow she forced the words past her lips. 'I'll do whatever you say.'

Sir Charles studied her in silence for a few moments. 'Do you know, I think you really mean it.'

'I *do* mean it. Just let me go now.'

'All right, I'll send my carriage at dawn. You have until then. Otherwise I'll make sure that everyone in Whitby knows the truth about you by breakfast.'

'I'll be ready.'

'Good. Then we understand each other. You won't get away from me this time, Ianthe.' His face seemed to sharpen suddenly, becoming pointed and falcon-like, before smoothing out again just as quickly. 'Now you'd better go and see to your guests. You don't want to keep them waiting.'

Chapter Eighteen

Robert staggered out of the tavern, clutching the door frame and wincing as the evening light assaulted his eyeballs. Perhaps that last cup of ale had been a mistake after all, he conceded. Not that he was completely drunk, not yet. He was still lucid enough to feel pain whenever he thought of his wife, which was still far too often, no matter how much he tried to drown her out of his thoughts.

Even now, he had the fanciful impression that one of the men walking along the quayside towards him had the same face as her, the same large doe eyes and dark blond hair. Even more strangely, the man was looking at him with recognition, too, as if they were already acquainted. He screwed up his eyes, trying to make sense of it. Was he imagining things now?

'Percy?' The answer hit him at the last moment. 'Felstone?' From the startled look on the youth's face, it was hard to tell which of them was the most surprised. 'Is that you?'

Robert felt a flash of annoyance. Of course it was him. Though he supposed he could understand the lad's confusion. He was still wearing his dishevelled clothes from the rescue, and as for his behaviour…well, he wasn't exactly his usual self-contained, respectable self. He couldn't remember the last time he'd been drunk in public—drunk at all, for that matter.

'What are you doing here, Percy?'

The youth's expression altered at once. 'I need to speak with Ianthe. Is she at home?'

'I expect so.' Robert heaved a sigh. 'We're having a dinner party tonight.'

'*You* are?'

He ignored the youth's sceptical expression. 'Some time around now, I should imagine. Come on, I'll walk with you.' He took a step forward and lost his footing, catching hold of the wall as the ground started to sway beneath him. For a fleeting moment he thought he was back on the lifeboat again. Before his world had really collapsed.

'I say, I think you might want to wait a bit.'

'You might be right.' Robert leaned back against the tavern wall, half-closing his eyes. 'So what's so important that you had to come in person? You didn't even come to our wedding.'

'No, sorry about that. Work, you know. As for now...' Percy's expression turned shifty. 'There's just something I need to tell her.'

'Such as?'

'It's private, I'm afraid... Ow!'

He yelped as Robert grabbed him fiercely by the collar and pushed him up against the wall.

'You know—' Robert's voice was a growl '—I didn't like you the first time we met. I didn't like the way you treated your sister then and I still don't like it now. So if you've come to upset her again, I suggest that you turn around and go back to London before I make you.'

'I'm not!'

'Then why are you here?'

'She's in danger!'

'What?' Robert felt his heart thud to a painful halt. 'What kind of danger?'

'I don't know. I'm not sure, but I think I've done something really bad this time.' Percy shook his head on a sob. 'You're right, I've been a terrible brother. I should have taken better care of her after our parents died. If I had, then maybe none of this would have happened.'

'*This?* Meaning me?'

'What? No, I had nothing to do with her marrying you. She chose you all by herself. She's a lot smarter than I am.'

'Then what are you talking about?' He gave the youth a small shake. 'What did you do?'

'I told someone something I shouldn't have and now I think they intend to use it against her.'

'Someone and something?' Robert was getting impatient. 'Percy, if my wife's in danger, I want details.'

'I can't tell you. I promised I'd never tell anyone, but Charles kept on giving me wine and asking me questions and it just slipped out. I shouldn't even be telling you this much, but now that he knows…'

'You mean Lester?'

'Yes. We were playing cards. I was in so deep and he said that if I just told him one thing about Ianthe, something she might not want anyone else to know…something secret…'

'Then he'd clear the debt?'

'Yes.' Percy hung his head miserably. 'He's been in a foul mood for weeks, ever since you two got engaged. We had a bit of an altercation about it, truth be told. I've been trying to avoid him, trying to get back on my feet, but he seemed to be like his old self again. And I thought, *What's the harm in just one game of cards*…? I'll never play again, I swear it.'

'What did you tell him, Percy?'

'I can't tell you.'

'You can.' Robert's grip on his collar tightened. 'And you will. Now.'

* * *

'She *eloped*?'

Ten minutes later, Percy's words still hadn't sunk in, a combination of anger and all-consuming jealousy making it difficult to focus.

'Yes, but they didn't get far.'

'Eloped?'

'Yes!' Now it was Percy's turn to be impatient. 'I say, if you're going to march around ranting all day, I should get going.'

Robert came to an abrupt standstill. That last cup of ale had definitely been a mistake. He was still struggling to take in everything Percy had told him, as if his brain were having trouble keeping up with his hearing. He couldn't comprehend, let alone believe it. It just wasn't possible. They had to be talking about different women. His prim and proper, respectable wife would surely have never done anything so scandalous. And yet…a faint memory tugged at the edge of his consciousness. Something Percy himself had said that first day they'd met on the train—something about a scandal…

'It's not true.' He still refused to believe it.

'We've been over this.' Percy sighed with exasperation. 'It *is* true. And now Charles knows it, too.'

The words acted like a bucket of water over his head, sobering him instantly. 'You really think she's in danger from him?'

'I'm not sure, but you know he always liked her. He wanted to marry her before you came along, but I thought he was over it. There was just something odd about his expression when I told him, menacing almost, as if he intends to use it against her.'

Robert's brows knit together darkly. Blackmail? That sounded like something the Baronet might stoop to. As for what he'd want in return…

'When was this?' He spun on his heel, starting up the hill with a sudden burst of energy.

'I say, wait for me!' Percy trotted alongside. 'It was two nights ago. I went back to his house the next morning, to ask him not to say anything, but they said he'd already left for Bournemouth. That's when I really started to worry.'

'So why didn't you come straight away?' Robert threw him a savage look.

'I had to go to work. Then I had to practically beg them to let me go today. They're none too pleased with me, I can tell you.'

'I know the feeling.'

Percy flushed. 'So what are you going to do?'

'With Lester? If he touches so much as a hair on her head, I'm going to throw him into the harbour personally.'

'Not with him. With Ianthe?'

Robert didn't answer. What *was* he going to do with *her*, the woman who'd kept not just a secret, but a whole scandal hidden away from him, one that would destroy both their reputations if it ever got out, not to mention his plans for the shipyard? The woman who'd had the nerve to say that *he* wasn't worthy of her love?

No. His step faltered momentarily, memories of that morning piercing the fog of his consciousness. She hadn't said anything like that at all. He'd simply assumed the worst for himself. She hadn't given him any convincing reason for her change of behaviour. She'd actually seemed more concerned about the dinner party than anything else, adamant that it go ahead, as if buying Harper's shipyard meant more to her than it did to him. She'd said something about fulfilling her side of the bargain, too—words that had struck him as odd at the time—as if she'd been afraid of letting him down. As if she'd felt...guilty?

'It's not really so bad when you think about it.' Percy sounded anxious. 'It's true that she eloped, but she never shared a room with the man or anything like that.'

'Do you think people care about those sort of technicalities?' He threw him a scathing look. The thought of her sharing anything more than a handshake with another man wasn't something he wanted to think about.

'No...I suppose not, but it was really my fault as much as hers.'

'What do you mean?'

'I pushed her away. After our parents died,

it was just so much responsibility all at once. I didn't want to deal with it. I made her feel unwanted, I suppose. I knew she was lonely in Bournemouth, but I didn't do anything to help. It's no wonder she ran off with the first man who came along.'

Robert felt a fresh stab of jealousy. 'That doesn't explain why she didn't tell me.'

'Maybe she thought there was no need. It was all hushed up, after all. I'm the only one who blabbed.'

'Quite.'

'Look…' Percy sighed '…I don't know why she didn't tell you, but I know she was a different person after Bournemouth. When she went there she was in mourning, but she was still my sister. When she came back she was someone else, like she'd turned to stone or something. She was so full of life before, always loving and laughing and happy.'

Robert felt his stomach clench. That sounded more like her—the elusive woman behind the respectable façade, the one he'd caught fleeting glimpses of over the past few weeks. He felt a surge of relief, as if a weight had been lifted. If that was the real Ianthe then perhaps there was a chance for them after all. *That* was the woman he wanted, the woman who'd gone to bed with him, not the one who'd pushed him away, the woman with a scandalous past and the ability to destroy everything he'd built in less than a day—the woman he loved despite any of it.

'Come on!' He seized Percy's arm, breaking into a run. 'It'll be quicker if we go in the back way.'

'Mr Harper.' Ianthe fixed a smile to her face as she entered the small parlour, trying her best not to show that her world was tumbling down around her ears.

'Mrs Felstone.' Mr Harper looked distinctly unimpressed. 'I was starting to think that you and your husband had forgotten us. Where is he?'

'I'm afraid he's been delayed at the yard. After the storm and shipwreck last night he had a lot of work to do there today, but I'm sure he'll be here as soon as possible.' At least she hoped so...

'I'm hungry. If he wasn't going to be on time then he should have cancelled.'

'Oh.' She blinked in surprise. Somehow she'd assumed that saving the lives of twelve men might have been a reasonable excuse for tardiness. 'In that case, shall we start without him? I'm sure he won't mind as long as you don't object to my company? And the Lovedays will be here any moment.'

'Of course we don't object,' Violet interjected hastily. 'Everyone's been talking about the rescue last night and how brave he was, but you went with the lifeboat, too, I understand?'

'Yes, though I stayed on the shore. I helped to look after the rescued crewmen.'

'Common sailors?' Mr Harper gave her a disapproving look. 'Hardly a fit task for a lady.'

'I think you were very courageous.' Violet's eyes shone with admiration.

'Thank you, though I'm sure you'd have done the same under the circumstances.'

'Her?' Mr Harper snorted. 'She'd have to get her head out of a book first. Do you know she needs to wear glasses now? Glasses! On a woman, ha!'

'I'm sure she'll look just as lovely as always.' Ianthe bit the inside of her cheek in restraint, shocked by the old man's insensitivity. Poor Violet looked mortified.

'Shall we eat?' She took the other woman's arm pointedly, leading her ahead into the hall. 'I'm famished, too.'

'Yes. Thank you.' Violet's stricken expression didn't alter. 'Though perhaps we might talk afterwards?' She threw a quick glance behind before lowering her voice. 'In private?'

'Of course. Is something the matter?'

'I'm not sure. It's just something my father said.'

'Then of course we'll…' Ianthe faltered mid-sentence, distracted by a commotion coming from the back stairs to the kitchen. Raised voices and running footsteps and…

'Robert…! *Percy?*' She dropped Violet's arm as the two men charged, panting and breathless, into the hallway.

'What's the meaning of this?' Mr Harper sounded indignant. 'Mr Felstone, this is most unseemly.'

'Ianthe…' Percy started towards her first. 'I'm so sorry.'

'No!' She put her hands up to fend him off, suddenly realising just how the Baronet had found out about Albert. Until this moment she'd refused to consider the obvious answer, that her own brother had betrayed her. Now there was no way of denying it. But what was he doing with Robert? What were the two of them doing *together*?

'Why, Percy.' The Baronet's distinctive drawl from the drawing-room doorway made her heart sink to her feet. 'I didn't expect to see you again so soon.'

'I say…'

'Get out.' Robert advanced forward threateningly. 'Get out of my house now!'

'Mr Felstone!' Mr Harper looked positively outraged. 'Mind who you're speaking to, sir! Good evening, Sir Charles. It's an honour to see you here.'

'I don't give a damn who I'm speaking to.' Robert's voice was tight with barely restrained fury. 'I told him to get out.'

'I'd think very hard about what you were saying if I were you.' The Baronet's confident manner faltered as he took half a step backwards. 'If our friend Percy here has apprised you of certain *events*, then you ought to be extremely careful about what you do next.'

Ianthe felt her heart start to thud erratically, gripped by a sudden rush of panic. Sir Charles was talking as if Robert already knew the truth about her past—as if Percy had told him, too! In which case... She dragged in a wavering breath, feeling as if there weren't enough air in the room to breathe any more. She wasn't even going to get the chance to tell him herself. This was awful— more awful than she'd even imagined. If Robert knew, then no wonder he was so angry. He looked absolutely livid, his eyes blazing with fierce, fiery emotion. In another moment, he'd turn that face on her!

The doorbell rang again and she whirled towards it. This would be the Lovedays—more witnesses to her shame, as if there weren't enough already! Quickly, she picked up her skirts, unable to bear the atmosphere in the hall a moment longer, charging out of the front door, past Kitty and Giles and down the marble steps, hurtling blindly through the ornamental gardens towards the promenade. She had to get away—couldn't just stand there and watch as her past brought the present crashing down on her head! It was too late now to undo any of the damage she'd caused. Harper would never sell to Robert now. And Robert...surely he'd never forgive her!

'Ianthe!'

She heard him call out behind her, but she kept running, her whole mind fixed on escape. If Percy had told him about Albert, then it was too late to make excuses or to defend herself. Not that she could anyway. Everything was ruined and it was all her fault!

She skidded to a halt at the end of the promenade. Below her the sea spread out like a sparkling green blanket, rippling in gently undulating waves all the way to the horizon. Maybe if she sailed across it then she could find a new home, a place where no one would care about her past, where she could make a new start and try to bury the fact that her heart was breaking...

'Ianthe, get back!' Robert's voice sounded alarmingly close.

'Go away!' she shouted over her shoulder, still refusing to look at him.

'I won't come any closer, but come back from the edge, Ianthe, please. The soil might be unstable after last night.'

Edge? She looked down, surprised to find her toes pressed up against the very brink of the precipice. In her haste she hadn't noticed how very close she'd come to the edge, but now she was alarmed to find that he was right. The rim of the cliff looked as if it were sagging, in imminent danger of collapse, with small fragments of rock and soil already starting to crumble into the waves below.

She shifted her weight backwards, turning around to find Robert standing only a few feet away. He was watching her intently through the drizzle, his whole body poised as if making ready to spring forward and catch her.

'Take my hand.' He advanced another step closer, moving slowly as if he were afraid of startling her.

'No.' She ignored his outstretched hand. 'I'll come back from the edge, but you need to go first.'

'Just take my hand, Ianthe.'

'You don't understand!' she wailed at him. 'I've ruined everything. I didn't mean to, but I have. It's over, Robert! Just leave me alone, please.'

'No.' He shook his head stubbornly. 'Percy told me everything and it's all right, I don't care.'

'What?' She felt her heart leap into her throat.

'He told me what happened in Bournemouth and I don't care.'

'How can you *not* care?'

'Because I don't. Not as much as the thought of losing you anyway.'

'But I behaved so shamefully.'

'You made a mistake.'

'I'm not respectable!'

'Neither am I!' He gave a strained smile. 'I never was, not really, but I don't care any more.'

'Aren't you angry?'

'Furious, but that doesn't matter.'

She shook her head, resisting the temptation to believe him. 'I should have told you. I knew I should have, but I couldn't bear to talk about it. I didn't realise how important respectability was to you at first and then…then I thought that if I could be the woman you wanted, it wouldn't matter.'

'You *are* the woman I want, Ianthe. I love you.'

'But Sir Charles knows, too, and he says he'll tell everyone. There'll be gossip!'

'Let them gossip.'

'Harper won't sell you his yard!'

'If he thinks we're not good enough for him, then he can keep his damn yard. We can't help our pasts, I know that now, but we can bloody well decide our own futures. I won't let the likes of Harper and Lester ruin it.'

'So…you still want me?' She could hardly believe it…

'Yes! With all my heart, Ianthe. Just take my hand.'

She let out a sob of relief, stretching her fingers out towards him just as the ground beneath her feet started to quake and disintegrate. Startled, she tried to fling herself forward, but she was already falling, sliding into thin air as the edge of the cliff gave way.

'No!' Robert's hand clamped around hers in mid-air. 'Hold on!'

'Ah!' She cried out in pain as she swung against the side of the rock face, her fingers already slipping through his.

'Reach up to me!' He lay face down on the ground, straining to hold her.

'You're too far!' She swung her empty hand up and missed. 'Robert, you need to let go. I don't want to drag you down!'

'If you fall, then I'm coming down with you!' His tone was implacable. 'You're not giving up, Ianthe.'

'I don't want to give up!' She looked down, catching a glimpse of the waves crashing against the rocks two hundred feet below. They seemed to be getting taller and more threatening, as if they wanted to reach up and pull her down with them. No, she didn't want to give up. If Robert still wanted her, then she wanted to show him how very much the feeling was mutual. He was right about the past. She'd made a mistake with Albert. One stupid mistake. Why should it have the power to ruin the rest of her life? If Robert could forgive her, then maybe she wasn't so bad after all. Maybe she could let go of all the shame and self-recrimination and be herself again after all—the *her* she wanted to be...

She swung her hand up again, throwing all her strength into one last desperate attempt to reach him as their fingers touched. And held.

'Hold tight!' Robert heaved on her arms, hoisting her up and over the side of the cliff, back on to the grass.

'I thought I was going to lose you.' He caught her in his arms the moment she was safe, rocking her back and forth as she clung to him, waiting for the fearful trembling sensation to subside.

'It was an accident. I didn't mean to get so close to the edge. I was just running, trying to get away.'

'You have to stop running, Ianthe.'

'I know.' She pulled her head back. 'But I was so scared that you'd hate me. That was why I behaved the way I did this morning. I didn't want to deceive you any more, but I was too afraid to tell you the truth. I knew that I had to, but I thought that if I could just convince Mr Harper to sign the papers first then I wouldn't have failed completely.'

'You haven't failed me, or if you have, then I'm glad that you did.'

'You're *glad* I deceived you?'

'I wouldn't go that far.' He gave a terse laugh. 'But if you'd told me the truth at the start then I might never have taken the chance to get to know the real you. I thought that it mattered what society thought of me, what men like my father thought of me, but it doesn't. All that matters now is what *you* think of me. Tell me the truth, Ianthe. Tell me how you really feel about me. If you can love me, then I don't give a damn about anyone else's opinion.'

'Of course I can love you!' She tightened her arms around him. 'I *do* love you!'

'So do I.' His voice sounded hoarse. 'Strange as it sounds, I think I did from the first.'

'You called me a schemer!'

'A schemer I still asked to marry me. I must have had a reason, even if I didn't realise it at the time. The only mystery is why you said yes.'

'Oh…' She bit her lip, reluctant to tell him the story, but knowing that she owed him the whole truth. 'It was Sir Charles. He followed me to Pickering Castle the morning after the ball and attacked me. He said he'd been in love with my mother for years—that if he couldn't have her then he'd have me instead. He was obsessed.'

Robert clenched his jaw angrily. 'Percy said something similar.'

'Percy? Wait till I get my hands on him…'

He pulled her close again, pressing kisses into her hair. 'I wouldn't be too hard on him. If it hadn't been for him, I'd probably still be drinking in a tavern on the quayside.'

'Is that what that smell is?'

'I'm afraid so.' He made a wry face. 'Apparently I'm perfectly capable of ruining my own reputation without you. But I think Percy's genuinely sorry.'

'He ought to be.' She felt a fresh flicker of panic. 'What about Lester?'

'Yes.' The Baronet's voice behind them was positively glacial. 'What about Lester? Touching though this scene is, it doesn't change anything.'

'It changes everything.' Robert set her to one side, pulling himself slowly to his feet. 'If I were you, I'd walk away now.'

'I've every intention of walking away.' The Baronet pulled a small pistol from his jacket pocket. 'But I'm taking your wife with me.'

Ianthe cried out in horror. The Baronet was pointing the gun straight towards them, standing with his back towards the crescent. Anyone looking out of the windows wouldn't be able to see the weapon at all. They wouldn't come to help. On the contrary, they'd think that *he'd* come to help them.

'I'm tired of waiting, Ianthe. You're coming with me.'

'She's not going anywhere.' Robert stepped in front of her, shielding her body with his own. 'You can spread whatever rumours you like.'

'I'm prepared to do a lot more than that.' The Baronet jerked the pistol threateningly. 'It would be such a shame if you fell over the cliff, especially having just saved your lovely wife, but then, accidents do happen.'

'If you shoot me, I'll be washed up on the shore. They'll find the bullet.'

'They might, or they might be convinced not to notice. I have powerful friends. Now step aside.'

'No.'

'Robert...' Ianthe put a hand on his arm.

'You're not going anywhere with him!'

'I won't let him shoot you!' She rushed past him quickly, moving to stand beside the Baronet. 'You don't know what he's capable of!'

'And that's supposed to convince me?' Robert's face was like thunder.

'We don't have a choice!'

'You should listen to your wife, Felstone. She's a smart woman.'

'That explains why she never wanted you.'

'How dare you?'

The Baronet's finger twitched, and Ianthe reacted instinctively, hurling herself sideways at the same moment as Robert charged forward, barrelling into the other man with such force that it knocked them both off their feet.

Quickly, she lunged for the weapon, but Robert got there first, clamping one hand over Sir Charles's wrist as they both fought with the other, rolling closer and closer towards the edge of the cliff.

'Look out!'

She screamed and saw Robert lift his head at the warning, saw him register the danger a split-second before the Baronet slammed a fist into his jaw. Horrified, she saw him slump to one side, just as Sir Charles lifted the gun again and took aim, staggering back to his feet and heedlessly towards the edge.

What happened next seemed to take place in slow motion. One moment, Sir Charles's face was contorted with a look of hate-filled triumph, the next he simply looked surprised as the gun fired and he tumbled backwards off the edge of the cliff into thin air.

'Robert!' Ianthe threw herself to the ground beside him. 'Are you hurt?'

'What happened?' He pulled himself up to a sitting position, tenderly rubbing his jaw.

'Did the bullet hit you?'

'Bullet?' He seemed slightly dazed. 'No, I don't think so.'

'You don't *think* so?' She ran her hands over him, frantically checking for blood.

'I'm all right, Ianthe.' He laughed hoarsely. 'There's no need to grope me in public.'

'What?' She punched him hard on the shoulder. 'I'm making sure you're all right! Ingrate!'

'What happened to Lester?'

'He fell.' She shuddered. 'He was going to shoot you and he fell.' She punched him again.

'What was that for?'

'Because you almost got yourself killed. You

could have fallen off the cliff *and* been shot into the bargain. You should have let me go!'

'Never again.' He dragged her into his arms, clasping her tightly to his chest. 'You're all I want now, Ianthe. You can be whatever version of yourself you want to be, just don't leave me again.'

She held out for another moment before throwing her arms around him too. 'You're all I want as well. I love you, Robert. Let's go home.'

Epilogue

January 1866

Ianthe looked around the large, desk-filled room with a sigh of contentment. The new school had been open for a week and she had thirty pupils already, most of them the children of families who worked in the shipyard, though she'd had enquiries from others in the community too. At this rate, she'd have to find bigger premises.

'All done.' Robert climbed down from the ladder where he'd been hammering a blackboard on to the wall. 'Now, is there anything else I can do to assist you, Mrs Felstone?'

'I think you've done quite enough for today, thank you, Mr Felstone.' She gave him a teasing smile. 'Until we get home anyway.'

'Sounds intriguing.' He sauntered slowly towards her, grey eyes darkening seductively. 'Why not here? These desks look quite sturdy.'

'Because Violet will be back at any moment!' She feigned outrage. 'She only went to collect some more books.'

'I could lock the door...'

'Stop it!' She laughed as he curled his arms around her waist, pulling her tightly against him. 'Don't you have a shipyard to run? Besides, I'd have thought you'd be tired after this morning.'

Robert grinned wickedly. 'I'd have thought so to, but I can't seem to get enough of you these days. I think I'm still making up for lost time.'

She raised her hands to his chest, half-heartedly fending him off. 'There's something I need to tell you anyway.'

'Mmm?' His lips traced the curve of her throat. 'I'm all ears.'

'It's about Harper's yard. Violet says he's found another buyer.'

'I know.'

'You *know*?'

His mouth trailed an idle path up her neck towards her mouth. 'There've been rumours for the past month.'

'And why didn't you tell me?'

'Because we've had far more interesting things to talk about.' She could hear the smile in his voice. 'And because I don't care, remember?'

'Are you sure?'

'I'm positive. Marriage is far more distracting than I'd anticipated. If I'd bought Harper's, then

I'd have had to spend even more time at work and for some reason I prefer to be at home these days.'

'I prefer that, too.'

'Good. And since we're telling each other things, you ought to know that I had a visit from the local magistrate this morning. He says they won't be investigating Sir Charles's death any further.'

'So they're going to declare it an accident?'

'They already have. There were enough witnesses who saw him point the gun at me before he fell. Percy's testimony about his state of mind helped, too.'

'You're quite his champion these days, aren't you?'

'Credit where it's due. He's turned out to be an excellent clerk.'

'I'm glad he decided to stay in Whitby.' She pressed her forehead against his with a sigh. 'And I'm relieved it's all over. Maybe now we can find out what a normal marriage feels like.'

'You know there'll still be talk.'

'I'm getting used to it.' She shrugged. 'Why? Do you think some people will still blame you?'

'Maybe, but it's no great loss. The people who matter know the truth. The rest were always going to hold my past against me anyway.'

Though thankfully not hers as well, Ianthe added silently. Sir Charles had taken that secret with him.

'Besides—' grey eyes smouldered into hers '—there *are* benefits to being a social outcast. Now that I've regained the thoroughly disreputable reputation I deserve, nobody bats an eyelid at how much time I spend with my wife. It's quite liberating really.' He trailed a hand suggestively down her back. 'We might not be the most respectable couple in Whitby, but we're certainly the most interesting. Now will you give me one kiss at least, or is that too scandalous for you?'

'You know I don't care about such things any more.' She smiled gleefully. That was true. In the past few months, Robert had positively encouraged her to be scandalous. If she wasn't careful she'd give in to him now and really shock poor Violet. Tenderly, she wrapped both arms around his neck, kissing him so deeply that she felt both their bodies start to respond.

'There's always my office.' Robert's voice was dangerously tempting. 'If you'd care to stop by for a visit this afternoon? My desk is bigger, after all.'

'Perhaps.' She smiled against his mouth. 'What exactly did you have in mind?'

A shocked squeak caught them both by surprise.

'Oh, Violet!' Ianthe dropped her arms and cleared her throat hastily. 'We were just… That is…'

'I was just saying goodbye.' Robert made an

ironic bow. 'Though I ought to put that ladder away first. Excuse me, Miss Harper.'

'I'm sorry, Violet.' Ianthe covered her face with her hands, peeking through her fingers with embarrassment as the door closed behind him.

'Next time I'll remember to knock.' Violet giggled. 'I should have known better than to leave the two of you alone together.'

'Oh, dear. Are we really so shocking?'

'You're perfectly incorrigible, but you seem very happy together. That's what matters, isn't it?'

'You're right. I never imagined I could feel this happy.' She beamed. 'Thank you for the books, by the way, but doesn't your father mind you coming here to help with the school? I know he doesn't approve of me any more.'

Violet flushed guiltily. 'He doesn't know. He's bedridden most of the time now. I tell him I'm out making calls.'

'What if he finds out?'

'Then I suppose I'll have to tell him the truth. It won't matter for much longer anyway.'

'Is he so very poorly?'

'Yes, but it's not that.' Violet's voice shook slightly. 'He says he's arranged a match for me.'

'A marriage?' Ianthe gasped in amazement. She wouldn't have thought the old man would ever let Violet go. 'Who to?'

'That's the worst part. He won't tell me. He just expects me to agree.'

'When?'

'After the funeral.'

Ianthe blinked in confusion. 'Whose funeral?'

'*His*. He says it won't be long and I think he's right. He has everything planned out. I know he's doing it out of love, because he wants to be sure I'm taken care of, but I just wish that he'd ask me what I want for once.'

Ianthe bit her lip. She had the strong suspicion that Mr Harper had never known what love was. Now it seemed he intended to keep on controlling his daughter even after he was gone. The thought sent shivers down her spine. No matter how overly romantic her own parents had been, at least they'd given her the freedom to choose her own path—even if she had made a faltering start on it. All of the bitterness she'd felt towards them was gone, replaced by a dawning suspicion that they might have been right all along...

'Can't you just refuse?'

Violet shook her head. 'No one says no to my father. But I was thinking...' Her words trailed away as Robert came back into the classroom.

'What were you thinking?' Ianthe prodded her.

'It doesn't matter.' Violet's face took on an oddly determined expression. 'I ought to get back before he misses me. I'll see you tomorrow. Good afternoon, Mr Felstone.'

'Something I said?' Robert lifted his eyebrows quizzically as Violet brushed past him. 'She looked like she was about to cry.'

'I think she was, but I'll tell you about it later.' Ianthe heaved a regretful sigh, wishing there were something she could do to help. 'Are you finished?'

'With the ladder, yes. With you, not even close. And now I have you all to myself again, you were saying something before about having a *normal* marriage. Care to define those terms?'

She gave him a pointed look. 'I thought we agreed that marriage wasn't a business.'

'Shame. You know I always enjoy negotiating with you.'

'Negotiating?' She pursed her lips and clasped her hands in front of her, putting her respectable mask back on again. 'Honestly, Mr Felstone, who would have thought that the hard-headed businessman I met on that train would turn out to be so thoroughly disreputable?'

'Insatiable, too.' He gathered her into his arms.

'Relentless.'

'Irresistible?'

'Perhaps.' She brushed her lips against his.

'I think we're both different people now from the ones we were that day.' He cupped her face in his hands. 'I like us better this way.'

'Maybe we're the same people we always were underneath. We just needed each other to bring them out.' She gave a dazzling smile, letting her real self shine through. 'And there's nothing remotely respectable about either of us…'

* * * * *

If you enjoyed this story,
you won't want to miss Jenni Fletcher's
enchanting Historical Romance debut,

MARRIED TO HER ENEMY

MILLS & BOON®

HISTORICAL

AWAKEN THE ROMANCE OF THE PAST

A sneak peek at next month's titles...

In stores from 29th June 2017:

Ruined by the Reckless Viscount – Sophia James
Cinderella and the Duke – Janice Preston
A Warriner to Rescue Her – Virginia Heath
Forbidden Night with the Warrior – Michelle Willingham
The Foundling Bride – Helen Dickson
From Runaway to Pregnant Bride – Tatiana March

Just can't wait?
Buy our books online before they hit the shops!
www.millsandboon.co.uk

Also available as eBooks.

MILLS & BOON®

EXCLUSIVE EXTRACT

Five years after Viscount Winterton abducts her by
mistake, Lady Florentia Hale-Burton discovers her
kidnapper is alive—and as dangerously handsome as
she remembers!

Read on for a sneak preview of
RUINED BY THE RECKLESS VISCOUNT

'Lord Winterton graced the ball this evening, Florentia,
and the Heron girls were all over him, though in truth
I did not see him complaining. I think he had danced
with each of them by the end of the evening.'

'Winterton is the viscount newly home from the
Americas?' Flora had heard of the man, of course. He
was the newest and most interesting addition to the ton,
a soldier who had made his fortune in the acquisition
of timbers from the east coast and transported them back
to London town.

'That's the one and he is every bit as beautiful as
they all say him to be. It's his eyes I think, a true clear
pale green with the darkest of lashes. You would love
to paint him, Flora, but that's not my only news. No
indeed, my greatest morsel is that the oldest Heron girl,
Miss Julia, apparently told Winterton that Mr Frederick
Rutherford would be painting all three daughters at their
town house in Portland Square across the next few
weeks.'

Florentia put down her book. *A true clear and pale green.* The world tilted slightly and went out of focus, so much so that one of her hands twisted around the base of the chair on which she sat in an attempt to keep herself anchored.

'Are you alright, Flora, for you suddenly look awfully pale.' Her sister moved closer as she made an attempt to smile.

'I am tired, I suppose, for London is a busy and frantic city when you have been away from it as long as I have.' Her heart was racing, the clammy sheen of sweat sliding between her breasts. Could it be him? Could her kidnapper have survived? Was he here now in London, living somewhere only a handful of miles from the Warrenden town house?

Don't miss
RUINED BY THE RECKLESS VISCOUNT
by Sophia James

Available July 2017
www.millsandboon.co.uk

Copyright ©2017 by Sophia James

Join Britain's BIGGEST Romance Book Club

50% OFF your first parcel

- **EXCLUSIVE offers every month**
- **FREE delivery direc to your door**
- **NEVER MISS a title**
- **EARN Bonus Book points**

Call Customer Services
0844 844 1358*

or visit
millsandboon.co.uk/subscriptio

* This call will cost you 7 pence per minute plus your phone company's price per minute access charge.

CB3

MILLS & BOON®

Why shop at millsandboon.co.uk?

Each year, thousands of romance readers find their perfect read at millsandboon.co.uk. That's because we're passionate about bringing you the very best romantic fiction. Here are some of the advantages of shopping at www.millsandboon.co.uk:

* **Get new books first**—you'll be able to buy your favourite books one month before they hit the shops

* **Get exclusive discounts**—you'll also be able to buy our specially created monthly collections, with up to 50% off the RRP

* **Find your favourite authors**—latest news, interviews and new releases for all your favourite authors and series on our website, plus ideas for what to try next

* **Join in**—once you've bought your favourite books, don't forget to register with us to rate, review and join in the discussions

Visit **www.millsandboon.co.uk**
for all this and more today!